Spense woke to small and light ticklin... ...reeze. The tickling increased. It was quite pleasant, much more so than the roots and pebbles digging into his ribs as he found consciousness.

He fluttered his eyes and stretched his still sleepy arms, expecting to reach the leaf or feather, but instead, his fingers brushed the form of a person. Hair like gossamer shifted in the light morning winds. Spense blinked rapidly. Tiny freckles accented a girl's fine features like kisses of sun.

Spense bolted awake and scuttled crablike away from the girl. She widened her eyes and tilted her head to the side, as if surprised that the rare creature she'd been inspecting had moved. Her hair shifted and revealed delicate, pointed ears sticking out from her unbound tresses. "You...you're a faerie!"

She giggled, but not like the coquettes of the Telridge court who were always trying to attract attention from his older brother. Her smile was playful and enchanting, at once both kind and menacing. "Oh no, silly, I am Fae."

Praise for J.A. Nielsen

From the Winner of the 2020 Pacific Northwest Writers Association Literary Contest - YA Category

"Plainly put, this is a phenomenal story. From start to finish, I was hooked the entire way…Each character was diverse, deep, and delicious. The descriptors are elegant, but not overbearing, and the entire story begs for more. More Dewy, more Spense, more, more, more. I cannot wait to read the next, hopefully many, installments. But overall, this was truly exceptional. [J.A. Nielsen has] an amazing way of painting a picture with words and filling it with lovely characters that connect with the reader instantly."

~ Joshua Roots, author of the The Shifter Chronicles

"War, forbidden magic, and a sprinkling of innocent romance make for a fantastic debut sure to delight younger YA readers and anyone young at heart."

~ Dan Rice, award-winning author of Dragons Walk Among Us

"With *The Claiming*, J.A. Nielsen takes us on a magical journey filled with political intrigue, richly drawn characters and a beautifully imagined world. Fascinating interactions between faeries and humans, along with a brilliant lyrical style, create a gorgeous page-turning adventure—I could not put it down."

~ Award-winning author, Laura Reeves

"An enthralling debut by J.A. Nielsen! With well fleshed out and relatable characters, elegant descriptions, and an engaging adventure the pages just flew by! I loved her unique take on the fae and can't wait for the next one!"

~ C.E Brown, author of Seeing Gray

The Claiming

by

J.A. Nielsen

Fractured Kingdoms

The Claiming

Cover Art by *Jennifer Greeff*

The Wild Rose Press, Inc.
PO Box 708
Adams Basin, NY 14410-0708
Visit us at www.thewildrosepress.com

Publishing History
First Edition, 2023
Trade Paperback ISBN 978-1-5092-4622-9
Digital ISBN 978-1-5092-4623-6

Fractured Kingdoms
Published in the United States of America

Dedication

To Jamison, Scott & Paige

You've forever claimed me

Chapter 1

Dewy raced along the moss carpeting of The Vail's grand promenade on her way to her weekly scolding. She was late. Really late. And she didn't think her aunt—Lady Radiant, the Revered and Glorious Queen Regent of Summer—was going to overlook this transgression. The delegation from Winter was supposed to arrive today. And receiving those frosty dignitaries was mandatory for all members of the Summer nobility.

Dewy's mother might've argued that the first priority of any faerie was to bring joy to all things living. When Dewy had awoken to afternoon sun filtering through aged oaks in the wood faerie quarters, faeries lay about, muggy with sleep and the aftereffects of the draughts consumed the night before. They were nestled—in pairings and trios—in hanging bowers, on pine-filled cushions, and wrapped in downy coverings. The self-satisfied, sleepy smiles of the faeries were evidence that there'd certainly been joy at the nightly dance. In her mother's mind, officious responsibility to the Court came *after* celebration.

But Lady Radiant didn't see it that way.

Small gray birds twittered their songs from high in the corridor treetops and swooped down in front of Dewy's face. She wiggled her fingers at the chirruping chorus and shook her head. *Not today, friends.* Her mother would be disappointed. But she was long gone, and Lady Radiant was both very present and occasionally prone to temper. Dewy picked up her flowing skirts and bolted along the shadowed path.

When she approached the archway of tall aspens that led to the royal chambers, Dewy slowed her steps. Her bird friends circled above and retreated back to their nests, as if they knew what was coming.

She smirked at her meek companions and padded on bare feet to the open arch.

Soft voices whispered inside the chamber. Dewy peeked around one of the aspens, wrapping a hand around the trunk. Late afternoon light shone through dappled silver leaves. Her aunt spoke with a cloaked person, tall and statuesque like the aspens surrounding them. "I offer my sympathies to you and your court."

Dewy leaned closer. The dark-hooded person hissed something in return. Though most of the stranger's face was shadowed, Dewy could make out the flashing of white teeth as he spoke.

"You know I cannot—" Lady Radiant gently reached out. "—though I will not interfere in your efforts to find peace in this matter, Lumine."

The cloaked person stood still and silent. *Lumine? The Winter King?* Five heartbeats later, he nodded with a sharp jerk of his head. Dewy's breath stuttered in her throat.

"Grace be with you," Lady Radiant murmured.

King Lumine raised his hand in farewell and turned to exit. In a swirl of shimmering dark robes—indigo, purple, and black—the royal Winter procession glided through the woven archway. Dewy scooted behind a tree, hiding in the afternoon's lengthening shadows. As the king and his attendants passed, she inhaled the scents of edelweiss, pine, and snow, but the refreshing breeze did nothing to slow her heart or cool her inflamed cheeks.

She'd missed the *whole* thing. Dewy closed her eyes and waited four breaths before creeping from the shadows. This wasn't going to go well.

"It is impolite to skulk in doorways Lady Dew Drop," her aunt said. She was using her *queen voice.* "Enter."

Dewy slid to the entrance of the royal chamber and peered through the archway as Lady Radiant settled herself onto a seat woven of blooming camellia branches—the royal throne. Someday, her throne. Attendants and courtiers swanned around their queen. Some reclined on smooth stones at her feet. Others carried sparkling refreshments throughout the forested chamber. The movement of the court was like a summer sunset, gradual and deliberate. Never rushed.

Dewy pressed her hand against her own racing heartbeat, willing her breaths to slow. Her aunt caught Dewy's movement and lifted one brow.

Here we go.

"Dew Drop." Lady Radiant gripped the arms of the camellia throne.

"Yes, My Lady?" Dewy approached her queen, touched a knee to the ground, and bowed her head. The perfume crush of the sugar-sweet blossoms fell upon her.

"Do I *want* to know where you have been and why you were not here when I expressly commanded it?"

Dewy peeked up. Lady Radiant had little patience for the celebrations of the nightly dance and never participated herself except to bless the beginning of the festivities. "Umm...I am thinking no, My Lady."

Radiant rolled her eyes and waved at Dewy. "Rise,

girl."

Dewy bolted up right and met Radiant's gaze.

"This is not a conversation I like to have," Lady Radiant said, raising her voice. She tapped one finger on the arm of her throne. "I am especially not fond of having it *repeatedly*."

Dewy held her tongue, waiting for Radiant to get through her standard lecture.

"Your behavior is an example to others—whether you like it or not." Lady Radiant sighed heavily.

This line was one of Radiant's favorite refrains, reminding Dewy that she was a *princess* with *responsibilities*.

"I expect more from you—*need* more from you, and when you shirk your duties…for inappropriate entanglements…" She lifted her arms, palms open at her sides.

Radiant also had firm opinions about noble-born— the Fae—and common faeries inter-mixing too much. Given that Dewy herself was the product of such a union, she felt honor-bound to disagree.

"You realize I have to discipline you—publicly—is that what you want?"

"No, My Lady."

"Then do not disappoint me. Do not disappoint this court."

"I try not to—"

"No." Lady Radiant pushed herself from her seat. "Perfection. In *all* of your responsibilities. At *all* times. That is what is expected of you."

Dewy held her breath and slowly, slowly let the air out. It wouldn't serve either of them to retrace old arguments. "Yes, My Lady."

"Especially at times such as these, the *Court* must behave in a manner above reproach. Your father understood that—Grace be with him."

"Of course, My Lady." Dewy scowled and fisted her hands into tight balls. Radiant invoking the ghosts of her dead parents into this rebuke was hardly fair.

Her father, the Crown Prince of Summer, had dearly loved her mother Hopberry, and even married her, common though she may have been. Her mother had helped balance the priorities for her father. He had love and laughter and joy. Dewy wished that Radiant would remember these important truths about her father along with his commitment to duty.

The queen narrowed her eyes and tilted her head. Dewy attempted to school her thoughts, knowing her gifted, intuitive aunt could pluck other's emotions like ripe pomegranates. "Tonight, you will water the marsh grasses and shrubs near the River Selden."

Dewy clamped her mouth shut tight. This was a lowly punishment, much more so than usual. It meant entering *human* territory and risk encountering one of the barbaric louts. She had underestimated her aunt's disappointment.

"You're dismissed," Lady Radiant said, her voice cool as summer rain. "I will see you at dawn. *After* your chores are complete."

Dewy bowed. "Yes, My Lady."

She slipped through the archway, and made her way through the treed palace, clenching and unclenching the fingers she'd tightened into fists. How had her parents ever lived like this? The noble play-acting? Her mother was a creature of laughter and sunlight, not stiff responsibility.

If only she could flee The Vail and her aunt's disapproval, live free with no duties, no obligations, and no expectations like so many of the other faeries.

A gray dove cooed overhead. Dewy looked up and smiled at her friend. She lifted her hand, and the bird alighted on her extended fingers. It tilted its head and blinked its bright eyes. They both knew it wasn't so easy. She shook her head. Some stinking marsh grasses were waiting for her.

Chapter 2

Spense hefted the copper basin and angled it so that his latest ruined potion could slide in oily clumps down the drain. Not quite the "satinous" texture his alchemy book directed. He rubbed his forehead with the back of his wrist, careful not to drip any of the noxious mixture from his gloved hands onto his face and muttered under his breath—something also *not* satinous.

Three blooming hours wasted. Not counting the two hours already lost when his first attempt was less foul and more...incendiary.

Mum was going to kill him.

He heard footsteps and looked up from his precarious, potion-disposing stance. The steps were heavy and thumping and not—he thanked Grace—the assassin-light movements of his mother. A moment later his older brother, Dirk, ducked through the low door lintel and into the makeshift laboratory. Spense never had to stoop.

"There you are!" Dirk twisted his lips into a smug grin as he tromped the last few feet to Spense. "Playing cook again, spindly?"

Spense cringed.

"Shouldn't your mum be helping you with that?"

"My Lord," Spense said. He should have bowed. Dirk was, after all, nobility. Half-brother, but still royal. Spense tilted his head and repositioned the dented metal pot.

"*Sweet Spring!* What, dear brother, is this—" Dirk sniffed, breathing in the mixture's sulfur and burnt-toad-skin aroma. "—failure?"

Failure. The word circled around Spense's head, coming to rest like a dead weight. Spense lowered his gaze to the last globules of the useless potion making their way to the drain. Slowly, as globules are wont to do. The sewers would carry his potion far, to the delta of the River Selden, where the cleansing waters would turn his failure into nothing but a bitter memory. But in the close space of his laboratory, the lingering odor felt like an accusation. "I attempted a healing mixture."

"Isn't that advanced magic?"

Spense startled and pulled back.

"Don't look so surprised. I know a thing or two about the magic you practice—or try to. Would Father do something like this?" Dirk pointed to the nearly empty pot.

Spense shook his head. Lord Ferrous was the most adept seer Telridge had known for a century. He would never do lowly spell work or brew potions. That was for the likes of Spense—gifted but only in the elemental arts. Unrefined. Faerie-like.

But at least he *had* magic. His older brother had none—sometimes that happened even with the most talented of parents. What Dirk lacked in magic, he more than made up for in military skill, strength, and according to certain gentle ladies, charm. Spense couldn't claim any of those qualities.

"Why would you try something so…?" Dirk's face cleared in sudden understanding. "Ah, I see. You were trying to *help* someone. What sort of wastrel was it this time?"

"One of the miners' children—he showed signs of infection."

"And what? You're a surgeon, now, too?"

"Hardly." Spense scowled. He was nothing like the barbarous surgeons, with their bloody lancets and steep prices. Too often, families were forced to choose between a cure for one child or food for the rest. Spense wanted to heal people.

Because what Dirk didn't understand was that Spense was one of them—the wastrels. If they didn't look out for each other, who would? People like Dirk were occupied with bigger concerns.

Before he could say as much, Dirk waved him off. "It doesn't matter. It seems our father has a use for you."

Spense straightened up. "Truly?"

"If you'd been at training, instead of down here with your little experiment, I wouldn't have to come fetch you." Dirk folded his arms over his muscled chest.

"There's no point and you know it. Most of the new recruits are a head taller than me." The armorer hadn't been able to find a kit in Spense's size. The chain mail he'd been issued dragged on the ground and hung around his wrists. Not great for sword fighting.

"Not true. Many of my soldiers have started out almost as wimpy as you. And *they* made it through. Clean yourself up, dispose of this—" Dirk waved at the cauldron. "—catastrophe. And get to Father's study by the second dinner bell."

"What does he want with me?"

"No idea—something about the river."

Spense frowned. That didn't explain...well, anything. But Dirk was already moving. Having delivered the message, he pivoted and launched himself back up the steps. "Don't be late!" he called out.

Spense shucked off his gloves and glanced at the empty pot.

His failure. It now flowed through sewers. The river would bear it away to the frothy currents of the sea and carry on.

As would he. Some basic magic and another failed experiment. That was what he had. He had to make that count. Had to make it mean something. Because no matter how much he trained, he could never be one of Dirk's soldiers, and definitely not a Knight.

Dirk was the Commander. One day he would inherit a crown. His skills were useful, and his birth was a joyous event for the kingdom of Telridge—celebrated throughout the land and in neighboring countries as well, human and faerie alike. Spense's birth was a bit of a scandal. Hushed up. Spoken of only in whispers in shadowy corridors. Not for polite company. The most Spense would ever inherit was his Grandfather Clove's isolated cottage and the orchards surrounding it.

By Grace, someday Spense would overcome that. And if Lord Ferrous had a use for him, maybe it would be today.

Chapter 3

Lord Ferrous paced in his private study, one of the few places he could be at peace—or not be at peace—without a court full of onlookers and gossipers watching. He passed in front of the stone-framed windows, in and out of the sun's last rays, pivoted and retraced his route. Each sharp turn caused the fraying window hangings to flap at his ankles. The late Lady Iris insisted upon them. If they were to spend long nights writing up legislation and official decrees, they could do without a draft, she'd said.

Ferrous paused mid-stride and breathed in the dust of the old brocade. *Iris, what I wouldn't give to have you still by my side. I fear I am facing war, my dear. Would this have happened if you were here?*

But his dead wife's embroidered silk roses offered him no answers. He retreated to the back of his desk and rested his elbows on the wide wood surface, steepling his fingers over a letter—correspondence from Lumine, the Winter King.

Lumine had the audacity to ask for a favor, after all they'd been through. The Kingdom of Telridge's official policy was that it did not maintain alliance or keep correspondence with the Winter Fae anymore. Privately, things were more complicated.

But Ferrous knew the cost. He'd paid the price. And the one time Ferrous reached out ended with a hastening of his wife's death. Dirk, still a small child, had been left motherless. There was a reason the Winter faeries were also called the Dark faeries, but at the time Ferrous had been too desperate to heed the warnings.

No, he wouldn't provide aid to *that* court, no matter how fervently they asked.

Ferrous re-read the response he'd penned, denying knowledge of the person King Lumine sought and certainly not permitting him access to practice his dark faerie magic within the borders of Telridge. He added a few further lines but offered no assistance. Lumine could solve his own problems—and he could do it in his own kingdom. He hoped his wording wouldn't prove too disastrous. Lumine was notoriously unpredictable.

He braced his head with his hands and groaned. He didn't need this on top of the many convoluted omens he'd received—that an ally would betray them, a dear one would go on a journey, and dark magic would again rear its mischievous head, causing disruption to his people and his land.

A tentative knock on his office door broke into his brooding. It was followed by several door-shaking thuds. Ferrous lifted his head and ran his fingers through his hair. He settled his breathing and forced his face into a calm mask in preparation of his sons' entry. They couldn't be more different—in looks, talent, and temperament. But the omens told him they would *both* be needed in the days ahead.

Chapter 4

At their father's gruff command to enter, Spense reached for the door handle, but Dirk bouldered his way past him and yanked the door open. He glanced at Spense before pushing his way in. "You missed a spot."

He took quick inventory of his hands and arms, scrubbed his face and hair, and smoothed out his tunic and trousers. He thought he'd gotten most of the potion wiped from his face and had donned a clean set of clothes. There wasn't much he could do now. "My Lord," Spense bowed just inside the door.

"Sit down. We have matters to discuss," Lord Ferrous said, already behind his large, solid desk, as much a presence seated in his study as on his throne. The king—his father—filled every space he occupied.

His father tilted his head and looked Spense over briefly, eyes glinting. Ferrous encouraged Spense's practice in alchemy and the magical arts—even if it was elemental—and gave Spense room and materials to study, alongside his general pursuits in mathematics, history, and literature. Spense hoped his fitful progress would be enough to grant him admission to the Academy. He thanked Grace every time Ferrous found his failed experiments amusing rather than simply disappointing. Spense double-checked his boots—not wanting to get anything on the faerie-made carpets.

Dirk commandeered an armchair facing Ferrous's

desk. "My Lord? You called for me?"

"I called for the *both* of you."

Dirk quirked an eyebrow at Spense, loitering in the entrance to the study—unlike his noble half-brother, Spense spent little time there. He took in the large room, the stone fireplace and polished wood paneling. A set of window coverings hung behind the desk—he happened to know they were a frustration to the head housekeeper. The thick fabric was embellished with a repeated pattern of winding roses. Deep red on a background of ivory. Dingy and worn near the floor. Overdue for replacement. But until they were so threadbare that they fell from their hangings, his father would leave them as a remembrance of his late wife, and the housekeeper had to cope.

There was nothing in the study to hint at a brief dalliance with the head cook. Not that Spense would have expected anything. His parents didn't have that type of relationship. They were on cordial enough terms, but Lord Ferrous's heart would always belong to Lady Iris. Everyone understood that.

"I fetched *him* as you asked," Dirk said, "but Father, what could we possibly need to discuss that would include Spense?"

"Be patient. I'll explain soon enough." Lord Ferrous glowered. As large as Dirk was, Ferrous still had the capacity to make most men feel smaller. He turned to Spense, "Son, shut and latch the door, then do, please, take a seat."

Ferrous waved at a second chair, and Spense scrambled to obey. "I have unfortunate news regarding the borderlands."

"What news?" Dirk scowled. His chin wrinkled as he frowned. "I have Knights patrolling deep into the

White Rock Mountains. I haven't heard a thing."

"Your Knights—talented as they are—cannot observe everything. There are some who move beyond them."

"I don't know what you mean," Dirk bit back.

Spense could understand Dirk's defensiveness—though *he* would never challenge their father. Leading soldiers was something Dirk performed well. His Knights were the envy of any country—disciplined, skilled, and loyal. But even Dirk had to know that some things could not be battled with a sword or learned from a spy.

"Fae?" Spense guessed, his voice no more than a whisper. He looked up to catch Ferrous's gaze. "I thought we were at peace with The Vail."

"We are," Ferrous said. "I've no quarrel with the realm of Summer and the Light Fae. But the Dark Fae of Winter have communicated displeasure. I don't see that relationship improving any time soon. And I have received a number of omens recently—one of which suggests we may be challenged from a rival. From our human neighbors."

"Who?" Dirk asked.

"It could be anyone." Ferrous lifted his open hands. "Breckenview, The Peaks, even Verden. Our prosperity has made jealous neighbors. We need to strengthen our borders while I learn more."

Dirk whistled through his teeth. "What if the omens aren't trustworthy? I know that you are a gifted seer, but haven't you heard enough cryptic prophecies?" He jumped up and began pacing.

Ferrous tracked him with his eyes. "Those cryptic prophecies have proven valuable on many an occasion."

15

"So you say. What we need is *solid* information. I can send scouts. I can get that." Dirk pointed to himself.

"Son, while I appreciate that your trained scouts are quite capable—"

"They're more reliable than the messages you *receive* by fasting and combing through archaic books."

Ferrous stifled an additional rebuttal. Maybe because he knew that Dirk wasn't entirely off in his assessment. His mother's death had been hastened once magic became involved. Everyone knew the tragic story of the beautiful and elegant Lady Iris. Most blamed the Fae lord who came at Ferrous's request, the Winter King. Ferrous and Dirk lived with the consequences of that decision every day.

But perhaps Ferrous simply wanted his elder son's cooperation, and if he and Dirk began one of their frequent shouting matches, he would not gain it. Ferrous did, however, sharpen his glare, until Dirk broke and returned to his chair.

"Despite your willful agnosticism regarding the magical arts, I value your many other assets and abilities."

Ferrous waited as Dirk clenched his jaw but refrained from speaking. Spense sank back in his chair. He had no interest in getting caught in the middle of this debate. He appreciated his own magical gifts—mostly because he didn't have much else to offer. But he understood the tension between those who were gifted and those who made their way in the world without such advantages. It must have seemed unfair. Especially to people like Dirk, who sweat and bled for every new skill.

"I *would* like you to deploy scouts and increase Telridge's Knights on watch," Ferrous continued. "But strictly military operations are not the only level of precaution we might set up."

Spense felt the heat of his father's direct gaze.

"This is where you come in, Spense."

Spense opened his mouth to speak, but Dirk barked. "What can *Spense* do? He's not even in The Academy yet. And I've seen his so-called laboratory. Except for the smell, it isn't impressive."

"*He* can perform a Claiming."

Spense's mouth and eyes opened wider. A Claiming was one of the few spells he could perform consistently.

Dirk collapsed back into his chair. "Wicked Winter," he muttered, as if he recalled the humiliation he'd suffered when Spense placed a Claiming on a drinking goblet.

It was a simple trick—at least for small items. Spense had grown tired of his big brother swiping his mead at parties. When Dirk once again reached for Spense's cup at the Spring Feast, the Claiming spell he'd placed upon it repelled Dirk with such strength he'd ended up spluttering on the floor. Dirk avoided touching any of Spense's possessions after that. If Dirk knew that the spell required illegitimate-common-half-brother saliva, that might've been as effective as the actual magic. To be fair, Spense wouldn't want to touch anything that Dirk had spit on either.

"Wh-what would you like me to Claim?" Spense asked. This was it. His opportunity to help Telridge and show his father, brother, and any who doubted him that he could be valuable for more than scandals, gossip, and minor laboratory explosions.

"A bridge—temporarily, of course. Our last defensible position at the River Selden."

Spense nodded, already deep in thought—a bridge was a much larger challenge than a cup. A test. If he performed well with the bridge…then who knew what might be next!

"I have soldiers who can hold that bridge," Dirk argued.

"Yes, but with a Claiming sealed into it, they will not have to. It is a straightforward spell. Spense has my confidence in this."

Spense felt as if he grew a little, though his brother's scowl deepened.

"And remember, I would much rather have your soldiers defend our people—the city dwellers, villagers, and farmers who live outside the castle's gates."

That was Dirk's job—defending the people. Spense couldn't reconcile how Dirk could be so good at it, and then dismiss those same people when Spense wanted to do something like cure a boy's fever. But it was one of the reasons that he revered his father—why everyone did—because he both knew his role and took seriously his responsibilities. There were no people in the kingdom who didn't matter to Lord Ferrous. But maybe it was like the magic, and some things just weren't passed down.

"When would you like me to perform the Claiming?" Spense asked.

"Tonight. Before the pink dawn."

"How do you know the dawn—never mind." Dirk pushed off the chair and strode out. "I'll put the Knights on notice, My Lord."

****

Spense rushed through the castle, down winding corridors and back to his lab, still in disarray after his earlier disaster, but there was no time to straighten. The sky had already darkened. It was high summer, and the night was short.

He flipped through his alchemy text and reviewed the description, not that he needed to. He knew this spell. *Must not forget the screech-owl feathers.*

Spense crammed supplies into a leather satchel, grabbed an overcoat, and bolted back up the stairs. When he reached the open courtyard, the waxing moon cast rays to lighten his path, and he broke into a sprint.

Chapter 5

Spense picked his way along the causeway, past waterlogged scrub grasses, watching his steps. Slick marshes had led to more than one watery incident. And though, it was growing later than he'd like, he was better late than sopping wet. Chattering teeth weren't great for his focus.

Nor was his thumping heart and heaving lungs. When he reached the expansive bridge, Spense collapsed against the stone and timber railing, trying to slow his pulse. It took several long moments before he could take in a full breath and let it out without stuttering. When he lifted his head, checking, the horizon betrayed a slivered edge of hazy pink. But he'd made it. The sun wasn't up yet.

He knelt to rummage through his dropped bag, pulling scattered papers, bundles of feathers, leaves, a few pebbles and a small, leather writing journal out onto the rough roadway of the bridge.

His bridge.

Or it would be soon. Once he got everything sorted.

A breeze came up from the River Selden far below, and he heard the faintest of splashes as one of the river's many creatures broke the surface.

Musn't get distracted. He needed to be clear. Focused. Or this would never work.

As he settled, Spense let his senses extend.

Registered the plaintive twitters of night creatures, felt the soft summer wind whispering his clothing and the fine hairs on his arms. Noted these things and let them go. The planks and stones warmed beneath him, resonant with their nearly forgotten life. It was still there, long buried, but not gone. Not at all. He licked his fingers, and reached farther out, dragging his damp fingertips over the wood, smoothed from years of use and exposure. The life force was strong. Tendrils of heat leapt into his outstretched arms.

Too strong? He felt not the near dormant flicker of life one would expect from old wood, but heat strong enough for growing, rooted trees. Maybe he *was* becoming more adept.

Spense closed his eyes and began the words for the Claiming.

****

Dewy looked up at the night sky. Stars flickered and dimmed. She took a water-filled breath and released it, watching the mist dance in the air in front of her.

Time for her punishment.

One harmless night of flirtation with the wood faeries, a missed diplomatic meeting and Dewy got to spend her evening watering the marsh plants. And she'd so looked forward to tantalizing one of the aforementioned wood faeries at the nightly dance.

She stooped to brush her hand across the green grasses that grew along the river's edge, bending the tender shoots and weighing them down with her touch. She left her mark, weaving a watery path. With every inhalation, she drew in droplets of water from the air, felt it wandering coolly over her belly and limbs and let it pass through her fingertips. Out. Onto the reaching water lilies. To the cattails and short grasses. Scrubby bushes shook and stretched, sighing for her touch. Dewy flicked a couple of watery fingers in their direction until they settled back down. Little beggars.

Though demeaning, her job was easy. The air was heavy. No one would go thirsty this summer night. If she was quick, she could risk a swim before dawn. Before her duties at court began. She shook her head with mock pomposity, watering as she went, mimicking court life. She might have giggled a little.

Until a crash upriver pulled her from her work.

Dewy whipped her head at the sound. A cacophonous and clumsy creature headed her way. *A human.*

She flitted her fingers through the last blades of marsh grass and sprinkled a few extra drops to the pathetic little bushes upriver. They wiggled appreciatively. She used the sound of their rustling to mask her plunge into the river and drifted soundlessly beneath a human-made construction of stone and felled trees.

Moonlight filtered through the gaps in the bridge supports, while the stumbling creature moved about far above. Dewy slid farther under, backing into river reeds. They swayed and caressed her shoulders and back. She reached out a hand, stroking their long spindles, saying hello. With the other hand she held her finger to her lips, hoping the reeds understood her caution. Humans may be blundering and oafish, but they could also be dangerous.

This one moved awkwardly, setting out oddities from his satchel in a rough half-circle and muttering to himself. He lowered himself to the center of his ephemera. She heard him make a sucking sound through his teeth and spit onto the railings.

Dewy flinched into the reeds as a sticky warm something misted her skin from overhead. *Eww. Human juice.*

Dewy jerked her arm. Ripples and drops crashed around her. Steam rose from her body. Dancing flames licked through her arm and shoulder, hottest at the point where the human's saliva landed.

Wafting steam tendrils reached for her, coaxing and pulling, growing hotter still. Her heart pounded with the heat, swelling, releasing.

Dewy collapsed into the river. The river water soothed her near-scalded arm, but warmth still flooded through her. It was different from the cool water she was used to. Not painful or unwelcome, but…foreign.

The warmth drifted along her arms, shoulders, neck, and hair, in a close embrace. A cocoon of rightness. She wanted the heat, needed it, didn't know how she'd ever lived without it.

She raised her eyes to the human above her, still and poised on the bridge. He no longer seemed so brutish. What brute could sit unmoving for so long? She watched as the wind caught his loose clothing and dark, waving hair, cut just below his rounded ears. Dewy glided through the currents in the center of the river, away from her sheltering reeds.

Moonbeams shone through the railings at an oblique angle, but they were no match for the rising sun. Light moved over his smooth cheekbones and not quite straight nose. His mouth was closed, but relaxed. He opened his rich, brown eyes onto a pink dawn just as the sun revealed it. Dewy stared, holding her breath, wondering what about humans she'd ever thought was dangerous. This one was...beautiful.

Chapter 6

Flora breathed in the woodsy air, the acerbic pine layered with the rich, textured smell of decay that made way for new growth. Flora dropped her gaze to the forest floor, searching. *There.* She spotted it, a twisting, glistening rope of fox scat. Fresh. The mangy thief was nearby.

She crept farther into the scraggly brush surrounding her family's farm and lowered herself behind a waxy-leafed bush. Their farm was remote, far enough out that the forest quickly grew wild beyond its border, as if the faerie people who dwelled there held more sway than the ordered civilization of Telridge, whatever the maps might say.

Flora waited. She had a full view of the chicken yard, the murderous criminal's likely target. Her quarry had been growing bolder and more reckless in the last few days. Her aunt chased it off during daylight hours when the scraggly black and red beast skulked within a body length of her cousin Rook's toddling child. Flora took over feeding the chickens after that. And made plans to rid her family of the threat, even if it took all night.

When the bandit fox finally made his appearance, she'd been crouching for so long that her foot had grown numb. She saw its eyes first, glowing a sickly orange in the moonlight. It didn't see her. Not when she shifted her weight—ignoring that pins and needles that shot through her calf. And not when she lifted her bow. The thief took a few furtive steps into the moonlit farmyard. Its matted, stringy fur on full display. Flora sighted down the arrow and settled her breath as she pulled back. In the next moment, her fingers released the string.

Whisper. Thump. Her aim was true. And it was over quickly. The fox didn't yelp or scream. By the time Flora shouldered her bow and left her hiding spot, the creature's eyes had rolled back, and its chest ceased moving. A trickle of dark blood made a crooked line across the beast's rib cage. Flora loped over to it and toed it with her boot. She'd removed her long knife from her leather belt, but there was no need to use it. The fox was gone.

"Rook!" Flora called. "You're up!"

Flora frowned. It was a sad victory. Almost too easy. The fox had grown desperate and careless, driven wild by hunger, mange, or perhaps something more sinister. Who knew how the fair folk influenced the natural order of the forest.

She heard the back door of the farmhouse creak open. The candlelight within silhouetted her cousin Rook. "You got it?" He asked from the open door.

"I got it." Flora didn't know why the fox had separated from its pack. But it mattered little. She'd done her job, protected her family's farm, and provided a merciful end for the pathetic beast. "You can skin it if you want. Not sure if Aunt Lily will be able to do anything with the pelt."

In a few long strides, Rook reached Flora and her kill. He examined the creature and frowned. "I see what you mean. You never know with Mum. She wouldn't

26

want us to waste it, though."

Flora nodded, wrenched her arrow from the dead fox, and left Rook to sort out the rest. She stomped her way back to the house, working out the last of the cramps from her leg.

Inside the back porch door, she removed her bow and quiver, hanging them carefully. She dutifully removed her boots and entered the safe, cheery atmosphere of her aunt's kitchen. Rook's daughter, Petal, patted a small round of dough next to Aunt Lily. A flurry of wheat flour burst into the air and the girl giggled.

Both her aunt and the little girl looked up as the kitchen door closed behind Flora.

Petal's eyes grew wide. "Did you do it, Auntie Flora? Did you save us from the monster?"

Flora smiled and nodded.

Petal rushed her and threw her flour-covered arms around Flora's neck.

Flora cradled the child's head. "I will always protect you from the monsters, Petal-girl."

Petal squeezed tighter. After a moment, Flora unlatched the girl's skinny arms and stared into Petal's young serious face. "Now, tell me, why are you up so late? Shouldn't you be fast asleep by now? You have a big day tomorrow."

"Oh, don't fuss." Lily said, "The child couldn't sleep with you out slaying beasts, so I figured I might as well put her to work." Her aunt gestured to the biscuits in progress. "She'll tire just fine now."

Flora ruffled her niece's curly head. "And you'll have fresh biscuits for your trip tomorrow. You might need them on the road to Telridge City. It's not a short walk through the forest. But don't worry, I've made it safe for you."

Safer, anyway. The forest had been stranger than usual recently. The old fox's behavior was one symptom.

Petal wrinkled her forehead and frowned, making her look more like a wizened old man than a four-year-old child. "The forest is sad."

"What's that?" Flora laughed. But before she could answer, Rook burst through the kitchen door. "Well, that's that!"

Flora elbowed her cousin Rook. "I'm the one who shot it."

"Hah. That was the easy part. Believe me."

Flora shook her head. "You try holding perfectly still and making no sound, waiting for your shot—see how you like it."

In truth, Rook was a fine huntsman. But he preferred bigger sport, like deer and elk, and left the rabbits and foxes to Flora.

"Hush, the two of you." Uncle Mason's rumbling voice came through from the next room, followed closely by the bearish man, himself. "You sound like boasting peacocks. Rook, you might want to remember that you're a father and get that child to bed."

His own father's gruff words didn't diminish Rook's glee in the slightest—likely because he knew Mason was teasing. "Right-o. Come, little one. Bedtime."

Flora watched as her cousin lifted the little girl into his arms, their heads bowed toward each other, making their curly locks meld into one unruly mop on two heads. Petal was her father Rook in miniature—except for the ears, the only sign of Petal's mother, whoever she was. A weekend "adventure on the border with the lads" and nearly a year later, an infant daughter showed up in a faerie-made basket. A small note read, *She is yours. Her name is Petal.* One look at that dark crown of curls and there was no doubt.

As the pair drifted to the sleeping area of the farmhouse, Flora leaned toward her aunt. "It doesn't worry you, the things she says."

"You know Petal. She's always saying things like that. She's intuitive, that's all."

"I know. That's my point. Best keep her quiet while you're in town. And cover those ears. You know how people are."

Her aunt waved her off. "She'll be all right. Folks have more to concern themselves with than the wide-eyed observations of a small child, no matter how canny. You worry about your own business tending this farm for several days all by your lonesome. You sure you don't mind?"

"Of course not, Aunt. I'll be fine." The truth was that Flora was looking forward to the quiet. As much as she loved her family—her remaining family—there were times when the constant presence of so many other people wore on her. She was happy to leave all of the market day excitement to others. And she found solace in the peace of daily chores in their forest farm, far away from the goings-on and noise of Telridge Castle.

Chapter 7

Dirk lunged and cut across.

"Oy! Take it easy, princeling—it's just practice." Sir Gervais—Gerry to most of the other Knights—parried Dirk's aggressive slice. Their swords slid, the blunted metal scraping and clanging as their hilts hit, and Gerry shoved him back.

He took half a dozen stumbling steps away and held up his free hand. "Sorry."

"Sweet Spring, Dirk. What gives?" Gerry held his blade out wide. "Someone sour your honey mead?"

Dirk cleaned his blade with a rag and tossed it into the rack of practice weapons. "Something like that."

The Knight followed suit. "You going to tell me or do I have to guess?"

"It's nothing. Just...Spense."

"Your half-brother? What's he done?"

"Nothing, really." Dirk shrugged. "I guess I just got used to him being the little guy no one paid any attention to. But Father asked him to perform a spell for him—for Telridge."

"That's good, right? Gives the kid some purpose."

They made their way out of the dusty training grounds and back toward the barracks where they could clean up before snagging a late dinner. Gerry was generous enough to postpone his evening meal when Dirk asked him to spar. They'd known each other long enough the Knight recognized Dirk's need to vent some frustrations. Lady Xendra, the third member of their trio, would've made him talk first. Gerry knew better.

"I always figured my father would look after him, maybe help him get into The Academy or something, but having him in the study with us, discussing Telridge's security...I don't know. It was weird."

"Getting a little above himself, huh? Is that a problem for you?" Gerry raised his brows.

Dirk nudged him as he neared the outdoor wash area of the barracks. He flicked a silver spray of water on the Knight. "Come on. You know me better than that."

"You've put up with my sorry commoner ass for years—but it'd be just as weird if I was in that study with the wise and noble Ferrous family."

"I don't know—maybe."

"Or maybe you don't like your dear papa showing favoritism to the little brother?"

Dirk scrubbed his face with the brisk water from the pump. "I'm not that shallow, am I?" Excess water trickled down his overheated neck and shoulders.

Gerry shrugged. "Not usually—I mean, you're awfully picky when it comes to your horse's saddle, and just how shiny does your dress uniform need to be, really?"

"That is not by my choice."

"Yeah...but I don't see you moving out of your fancy rooms in the castle, either."

"I enjoy my privacy." It was one of his places of refuge. He'd prefer the stables or the training grounds, anyplace where he could move around with ease and not worry about breaking some priceless gift from a foreign ambassador.

Gerry guffawed and slapped Dirk on the back with a damp hand. "Is that what we're calling it? All right. Sure."

He chuckled. Gerry was always good for a perspective shift.

"You know…if your little half-brother is going to be more involved in things, he may need a proper welcome." The Knight's dark eyes sparkled with mischief. His pranks and hijinks were known among the Knights. Every time a new trainee was inducted into the Knighthood, they found themselves honored with a "welcome," courtesy of Sir Gervais.

"What did you have in mind?" Dirk slid his eyes to his scheming friend.

He rubbed his hands together. "Oh, I've got some ideas. Find me some food and I'll tell you all about them."

Chapter 8

Soft words. Strong will. Spense focused on the *life*. It felt like water and wind. Cool. Lapping along his arms.

Steamy, woody mists surrounded the bridge. Every breath was wetter, thicker. He focused his will, whispered, breathed.

It was complete.

Spense puffed out his cheeks like a fish before he exhaled. He'd done it. The latent life force thrummed through his fingertips.

Finally.

He'd performed a spell useful for the castle, for his country, for his father. And even for Dirk. No army could reach Telridge Castle without crossing the River Selden. Its churning waters and the marshes that spread out like fingers from its banks made for all but impassable terrain. Spense's spell would close off this access point. A whisper of a smile tickled the edge of his mouth.

Spense gathered the items that lay around him and put them into his satchel. Pushing off from the deck of the bridge, he glanced over his shoulder to the lightening sky. Streamers of pink and orange danced amongst the clouds. He wanted to breathe it all in, the colors and the light, the feeling of having done something right for once, for not having to apologize. He skipped off of the bridge and headed back along the causeway, through the city, and to the castle.

When Spense reached the gates, still locked closed for the night, he knocked on the side door. Two brisk taps. He listened for the sounds of shuffling, waiting for the watchman on duty to admit him. He might have whistled a little.

"Come on, Sern. Open the gates," Spense muttered. His warm bed beckoned, and he succumbed to a wide yawn.

When the small window slid open in the side door, Spense started at the face smirking back at him. Not Sern, the aging soldier, but Saylor, one of Dirk's deputies. What was *he* doing taking gate duty?

"Sorry, Master Spense," Saylor said. "Commander's orders. No admittance until morning watch."

"What? But I *live* here. Saylor, you *know* me."

"Aye. That I do."

"And it is Sir Saylor to you, young Master." Another Knight popped up alongside Saylor. Sir Gervais, one of Dirk's closest lieutenants.

The Knights chuckled and snapped the window shut.

Wicked Winter! Spense stumbled back a step. He shook his head, open-mouthed. He wanted to tell Saylor and Gervais what he'd accomplished. Maybe it would make the Knights see him differently. But he knew it was no use, and his chambers for the night were going to be found outside the castle.

His chest deflated as he considered his options. He could ask at an inn, but it was far too late and even the taverns had long since closed. And anyway, he had no coin. His grandfather's old cottage was available, but even the thought of that hike wearied him. The orchards would have to do.

Spense turned and circled the towering stone walls, kicking at small pebbles as he went. It wouldn't be the first time he'd slept outdoors. He wound his way through the orchard trees until he found a mossy bit of ground—not so good for the arborist, but it suited him well enough—and settled down, stuffing his satchel beneath his head.

His mind and emotions raced with excitement at his accomplishment and frustration at his present position. But his body was exhausted from the spell work. It wasn't long before his breathing slowed and he drifted. Images of the swirling orange and pink dawn filled his vision, and warmth from the lingering Claiming spell crept through him. He hardly felt the chill early morning air.

Chapter 9

Dewy had heard that most humans stubbornly rested behind dead wood and stone walls—like the great construction shadowing the human city. But as the pink dawn rose higher and she watched as the youth settled onto spongy moss in a grove of well-tended apple trees, she was happy to see the contradiction. A human appreciating the gifts of nature—*imagine that*!

She crept closer, weaving around one tree and the next. The orchard trees tilted their limbs at her touch, masking her movements by creating shadows and muffling her steps with whispering branches. She reached out her hands and sprinkled droplets of water onto their outstretched leaves, smiling as she shared her gift, grateful for their companionship.

As Dewy approached the sleeping youth, she wrapped her arms around a nearby tree. Did she dare go closer? She was supposed to return home by dawn. She was supposed to fulfill her duties in court.

She frowned. The Vail required too much of their young nobles. And the human's eyes had gone soft. His lashes rested on the uppermost ridge of his browned cheeks. She slid to the side, but held on to a young leafy branch, stretching with her other hand for the next tree, *his* tree. It obliged by swaying just so, caressing her fingertips, leaning over the human, protecting him.

She left the safety of the shadows. In an instant, she

too, was surrounded and protected by *his* tree. It was old, had stood in this grove for a long time and witnessed much, but it was still strong and supple, still producing bounteous fruit. Dewy embraced its trunk and sank to its curving roots. The tree nodded over her, over them, and watched as he slept. No longer two separate beings. One human. One Fae. They were united. *He* made it so. And the tree, at least, approved of the match.

Dewy scooted closer to the human, sharing his repose. She relished this tiny space that was just theirs. *Could it be so?* Slowly, slowly, she placed one finger, and another, her whole hand along his arm, sliding to his hand and closing around it. He squeezed her hand in his sleep and pulled her closer, her fingers and arms warmed by his touch and his nearness. He smelled of the funny soap the humans made down by the river—tree sap and lye.

Dewy breathed him in as she settled. Not quite sleeping. Not quite awake. Watching and waiting. They breathed together.

Time passed, round and full and heavy. Pink turned to orange and gold. Dewy blinked languorously against the lightening sky and shifted to face the boy. She felt the little points where her skin came into contact with his. She wanted more of that. Maybe, if she leaned over a little.

Her face hovered above his and her hair blew in curtains onto his cheeks. His lips were full and parted, still exhaling sleep.

She wanted to know them.

Chapter 10

Something small and light tickled Spense's face. A faint sensation. A feather. A breeze. The tickling increased. It was quite pleasant, much more so than the roots and pebbles digging into his ribs as he found consciousness.

He fluttered his eyes and stretched his still sleepy arms, expecting to reach the leaf or feather, but instead, his fingers brushed the form of a person. Hair like gossamer shifted in the light morning wind. Spense blinked rapidly. Tiny freckles accented a girl's fine features like kisses of sun.

Spense bolted awake and scuttled crablike away from the girl. She widened her eyes and tilted her head to the side, as if surprised the creature she'd been inspecting had moved. He jumped to his feet, knocking his head on a low branch. He winced and stooped to avoid another collision. "Wh-who are you? What are you doing here?"

The girl turned her face up to him. The tree-dappled sunlight and her freckles formed a mask of innocent concern. Her hair shifted, revealing delicate, pointed ears sticking out from her unbound tresses.

"You...you're a faerie!"

She giggled, but not like the coquettes of the Telridge court who were always trying to attract attention from his older brother. Her eyes sparkled with the early morning light and her smile was playful and enchanting, at once both kind and menacing. "Oh no, silly, *I* am Fae."

Icy fingers ran up Spense's spine, displacing the feathery warmth of only a few dreamy moments before. Encounters with the fair folk were troublesome. Everyone in Telridge knew those stories—days lost in the forest to dancing and wine, docile farm animals that turned vexing and recalcitrant or were turned loose, or brushes with elemental magic that came with steep and unexpected costs.

But faerie nobility...that was a type of trouble Spense did not need, the type that could get someone killed.

"You are hurt?" She asked.

"N-no. I am fine." He grabbed his satchel and shifted away from the Fae girl, pressing his back against the tree as he circled. She reached for him, but he stumbled even farther. "Don't touch me, and don't help. I don't need faerie help."

He got his feet underneath him, turned and fled the orchards, back to the safety and predictability of Telridge Castle. His thoughts raced with questions and fears. The obvious. *What is a Fae girl doing in Telridge's orchards?* The most insistent. *What does she want with me?*

Chapter 11

Lady Radiant, Queen of Summer, floated amongst the tree limbs. *Where has that girl gone?* It was not the first time that Lady Dew Drop had not returned to the grove of The Vail before dawn. Reckless shenanigans were her niece's forte. It was Radiant's habit to send her half-human pages to fetch wandering faeries back and let the ignominy of the apprehension serve to both demean and censure. It was the only time she allowed for the use of iron bands. Contrary to popular human lore—most likely perpetuated by faeries decades before her time— iron didn't actually kill faeries, but it had a weakening, nauseating effect. And it could slow healing and put a damper on magic. In short, it was humiliating, but not deadly.

The restrictions of a pink dawn would not allow her to condescend to her usual correction, however. Magic was heightened, and the iron's effects might cause actual harm. And that meant more work. It meant going herself. But perhaps she was overdue.

Radiant had heard giggling and followed in the directions of her niece's trills. She danced through the branches, tickling the leaves, more than once encouraging a young bud sprouting too near the ends of the limb. Her own gifts were strongest in the elemental magic of the earth, and too rarely did she have the opportunity to employ it out in the natural world. Too much time governing, too much time leaning into her other empathic gifts, reading the moods of Court members, the little tells indicating a lie or nervousness. Light filtered through the young leaves, sprinkling green and blue and gold light onto the dew below. At least Dew Drop had finished her chores.

Through a break in the attendant leaves, Radiant spotted a fleeing human youth. The human darted through the orchard, his bag made from dead animal skins clutched tightly to his chest. He dodged low-hanging boughs and tripped over unseen roots. Radiant sighed. Not the most fortuitous of human-faerie interactions.

The human youth was distraught. His hair was mussed from sleep, and his clothes were covered in dew, as if a certain young royal water faerie cozied up to the boy all night. *What torments is she causing now?* This was why Radiant cautioned all under her dominion to stay away from humans. It was dangerous for everyone. All of the Summer Fae knew how Dewy's parents had died.

Startling a human while he slept violated so many faerie restrictions, Radiant would be forced to put Dew Drop on muck-work for the next month. Telridge's southern lakes had been growing an unsettling amount of algae. Perhaps the green slime would serve as a punishment as degrading as iron, and the girl would finally take her role seriously. If only her late brother and his wife had been more cautious, perhaps they would not have been lost to a pair of human arrows. And perhaps Radiant would not have relinquished her true name and become Queen Regent. She straightened her spine. She would not lose her niece, too.

Radiant leapt through the branches. Each tree passed her to the next in a courtly dance, until she hovered above Dew Drop. She lowered herself into the boughs, slipped through the branches and touched down on the moss.

Dew Drop gasped. "My Lady!"

"Hush, dear." Radiant reached for Dew Drop's face. Just as her index finger traced the girl's chin, a sharp jolt caused her to recoil.

"Oh, My Lady, please don't be angry."

"Dew Drop?" Radiant frowned, analyzing her smarting fingertips. "What is your relationship with that human?"

"I hardly know myself. It all seems so mysterious and romantic and confusing." Dew Drop blushed and wrinkled her forehead, looking down into her hands. "I just *know* that I belong with him."

"Dewy dear." Radiant struggled with her words. "Have you noticed that *he* doesn't seem to share your conviction?"

"Well, yes." Dew Drop twisted her fingers into the ends of her coppery hair, gazing off down the path the boy had run. "That is why this is so very confusing."

Radiant settled herself next to her young niece, folding her hands into her lap, well away from contact with the girl. "Perhaps you should start from the beginning. When did you first encounter the human?"

"Only last night, just before dawn." Dew Drop explained what followed after. Her story left the queen feeling cold and stiff. The familiar words of enchantment, the rituals of a mage, and Dew Drop's obsession all led to one dangerous conclusion. Her niece had been Claimed.

Chapter 12

Lord Ferrous squinted as bright morning light filtered through his windows, pink and golden. He was consulting his scriptural texts when the dancing rays lured him from his early morning study. Such a dawn purported an auspicious day, full of wonder, the kind that often led his people to behave in erratic ways, careless and free. And while the magic lasted, everyone and everything was golden and shining. All seemed beautiful and right with the world. A truly dangerous state of mind.

A knock on his door pulled him from his thoughts. "Enter."

"My Lord." It was Lady Xendra, one the realm's most capable Knights, and a close friend of Dirk's. Her parents were among his most trusted ministers.

"Xendra, dear. Good morning."

She ducked her head with quick, military precision. "Good morning to you, too, My Lord."

"What can I do for you?" He closed his book and laid it gently on his desk.

The Lady hesitated, but no more than a moment. "I have word for you, My Lord. Of your son."

"Dirk?"

"Ah...no. Your other son."

Ferrous narrowed his eyes. "Go on." He knew that Spense never returned to the castle and had summoned an attendant to locate him and bring him in, insist upon rest—the spell had to have been demanding. It may mean his experiments would go untended for this day. He loathed sacrificing even a day of learning when the boy was progressing so much, but Spense was just old enough that the unpredictable magic of a pink dawn could impact him, and just young enough to have no ability to exercise restraint.

Xendra cleared her throat. "The…Knights played a small prank last night."

Ferrous arched an eyebrow. "And?"

"They locked the gates to the castle and refused Spense entry. Patrol guards spotted him in the orchards." Xendra directed her gaze to the floor. "I believe it was meant in jest, My Lord, but I heard that you'd been asking after him and thought you'd want to know…"

"Oh, I'm sure they thought it was all in good fun," Ferrous mused as his scowl deepened. "I suppose my elder son and Sir Gervais were at the center of this."

Xendra opened her mouth to speak, but Ferrous held her off.

"Never mind. I don't want to know." He turned, braced his hands against the window frame and peered out, scanning the city, fields, and orchards for signs of his younger son.

Lady Xendra joined him at the window. "There, My Lord." She pointed in the direction of the orchards.

Movement caught his eye near the apple groves. Sure enough, Spense stumbled free of the trees and zig-zagged toward the main castle keep. He looked as if he'd partaken of one too many of his mother's enriched mead cakes. Ferrous frowned as the lad tripped again, and landed flat out, but scrambled back up to resume his crooked path. Even from a distance, he could detect his son's enlarged eyes and heaving chest. Spense was not drunk from mead or the pink dawn. His son was frightened.

Ferrous turned on his heels, charging through his study and past Lady Xendra, out into the corridors where he signaled two attendants to meet his son at the front gates. Illegitimate or not, it was a father's duty to protect his children. He didn't care about the prank. This wasn't about that. And as Xendra had implied, it was likely meant in jest.

But something had happened to Spense overnight, and Ferrous intended to find out what.

Chapter 13

His footsteps were loud and his breathing heavy. Spense raced through the city, clipping elbows and extended feet of Telridge's workers and vendors along the way. It was a market day, and the city was bustling.

"Oy!"

"Watch yourself!"

"Hey!"

"Loony!"

The epithets continued as he tripped across stones, hoofs, barrels, and carts. Spense grabbed hold of a wood pillar with one arm, catapulting himself toward the most direct path that would lead to the castle. He didn't hear the words. Too many of his own echoed in his head.

Spense crashed through the iron gates, stumbling into the courtyard. No soldiers prevented his entrance, but more than a few onlookers stopped to stare. Some snickered, their titters echoing against the cobblestones. He lurched through the open courtyard as distorted faces spun past him. A group of soldiers clumped together near the stables. Groundskeepers, stable boys, and other palace staff swam in and out of focus. Kitchen maids and laundresses filtered into his periphery, but their faces morphed into *her* face. They wore *her* freckles. Their frowns became *her* lips. Spense swayed, blinking against the golden light.

Someone called his name. Shouted it. He couldn't

find the source. A crack sounded near his ear, and a slap pushed his face to the side. A warming heat grew in his cheek. He blinked and turned his head to the still-raised hand of his attacker. When he could focus, Spense met round brown eyes, slightly larger than his own, beginning to crinkle at the sides.

"Mum?" he croaked.

She raised an eyebrow over one of those brown eyes and grabbed his wrist—as if he was still a child toddling behind her. Spense groaned, and she and pulled him farther into the keep, away from the gawking onlookers.

His mother wrenched his arm, forcing him low—to her height—and hissed in his ear. "Wicked Winter, what has gotten into you?" She sniffed. "Are you drunk?"

"No, Mum." Spense shook his arm free. "Of course not."

"You expect me to believe that you are making this spectacle completely sober? Please." She reached for his arm again. "Come with me. I will get you cleaned up."

"Mum. Honestly, I'm not—" They'd not taken more than a few halting steps when they nearly collided with his *other* parent, Lord Ferrous, flanked by two attendants and a Knight, Lady Xendra.

"Steady now," the Lord grumbled.

"I apologize, My Lord." His mother ducked her head, and elbowed Spense to do the same. "Spense is out of sorts. I was just taking him—"

Ferrous held out his hand. "There is no need for apologies. Allow me to take over from here."

"But—My Lord!"

"Truly, Cait," he added more gently. "Allow me."

Spense's mother swallowed her next words and released him. She offered a quick curtsy to Lord Ferrous and darted down the corridor.

"You *are* out of sorts."

Spense felt the weight of his father's inspection. "A-apologies, My Lord."

"This way." Ferrous urged him along the corridor to his study. It would be Spense's second visit in less than a day, and more than he'd experienced in the previous year.

"Bring mulled wine and blankets," Ferrous directed his attendants. He pointed to a low sofa near the warming fire. "Spense, sit."

Spense obeyed. "Y-yes, M-My Lord." He hadn't noticed when he started shivering. The blankets draped around his shoulders and the spicy wine placed in his hands began to cut the chill, but his vision still swam with the golden light and the movement of the servants. He closed his eyes and steadied his breath. It made no difference. He still saw *her*.

"Can you speak of what happened to you this morning?" Ferrous's voice moved closer.

Spense shook his head, swallowing the warm wine. When he opened his eyes, Lord Ferrous crouched beside him on a footstool. The servants and Knight had vanished.

"Fae," he whispered.

His father sat back on the footstool and scowled. Spense knew his father's prejudices. This morning, he felt they might be warranted.

Chapter 14

The trembling in his son's body eased, and a bit of color returned to his features. "Fae," Spense said again, his gaze meeting his father's scrutiny. As if that explained all.

"Tell me," Ferrous commanded. He felt the rise of his old anger and dormant fears. First the letter, and now his son had a run-in with one of the faerie nobility. It couldn't be a coincidence.

Spense swallowed more wine. "I'm not even sure I know, My Lord."

"Think."

Spense's forehead wrinkled. The Ferrous Frown emerged, the one he and his sons all possessed, perhaps the only similarity the three Ferrous men held in common. As Spense began to weave his tale, the fright left his body and a story of wonderment took over. The more his son relaxed, the more Ferrous felt his stomach tighten and frown deepen. He gripped the edge of the stool.

"This faerie. Dark or Light?"

"Light, I think," Spense said, rising. "She was pale for the Summer faeries, though." His feet found his pacing path. "Her intentions did not seem harmful. Only curious. I suppose she just surprised me." Spense turned to face his father. "Please forgive me. I don't know what came over me. I should never have reacted so strongly."

Ferrous rolled his eyes. "Boy, do you think you are the first human to be undone by the presence of the fair folk? You are wise to fear them. They can be mischievous at best and lethal at worst. You know this. Everyone knows this."

Spense stopped his pacing. "Of course you are right," he murmured, more to his feet than his father.

"No more about this." Ferrous cleared his throat. "Tell me about the Claiming of the bridge. How did it go?"

"Really well…I think."

"You think?"

Spense paused, wrinkling his brow and chin. "It was…stronger than I expected. The life force." He met his father's gaze. "How old is the bridge? I thought your grandsire built it, but it felt more like—"

Ferrous started. "Like *what*?"

"Like the lumber had been felled yesterday. Like the stone was alive. I haven't felt that before."

Ferrous reviewed his son's comments, the pink dawn, and the troublesome Fae. A sickening possibility occurred to him. If Spense misdirected his spell, and Claimed something other than the bridge, or worse *someone*, the consequences could be disastrous. He could only pray the arrival of the Fae girl was a coincidence, but his senses rang with alarm, and his chest grew tight. "I think we need to re-visit the bridge."

"Now, My Lord?" Spense balked.

"Indeed. Now."

Chapter 15

Dewy scampered from her hiding place when she spotted the boy. The beautiful boy—*No! Young man!*—emerged with an older human gentleman. Several other humans followed them, all carrying and wearing iron. She shrunk back, smelling the rust and tasting the blood from their unnatural killing tools, even from her distance nestled amongst the trees.

If what Lady Radiant said was true, then she would have to survive among them and all of that horrid iron. She fought against the bile rising in her throat.

Banishment from The Vail. Life with humans.

She choked on a sob. As much as she resisted the life of the Summer Court and all of its responsibilities, permanent exile was worse than any punishment her aunt would have chosen willingly.

But there was no alternative. She *belonged* to this human youth, and one so enthralled could not live in the faerie world. The devastation of her new reality washed over her again. If not for her folly and missed obligations, Dewy would never have been punished. If she hadn't been carrying out her punishment, she would not have been in such proximity to the dangerous human. Just like her parents, her folly would cost her—perhaps her life.

Lady Radiant left her among the whispering trees, with no more than a few parting words of regret. Dewy's heart crumbled. She could not be comforted by her aunt or say her farewells with an embrace. The human owned her very touch. She seethed at the injustice.

But at the sight of him again—*her* human making his way along the causeway—it felt nothing but right. His steps were sure, so different from the bolting she witnessed before. And he was surrounded by an entourage, which was fitting, she supposed. Surely someone as beautiful and worthy as he should garner respect among humans and faeries alike.

Dewy followed their long march to the bridge where she'd first encountered him. The party tested the bridge for something, walking across it slowly, kneeling down, touching its planks. She could tell them the bridge was sound. Naught but one small corner showed sign of erosion. This human construction could stand as an eyesore—murdered trees and imprisoned stone—for another century, at least. But the older robed gentleman was not pleased. He punctuated frustrated words with sharp taps of his staff. The boy's face fell, and Dewy recoiled.

The boy nodded solemnly, while the older man turned away, whipping his long robes behind him. He barked a command, calling her human a "spense." Whatever was a *spense*? Some sort of servant? Surely not a name? Even humans knew better than to brazenly reveal a person's true name…right?

The human's chin sunk to his chest as the entourage retreated from him—her *Spense*. She tried out the word on her tongue a few times. Dewy could not reconcile the indignity of his abandonment. He drifted to the timber railings, bracing himself with both arms—such lovely, strong arms—but so sad, so alone.

After some moments spent gazing into the rippling river, the boy Spense pushed back and ran his hands along the railing. He closed his eyes. She watched as his long fingers caressed the old timber of the bridge. How she longed to be a dead tree at this moment! His beautiful full lips whispered to the wood. Dewy drifted closer. The wood hummed with life. And why wouldn't it? What she would give to hear those whispers spoken to her.

Chapter 16

"Do you hear it?"

Spense startled as a lilting, too familiar voice broke his concentration. He'd been reciting *The Rules*. Never had he imagined that he'd be in danger of breaking them. Spense repeated them as chants since he was a small boy. His father impressed upon him the serious responsibilities for wielders of magic, even when he could do no more than cast a minor heat spell.

Never harm another person.

Do not defy the laws of time.

Heal the sick, but do not revive the dead.

Never take willful control of another in mind or body.

But there *she* was. The evidence of his transgression. Standing before him in her sun-kissed, wild glory. "Do I hear what?"

"The wood, silly." The girl gestured to the old bridge. "It hums for you. Of course, it screams, too."

She glided to the railing where he stood and patted the edge with her freckled hand. Spense's mouth fell open as the girl carried on.

"It still remembers its murder," she whispered conspiratorially.

"Its what?"

"Well, what would you call the butchering that these poor trees endured? A willing sacrifice? A natural death?

Oh, no. These lovely friends were savagely murdered, just so some of your horses would not have to dampen their feet. But did you ask them? I really don't think they would have minded."

"The horses?"

"Of course, the horses. They are nature's creatures, too. How do you think they feel stomping over their dear fallen friends, day after day?" The girl leaned toward Spense, her eyes opened wide.

He breathed in her sunny woodsy scent, floral, sweet—and inviting.

Spense stumbled backwards, fearing what his father intimated. Terrified that he'd caused this attention from her, in the most unspeakable of ways. Ferrous told him to find the Fae, to determine the truth of the matter, and hope he'd Claimed something else, anything else, a fish, a marsh toad, a cluster of cattails. "What do you want from me?"

The Fae girl wrinkled her face in confusion. "From you?"

"Why are you bothering me? What are you even doing out here? Shouldn't you be hiding in the forest or something?"

Her face lit up. "Oh yes! And I am dreadfully tired. It has been a long night. But what a strange thing for you to ask me. You tease me? Is that it?"

"I assure you, My Lady, I do not."

The girl twitched her lips. "This is a fun game." She took another barefoot step toward him and laid her hand on his chest.

A resonant thrumming spread throughout his body at her touch.

"Do you feel that?" She stood on tiptoes to whisper

in his ear, her words feather-light and sweet.

He managed to nod, though most of his body had gone numb.

"Do you understand what it means?"

"Yes. I mean, n-no, My Lady."

"Truly?"

"I know better than to play games with the Fae." Spense considered her hand. His breathing grew shallow.

The girl stepped back from him and tilted her head to the side. "You have Claimed me—I belong to you."

"I—you—" Spense stumbled back a step, away from the girl's cool touch. He wanted to deny it, but the bridge…and her behavior…and what his father said. "I meant to perform a Claiming spell on the bridge." He thumped the railing with his open hand, insisting.

"Ah. And how well did that work?" She traced the railing with two slender fingers.

"Not so well, actually." Spense's heart collapsed, and he frowned at the still wood. When he turned his gaze to the girl, her coppery hair swirled around as a light breeze caught it, returning her floral scent to his nose. He shook his head. "But I would never—not a person."

"Well, you have. And I am." She lifted her arms, and then let them float down to her sides, her diaphanous clothing drifting to follow a full second later. "What's done is done."

A sinking, pressing sensation started in Spense's spine and roiled down into his heels.

The girl's face fell. She whispered, "So says Lady Radiant. And I *am* yours."

"No. This can't be." Spense brushed one hand through his hair. He held out an open, placating palm to the Fae girl and shook his head. He knew it made no difference. No matter how much he denied it, it wouldn't change the truth of what he'd done.

He had violated *The Rules.* He deserved the worst sort of punishment. Torture. Imprisonment. A lifetime binding sentence to dampen his magic—so that he could never hurt another.

But even if he were punished, it wouldn't matter. The damage was done. Whatever threat the Fae might have posed to the kingdom before, this offense would guarantee their enmity. By his folly—a simple mistake—he could be inviting an additional front to the predicted war. Tears formed in the corners of his eyes and were whipped away by the wind. He half expected a band of Fae warriors led by the Lady Radiant to burst from the forest. And he would deserve whatever retribution they brought forth. Even worse, he wasn't sure he could stop it. Magic for inanimate objects was different than magic for fully alive beautiful faeries.

Spense hung his head. "I don't know if I can reverse the spell."

"Do you want to reverse it?"

He snapped his head up. "Yes. I-I have to." He reached for her hands, urging her to understand through the pressure in his fingertips, the silent humming that surged between them. "I'm not sure how it happened, but I won't leave you like...this."

He scrambled for his satchel and pulled his notebook from it, scanning through his scribbled notes for the spell and its counter. The Claiming for the bridge was meant to be temporary. He'd removed the spell from other objects before. Maybe...

"Please, sit," he said. "I'd like to try something."

Spense crashed to his knees on the bridge, yanking

items from his worn satchel. The faerie lowered herself next to him, surveying the detritus he pulled from the bag.

"What's all this?"

"I want to try and fix it. It won't take long."

"All right." The faerie folded her freckled hands onto her lap.

Spense took a deep, settling breath. He closed his eyes and reached out. Leaning into his magic, while his physical senses grew quiet. He spoke the words to the counter spell he'd used many times before—when it was time to return the mead cup to the kitchen for washing, The Academy library book to its place on the shelves, or—once—the pie tin in which his mother had made a perfect ginger plum tart.

As he finished speaking the counter-spell, he opened his eyes. The faerie sat before him, still and waiting, the picture of serenity.

Spense reached out his hand. "May I?"

The girl nodded and slid her small hand into his. Immediately, he felt the thrumming as their two life forces joined. And he knew, if anyone else touched her skin, they would receive a sharp, repelling shock.

His heart sank, and he removed his hand from the faerie's. "I'm sorry. It didn't work…"

But he had piles of alchemy texts and ancient spell books in his laboratory, all cast-offs from The Academy. Surely somewhere in those stacks of ancient knowledge, there would be a solution.

"I'll need to go to the castle…and I don't think you'd want to follow me there. This castle—it's not a good place for your kind." Spense gestured to the distant stone walls and the iron gates.

"If it is where *you* are, it is the *only* place for me."

But he couldn't take her there. Too many distrustful eyes, people who would judge—his father included. A creature like her belonged in the forest, surrounded by green, living things, not cold iron and hard hearts. But there was a place…maybe his future inheritance was not so worthless after all. "There's another place I could take you. You'd be safer—will you come with me?"

The girl's green eyes welled. She nodded. "I will go anywhere with you."

Spense again took the faerie's hand as he guided her to her feet, trying to ignore the tingling in his fingertips where his skin came into contact with hers, or the way her sweet scent wafted through her coppery-golden hair—her entire being a contrast to the cold, gray surroundings of Telridge.

But it wasn't Telridge that she belonged to, who'd Claimed her. It was Spense himself, and there was only one place in this kingdom he could take her.

Chapter 17

Spense—*her* Spense—led her away from the castle, around the city, and into the woods beyond. Dewy shuddered, as if she could rid herself of the iron that festered like a disease in this human place. She couldn't breathe normally until they were well past the clanging city gates and beyond sight of the cold stone castle. The mere idea of all that iron left a brittle residue on her skin.

They followed a trail, not much more than a deer track, into old forest, well away from the cultivated orchards and gardens surrounding the human edifice. The woody tang tickled her senses, and she released a mist-filled greeting to the nearby trees.

Spense stopped. "What are you doing?"

Dewy wrinkled her brow. "I'm following you. Like you asked."

"No—I mean—just now, you waved your hand. What was that?"

"Oh, just saying hello to the trees. It has been dry in this part of the forest these past weeks, and they are ever so tall. And thirsty. Your people have stolen much of their natural groundwater to fill your stone tubes."

"Our stone what? You mean…our wells?"

"Whatever you call them."

Spense dropped her arm and rubbed a hand over his face. "I'm not going to get into an argument with a faerie over whether or not trees have water rights—my father

60

deals with enough of that as it is—between the farmers, the townspeople and the millers." He turned to look at her squarely—the first time he had done so without flinching. "*We* have more important things to deal with."

Dewy's mind went blank with confusion. What could be more important than protecting nature? Spense grabbed her hand again as if to pull her along. She planted her feet.

"Come on," he said. "It's just a little farther."

Dewy felt her chest squeezing, tightening.

"Are you...commanding me?" Dewy asked, breathless.

"What? Commanding? I just mean...we should...go."

"All right." She nodded and pressed a hand to her chest, but as soon as she lifted a foot to follow, relenting to the order, the tightness eased. Dewy let out a breath in relief.

"Did I...just make you do that?" Spense asked.

"I think so..."

"The Claiming? The spell?"

"Must be. It's strange. I *want* to be with you—more than anything. I *want* to do as you ask." It was true. She'd never felt this way about any of the wood faeries. Or been this obedient to anyone. Even her aunt.

"But for a minute there, you didn't?"

"No...but I do now, I think."

"That has never happened when I've Claimed a goblet."

"What does it mean?"

"I don't know."

She tripped behind Spense through dense forest, confused by her conflicting feelings, but warmed by the

61

hand that held hers. His fingers were slim but calloused, and his grip was strong, the type of strength that comforted, not the kind that punished. She knew enough of the human world to fear their brutality, but she was sure that her human—this young man who not only owned her touch, but maybe her will, too—was not of that sort. At least she hadn't seen any weapons on him, no iron blades, and no cruel bow.

They wound through ancient trees, each higher and wider than the last, until they arrived at a small orchard grove with three clustered trees at its center. The trees had grown together, limbs and trunks intertwining in their reach to the sky. At the base, a hollowed entry led to the trees' heart where a multi-level cottage lived, not a construction made from butchered wood, but one coexisting with the trees, leaning into and supporting it.

Nurtured and nurturing.

In harmony with the land around it. And it belonged to a human. Dewy had a feeling many of her assumptions about humans were inaccurate, and this was just the beginning.

Chapter 18

"What is this place?" Dewy whispered, as they approached the curving, graceful cottage snug in the embrace of the trees wrapping around it.

"It was my grandfather's home. It belongs to my mother, now."

Dewy opened her eyes wide as she faced Spense. "What is your mother?"

"Ah…well, she's a cook for the castle."

"A cook?"

"Yeah, she bakes the best bread in Telridge if you ask me." He shrugged. "The Head Cook, actually. An important role, at least for common-born folk like us."

At the arched entrance, he smiled, released the brassy handle, and pushed open the small door. "This was Mum's childhood home. It hasn't gotten much attention since my grandfather passed on, but you should be comfortable here, I think."

Dewy followed Spense through the tiny doorway. Only it wasn't tiny once she stepped past the landing. Three steps down led into a receiving room filled with delicate wood chairs and lounges, all crafted from existing shapes of the wood, molded, not assembled. Roots formed asymmetric bookshelves and small tables around the room. A staircase circled the walls leading to another story. Dewy peered up past the landing, surprised to find a third level above that. Dust danced in the sunlight, but otherwise the cottage was neat and orderly.

Beyond the main room, a small stone kitchen extended past the confines of the grove—perhaps the dominion of this cook woman. Dewy would never understand the human compulsion to brutalize food before eating it. Didn't humans know the sweetness of grass, the tang of a fiddle fern, a wheat head plucked from the field, rich and heady? No. Humans insisted upon rooting, stripping, beating down and then thrusting their food into hot ovens. Or hunting it. Dewy shivered.

Spense stepped into the kitchen and arranged dusky coal blocks in such an oven. Though the summer day had been warm, the subterranean space was cool. But that wasn't what caused her tremors. Dewy cocked her head, watching Spense whisper into cupped hands and then open them as he blew the invisible incantation onto the coal blocks. They sparked and caught. In moments, a small fire danced in the oven.

Spense smiled and shrugged. "Cheap trick."

Dewy stepped toward him and peered closer. "You practice fire magic?" She'd never seen anyone outside of the Winter Fae with such a skill. Perhaps human mages were more adept than she'd been led to believe.

"Sometimes," he said. "Small stuff." He turned and rummaged in the kitchen, pulling down two clay mugs and a copper kettle from the shelves, unearthing sachets of tea. He worked a brass-handled pump until water poured into a basin through bamboo tubes, at first in pops and bursts, but soon smooth and clear. Dewy touched her fingers to the stream.

"Sorry if I am stealing from the trees." Spense caught the water in the kettle—Dewy thanked Grace that it was not iron—and hung it above the flaming coals. "Shouldn't be long now. Would you like to sit down?"

Dewy whirled around, realizing the human had asked her a question. He gestured to one of the lounges, a piece of curving driftwood draped with a soft fleece. "Please," he said, almost but not quite touching her back.

She shuffled her feet forward, bent her body to fit the contours of the lounge.

"Are you sure *you're* human?"

"What? Why would you ask that?"

"You have elemental magic, and this home—it is *not* very human. There isn't any iron."

Spense glanced around the cottage. "If my granddad appreciated nature, then I can't be human?"

Dewy looked down at her hands, twisting in her lap. "Not in my experience, no," she whispered.

"Maybe your experience of humans is too limited."

"Maybe." Dewy fingered her skirt. "If I am to be yours, perhaps I should learn more about your kind."

Spense ruffled his already unkempt hair. "Hold on."

The kettle burbled, and he leapt to remove it from its hook. He returned to the main room a few moments later with two steaming cups. The fragrance of pine and verbena tickled her senses. "About that you-belonging-to-me thing…"

"Yes?" Dewy tilted her head.

"I *will* undo it—you believe me, right?"

"There is no undoing it—not according to Lady Radiant—I *am* yours. You saw that yourself when you tried the counter spell." Dewy scrunched her forehead and stared into the cup, replaying Spense's words. "But—why would you want to undo it?"

He spluttered. "Why? Because it's against *The*

Rules. I can't own you. It's wrong!"

Dewy felt something warm stinging her eyes. She tried to hold back the heat creeping into her cheeks and clamped her teeth tight to keep her chin from trembling. Spense was so adamant—she knew what he said was true—and yet she felt an unwelcome sting, at what he implied but did not say. "I understand," she mumbled.

"Do you?" He crouched in front of her, his face open and clear.

"I am a faerie—worse, I am Fae. What would a human want with that? You distrust, maybe even hate our kind. Of course you don't want me." Dewy bowed her head. An unchecked tear landed on her lap. She swiped at her eyes before more fell.

"No—no, that's not what I mean." Spense pulled a linen scarf from his pocket. "Here."

Dewy slid the square of linen from his proffered hand and dabbed her eyes.

"Believe me when I say that it wouldn't matter if you were a human, a goblin, a selkie, or any other being—it is not right to own another person—to take possession and make them an obedient slave. I didn't mean to, and I'm going to find out how to fix this."

Spense's brown eyes were pleading and sincere.

"You shouldn't belong to anyone but yourself," he said. "You are you. You're—"

"What?" she asked.

Spense twisted his mouth. He laughed. The brief sound was dry, with little mirth. "I don't even know your name."

"My name?"

"Yeah." He chuckled. "Most people have one. What's yours?"

"You're asking for my *name*?" Heat creeped up her spine and into her limbs. Her breath caught.

"Sure—for instance, I'm Spense," he said.

She nodded. That was what she'd heard on the bridge—the brazen use of his name. Heat continued to spread throughout her body, along with pressure, as if invisible bands were winding around her arms and chest.

"So, what's *your* name? Tell me."

Dewy flinched. She bit her lip to keep from speaking, but sharp, unwelcome heat licked through her veins—nothing like the comforting warmth she'd felt in the river. Needles pierced her chest, making it harder and harder to breathe.

"D-d-d…" Dewy panted, straining against the name that wanted out, that pushed and pushed, as pressure built in her head. She clamped her mouth shut and focused her stare onto Spense's alarmed face. But the bands grew tighter, squeezing, until there was almost no air. Flecks of darkness peppered her vision. Closing in, tighter and tighter.

And she lost the battle. "Dew Drop of the Morning Mist." The words—her full name—whooshed out in a rushed last breath.

Only it wasn't her last. The bands released and she drew in air. Her body toppled forward in hacking spasms, and Spense caught her before she hit the floor. Her tears streamed down her cheek, pouring forth as much for the lack of air as for the precious thing that she'd given away.

But Spense's arms were stable and supporting. He bore her weight as he would bear her name.

The coughing slowed, and she met his gaze. "Dewy. Call me Dewy."

Spense's return gaze was soft. "Honored to make your acquaintance, Dewy." He helped her back onto the lounge and arranged the fleece around her shoulders. "What happened? I only asked—"

"You asked for my *name*—not what I am called, but my true name. That is something no faerie willingly gives away. I didn't *want* to tell you."

"But you did?"

"Yes."

Spense's eyes widened. He slid to the floor. "Because I—I told you to 'tell me.' I commanded you again?"

She folded her shaking hands in her lap and bowed her head. "I think I'm beginning to appreciate your concerns."

Chapter 19

Dewy's countenance fell. Spense was sure his fell along with hers. He'd *hurt* her. Because of the Claiming. He compelled her to *do* something she didn't want to.

He grabbed tufts of his hair. "I don't want to make you do things," Spense mumbled. "I didn't mean to—just now."

Dewy jerked downward with her jaw. It might've been a nod.

"I'm sorry, so sorry. I want to make this right." Spense scrambled to his feet, pacing the main room of his grandfather's home. "You've got to believe that I don't want to hurt you or control you, Dewy."

"I know that you are everything that is good and right."

"No—no, I'm not." Spense knelt in front of the quivering Fae girl. "If you knew me, you'd definitely know that. If you think that, it's the Claiming talking—not you."

Dewy furrowed her freckled brow. Even huddled in a dim cottage, wrecked with grief and pain, and shaking with fear, she radiated sunshine. Little speckles of it danced across her face, winking as her expression changed shape. "You bring me to safety, to a place where any faerie would be comfortable—it is so different from your usual human constructions—offer me hospitality, and then, you kneel and apologize. To me. What is that but goodness?"

"Did you forget the part where I hurt you? Where I compelled you to do something you didn't want to?"

"No." Dewy rubbed her arms. "I am not forgetting. I don't believe that was your intent, but…"

"But how can you know what you really think and feel if you are…stuck to me?"

"This is terribly confusing."

"For you and me both." Spense grimaced, and then pushed himself off his knees. Away from the beautiful faerie before him, with her wide, adoring eyes. His feet found the pacing path again. His gaze followed his feet. "I need to return to the castle. I have work to do if I'm going to figure this out."

"You need to leave?"

"Just for a little while. You should be safe here—or maybe you can return to be with your people." Spense squirmed at the idea that he was abandoning Dewy, but what choice did he have?

"No, I can't," she said. "This is part of what it means to be *yours*. I must remain with you…among humans and…I already told you. I *want* to be with you." Dewy lifted her long arms in an exaggerated shrug and let them fall back to her lap.

Sweet Spring. Even her despair was graceful.

He tried to push back thoughts best left un-thought, as she emphasized how much she *wanted* to be with him. All of the first lessons in magic concerned self-control. He was beginning to understand now, as the embodiment of beauty offered herself so freely. Believing that she *belonged* to him. Spense's neck and cheeks flamed.

He took a couple of awkward steps away—from her and from the images his mind conjured—he'd never imagined himself as like some other men—those in the public houses or even Dirk's soldiers, supposedly so disciplined, but not so much after a few pints.

It suddenly became very important that his grandfather's haphazard displays of books get a little straightening. "There is no reason that you shouldn't be comfortable here," he said. He skipped farther away from Dewy's distracting floral scent and back into the kitchen. There must be something that needed tending.

Like the coal fire. He swung open the door to the oven to check. All good.

"There's...uh, extra coal in the bucket." He waved stupidly, obviously, at the tin pail located in front of the large oven. "You just add it in here." He pointed to the compartment at the bottom.

Spense blew out an exaggerated breath. There must be something else. He brushed his hands, and half turned in the kitchen, scanning the small space. He pulled open long-neglected cabinets and drawers.

"Right. So, not much in the way of food. Still plenty of tea. I can bring you something from the castle if you like—what do faeries eat, anyway?"

"I will be content—the forest provides all I need." She rose, drifting upwards like a floating dandelion seed. "Do you know when you will return?"

Spense edged closer to the earthy wall, creeping around her approaching form. He stumbled up the two steps into his grandfather's receiving room. "I am sure you will be...content," he choked. "Fine. I mean, fine. You should be safe."

"I have no doubt. You have provided a sound refuge." Dewy intercepted him before he got past. She placed a hand on his chest, as she had on the bridge. And just like on the bridge, he felt that warm thrumming in his chest.

Spense gulped. "I'll be back soon."

"Be safe." Dewy lifted onto the balls of her feet to place a tiny, feathery kiss on his cheek.

Spense closed his eyes. You be safe, too."

He turned and took a step away from the Fae girl. Then another. By the third long stride, he reached the door, and in another moment he was outside. The coin-sized spot on his cheek tingled. It felt cool and damp, as if he'd been touched by…dew.

Chapter 20

As good and right and wonderful as she was sure her Spense was, Dewy conceded that his actions were strange. One moment, gracious and hospitable—as if he'd been trained by Fae—and the next moment, he became fastidious about the house and then bolted to the door.

She wondered if there was something about *her* that made him uncomfortable. Dewy huffed, recognizing the feeling, and watched the closed door, hoping against reason that Spense might realize his foolish error in leaving her and choose to return.

The fire in the coal oven and the one candle grew dim before she abandoned her vigil. She had no concerns about darkness. More often than not, darkness gave her an advantage. Even other faeries lacked her keen eyesight—at least other Summer faeries. It was one of the reasons she was so well suited for watering duties, as it was a nighttime obligation.

Still, the little cottage wanted the warmth of candlelight to fill its round spaces. Dewy lifted the sputtering candle from its curled holder. "Where might your friends be?" she asked the waxy stub, rolling it between her fingers. Dewy tilted her head back and forth in rhythm with the slight rolls of the candle, letting the warm wax slip onto her fingertips. "Ah…"

She smiled and turned to a small cupboard, where

she found a box full of round amber candles and a stash of small disc-like holders. She plucked two of each from the cupboard, wedged the blunt end of the candles into their little trays, and caught each of their wicks from the stub she held in her hand moments before it guttered out.

Scanning her surroundings, Dewy roamed for a suitable placement, a golden orb uplifted in each hand. A glint caught her eye. There. Above a bookshelf hung a wide mirror speckled with age. She placed a candle at each of its farthest points, causing the little yellow flames to reflect and double their reach.

That done, she turned her attentions to the oven, shoveling another helping of coal through the hatch. Dewy placed her hands near the oven vents, delighting in the waves of heat.

Heat. She'd never had much use for it before. Not in Summer territory. Her life centered around cool water. But looking around the stone kitchen and the receiving room beyond, Dewy imagined she might understand what humans meant when they spoke of "cozy."

She made that her task. She would maintain coziness until Spense's return, when she could bask in the small warmth alongside him. Resolved, Dewy stalked into the sitting room, retrieved an old text from one of the shelves, and scooted under the fleece. It felt like a human thing to do.

The book used the common human tongue, and Dewy had to remind herself of pronunciation as she read the blocky script. The book was a history, describing the long-ago wars that resulted in the current human kingdoms, and the division of the Fae.

Light and Dark. That was how the humans described them. What did *they* know? Without the short cold days

74

and long nights of Winter, where was the value in a warm retreat? Without the chaos of an Autumn storm, how would the trees shed their leaves, seeds, and cones, and regenerate the forests? When the victorious humans forced the ancient faerie kind to divide their allegiances based on relationship to one solstice or another, they did no favors for anyone.

Dewy belonged to the Court of Summer—or at least she used to. She was considered *Light* by a human's reckoning. But her primary function—in addition to her courtly duties—had been to bring coolness to parched flora in the stillness of the night, at the darkest point, before dawn. In that way, she had more of an affinity with Winter. Even before banishment, she'd never quite fit in with her brethren. Add that she was an orphaned princess and had no real family but her aunt, and she was also the Fae Heir, set her apart amongst the faeries. Feeling odd and out of place was not a new experience for her. This situation with the Claiming spell was a new version of that same pressing feeling of aloneness.

With that not so happy thought, Dewy slid farther down on the lounge. She'd had no rest during the day— her usual sleeping hours—and exhaustion crept in. Lady Radiant—acting as Queen of Summer and not her aunt— stripped her of all responsibilities along with her title when she ordered her to accompany the human. At least the punishments were over—no marsh plants to water or even ordinary meadows to tend. No duties whatsoever.

She could get some rest. Like a little holiday. That never ended.

Chapter 21

Ferrous usually enjoyed his visits with The Academy Dean. It was a welcome time of respite, and reminded him of his time of learning, when she—Professor Stone—had been a young teacher and he had been a boy, wide-eyed and eager to learn, eager to master his gifts. But today he felt anything but restful. She was too shrewd not to notice.

She swirled her glass of amber liquid—one of their shared passions, along with philosophy and history—and tilted her head. "Something on your mind today, My Lord?"

He frowned deeply. "You know me too well."

Her blue-gray eyes glinted against a leathery, kind face. "Will you tell me or is it a secret of national importance?"

"I think I prefer when we discuss philosophy."

"Ah. Of course. Best stick to hypotheticals."

He chuckled at the veiled invitation and took a sip of his spirits, savoring the smoke and sugar flavors. "Hypothetically…how might The Academy handle a pupil who accidentally violated a Rule?"

"A Rule of Magic?" Her silver eyebrows rose.

"Hypothetically."

Professor Stone pursed her lips. "I suppose it depends on the infraction and how significant the consequences."

"Imagine they're significant—not fatal—but significant."

"We'll try to reverse the magic, of course, and after that…well, it's different for every circumstance but it can lead to a number of outcomes."

"Discipline at The Academy? Perhaps some sort of detention?"

"That would be one of the more mild consequences. Sometimes, we'll elect expulsion, and have even magically bound a student who couldn't or wouldn't control their abilities."

Ferrous took a deeper swallow of his drink. It burned his throat and inflamed his chest. "Even if it was an accident? A mistake?"

"If an arrow flies mistakenly from a bow, is the creature it pierces any less dead?"

"Point taken." He smirked. "You're always good for a life lesson."

She lifted her shoulders in a nonchalant shrug and finished off her drink. "I think I'll leave you to your hypotheticals—it seems you have much on your mind. Of course, you know where my office is located if you ever want to have a longer chat."

"Thank you, Professor Stone—if there weren't so many stairs to get up to your office, I just might consider it."

The Dean tutted and chucked him on the chin before taking her leave. She was very likely the only person in the whole of Telridge who could get away with that.

Soon enough, the warmth of her visit wore off and he was left alone with his troublesome thoughts. Ferrous stalked past his study windows. When he glimpsed movement at the edge of the forest, he moved closer to the glass, one hand holding on to the faded, rose-embellished curtains. He opened the catch, letting an unexpectedly cool breeze drift in. He watched the figure approaching the castle.

His son. Spense. Shoulders bent inward, but pace constant, as if he was deep in thought—solving a problem.

And that problem—from what he'd seen when he left his young son at the unclaimed bridge came in the form of a faerie girl. She was young, perhaps even Spense's own age. Even if she were Fae, as he'd reported, it was unlikely she was anyone of real importance. It wasn't like he'd cast his spell on Lady Radiant herself. But with the faerie folk, that may not matter. It was a grievous offense.

And it violated magical law. The boy Claimed a person. If he didn't resolve it soon, it would have to be reported to The Academy, to Dean Stone herself—that the situation had become more than hypothetical.

As frustrated as Ferrous had been—still was—over the failed bridge Claiming, he did not envy Spense the task before him now.

He rubbed his jaw and found his pacing path. One war brewing. The omens he read were vague—as usual—and he couldn't predict from what direction this new threat might come.

Another a possibility, depending on The Vail's level of offense.

A grave violation of magic.

And Lord Ferrous, high ruler of Telridge, mediator of peace between kingdoms, and skilled seer, had no idea how to fix it.

Chapter 22

Spense hurried back to the castle and his lab as quickly as his brooding thoughts would allow. He went straight to his shelves of books, pulling one down and the next. As old and crumbling as his collection was, most of the tomes were too new. They'd been written after the centuries old *Accords of Magic* had been dictated.

Several darkened volumes near the end of the middle shelf caught his eye. Spense yanked the first onto his workspace and flipped through moldering pages. The book might be ancient enough. Some of the alchemical incantations described crossed the line into darker magic. And provided counter-incantations. He pored through page after page. Antidotes to poisons. Curses and counter-curses. Death and death reversed.

He grabbed a volume with a crisscrossing pattern on the spine. More of the same. And the next. In the fourth, there was a curse for temporary mind-control, but no counter. And even if there had been, this was a small thing in comparison to the Claiming. He flipped more pages. He would find the answer. He had to.

"Have you been down here all this time?"

Spense jolted. He blinked and wiped a thin string of drool from his chin. Books lay open all around him. His head rested on one of them, pushing the limits of its creaking spine. A petite woman with a disapproving expression stood in the entrance to his lab. "Mum?"

She lifted one eyebrow.

"Sweet Spring! What's the time?" Spense pressed his thumb and first two fingers to the space in between his brows, kneading the unwelcome sleep away.

He wasn't sure when he dozed off. Somewhere in the middle of an old history text, describing the old wars and the Fae. Spense ran his hands through his hair. He still hadn't found anything more useful than the one spell about temporary mind-control.

"You have missed mid-day meal and afternoon chores. My ovens don't fire themselves, you know."

Spense glanced at the windows. Afternoon light slanted in the windows, making his workspace glow golden. The guttering candles in his lab were mere stubs. "Oh."

"Yes."

"Sorry, Mum. I'll get to the woodpile now. I'm not doing any good down here, anyway."

Spense pushed back from the table, strewn with papers and textbooks, just as Lord Ferrous entered his untidy workspace. Spense scrambled to form an awkward bow. "My Lord."

"Cait, I see you've located our wandering progeny."

His mother nodded and curtsied. Spense glanced between his parents, at their incongruous tableau. He supposed that most children were used to seeing their parents together, but it was disorienting for him. They were not a married couple and didn't exist as a pair. Most of the time, they lived and worked in such different spheres that it was as if one ceased to be when Spense was in the presence of the other.

"If I am no longer needed, I have a castle to bake for, My Lord."

"Quite." Ferrous's lips nudged toward a smile. "Thank you, Cait."

His mother dipped into another brief curtsy and then whipped through the doorway. Light steps tapped the stairs. And just like that, it was broken, the image of a small family, with two parents working together for the care of their almost adult son. No. His mother was a servant who'd taken up with a man, once upon a time, and like too many others, was left alone to care for a child. But unlike many of the fathers in those familiar cautionary tales, his father was the king. And everyone knew that Lord Ferrous couldn't marry a servant, no matter her respectability.

Spense turned to his father, steeling himself for the rebuke that was likely to come. "Apologies for my absence, My Lord."

"I see you are hard at study." Ferrous scanned the room. Spense cringed at his stacks of open texts and haphazard candles.

"Yes, My Lord."

"And you have found what you are looking for?"

"Not yet, My Lord." He shook his head in frustration. He hated not having the answer to a problem, but even worse, he hated having to admit that to his father. By now, he should be used to it. "I tried the basic counter spell, but, like you predicted, it didn't work. I don't know how to free her."

His father tsked. "Nor I. When generations are schooled in nothing but the light side of magic, a few things tend to get lost along the way."

Lord Ferrous wandered the shelves, running his finger along a row of dusty books.

"Ordinarily, I would say that that is for the best, but

in this circumstance, we find ourselves wholly unprepared." He turned to face Spense. "I don't like to be unprepared."

"No, My Lord." Given his father's ability with Sight, it didn't happen all that often.

"I can't help you with this faerie-girl, but I *can* prepare my fortress and people for a possible attack." Something in his father's phrasing grated. The dismissiveness of Dewy as just another problem to be solved in a list of challenges before the king.

"Yes, My Lord."

"You, Spense." Lord Ferrous pointed an imperious, ringed finger at his son. "You are going back to the bridge in three nights, and this time you will Claim it, and *only* it."

"Yes, My Lord—why three nights?"

"Because we will again have the blessings of a pink dawn to enhance magic and strengthen the spell. Fortune smiles upon us and gives us a second chance."

"As you wish, My Lord. I won't fail you." Spense met his father's gaze.

"No. You will not." Lord Ferrous didn't challenge the gaze. If anything, Spense thought his father's mouth might have twitched a little. "Take a rest, Spense. You look like you need it. You can work on your faerie-girl situation later."

"Yes, My Lord." He nodded to his father as Ferrous turned to leave. Something tickled his throat. Something foolish. "She's not just a common faerie, My Lord."

"Sorry?" Lord Ferrous swiveled back, in full authority.

"She's not a…'faerie-girl.' She's a person. And she's Fae. She's called Dewy."

Spense watched his father's eyes narrow and chin lift. "And you like her. Just when I thought the situation couldn't possibly get worse." He whisked his long coat behind him and made his way for the stairs.

Once he heard several steps retreat without pause, Spense sank down into the nearest chair. He should learn to ignore those stupid tickles in his throat that led him to speak recklessly. One of these days, maybe.

Chapter 23

Unable to find anything else useful from his books of alchemy and history, Spense made his way across the keep to the kitchens to help his mother as promised. Nearly there, Spense's legs flew under him, and his head came crashing to the unforgiving stones of the courtyard.

He moaned, wondering what he slipped on this time while his mind had been elsewhere. A forgotten log meant for the wood stack?

If only he could be so lucky. He rubbed his head, and slowly opened his eyes. A shadow—make that shadows—loomed over him. As he gained focus, he recognized Dirk's frown. Sir Gervais and Lady Xendra wore matching smirks.

"You should really watch where you are going little brother—a good soldier would never be caught off-guard like that."

Spense should have known. This type of thing had been going on for years as Dirk perpetually pressed Spense into one form of military training or another.

"Wicked Winter, Dirk—I'm not one of your soldiers and I don't have time for this." Spense pushed to a seated position, only to be returned to the ground by Dirk's boot.

"Oh, I think you'll find the time." Dirk pressed his heel, and Spense coughed. "We have some things we need to discuss."

Spense cringed. "Discuss" in Dirk-ese, usually meant something along the lines of beat until weeping. He read the anger on his brother's face, though. This wasn't an impromptu training exercise.

"What happened with the faerie?" Dirk pushed harder with his foot as he leaned forward.

"You heard about that?"

"Do you have any idea the danger that you've put *everyone* in?"

"I…uh…"

"No? Well let's see if I can impress the point?" Dirk tilted his head in pretended evaluation. His favorite methods of instruction often involved a kick or two to the ribs, or solid cuff to the jaw. Once, he landed a direct punch into Spense's nose. It never quite straightened out. He'd probably go for the kick, since Spense was already conveniently on the ground.

But today, he didn't feel inclined to be Dirk's student. Or a source of pitiable amusement for the on-looking Knights. He'd already been reprimanded by his father. And scolded by his mother.

Despite his poor showing as a soldier, Spense *had* learned some defensive maneuvers over the years. He was fast and could wriggle out of most situations. Dirk had learned a few things, too. There was a reason Lord Ferrous placed him in command of Telridge's army. And Dirk developed height and muscle that Spense hadn't.

There would never be any such thing as a fair fight between them.

Which was why Spense wasn't about to fight fair. He grabbed his brother's foot at the heel and toes and twisted hard, throwing him off balance. Dirk fell but turned it into a roll. Spense rolled the other way, scraping his hand along the loose gravel in between the stones before he got his own feet underneath him. Dirk lunged, and Spense threw a handful of sand. It hit Dirk square in the face. He screamed, pawing at his eyes and cursing.

"Aaaghh! You little…!"

Dirk dove for him, but Spense danced just out of reach.

"I know I messed up Dirk! I'm going to fix it!"

Dirk launched himself again and grabbed his tunic before Spense could dodge him. He jabbed his large finger into Spense's chest. "You'd better," he growled.

His brother pivoted hard and stomped away, cursing the whole time.

Spense didn't let out his breath until Dirk and his companions were on the far side of the courtyard. He limped the rest of the way to the kitchens and found his mother kneading bread. She was dusted in flour nearly to her elbows. A smear of it streaked her forehead. She nodded when he entered, but she continued her work.

"I heard you needed some wood chopped."

"This morning would have been nice."

She punched and flipped the mass of dough, causing flour dust to fly around her. Cait glanced up at him as he wove past her and the flour cloud to the back door.

"Oy! What happened to you?"

Spense looked down. His clothes were askew and covered in dirt from the courtyard. He felt the swelling growing on the back of his head and guessed that his hair was mussed.

"It's nothing."

She put her hands on her hips. "It doesn't look like nothing."

"Just…Dirk."

His mother's lips tightened.

"He wasn't too pleased about the Claiming situation."

"I guess not."

"Don't worry—I'm fine. You had work for me, remember?" Spense put his hands on his mother's narrow shoulders. Spense was not tall, but he had a good head on his diminutive mother.

"Wood pile." She nodded. "But maybe you should steer clear of Dirk."

Spense smirked. "Yes, Mum."

Outside the kitchens, there was a large stack of felled timber. The lumberman must have dropped a load recently. It cluttered up the back garden area.

He settled a round log on the chopping block and retrieved the axe from where it leaned against the shed. Spense gave a swing, up overhead and down cleanly into the log. About halfway. Not bad. Dirk could do it in one strike every time—when he felt the need to show off for his soldiers, not because he actually wanted to contribute to menial chores around the castle. It usually took Spense two or three tries. He lifted the axe, log and all, and brought it down hard, cleaving the two halves.

Spense set up again. Swung. And again. Soon he had a line of sweat trickling along his spine, and a pile of split logs strewn about the yard. He kept swinging. His body found a rhythm and his mind began to work. Both parts worked more fluidly when working in tandem. The tedium of the task focused his thoughts, and his attention to a mental task gave heft to his swing.

He thought about the Fae, how once upon a time, they'd been one people, not divided into Light and Dark, Summer and Winter. He wondered if humans had ever known a period of unity, or if there'd always been this tendency to posture and spar—little skirmishes and major battles. Thousands dead, maybe millions, over centuries of conflict. For what? A bit of land? Power?

He continued splitting the logs, ignoring the twinge in his arms and small ache in his back. When the logs ran out, he hadn't come up with any solutions, not for his current dilemma or for the years of conflict that never quite ended. He knew his father spent hours in his study, meeting with emissaries from neighboring lands, praying to keep the peace for a little longer. He knew it wore on the king. But he kept doing it. Lord Ferrous put his people first. And he met each challenge as it came. That's what Spense needed to do. One challenge at a time. He stretched his arms overhead. What challenge could he solve *now*?

He turned when his mother cleared her throat. She held a basket filled with bread and fresh greens.

"What's this?" Spense asked.

"I thought your faerie might be hungry. It is the way of the Fae to offer hospitality. The least you could do is give the girl something to eat." Cait lifted the basket.

Spense inspected the offerings. In addition to what he could initially see emerging from the basket, his mother included a passel of nuts and several pieces of fresh fruit. Except for the bread, all raw. "Thank you. That was thoughtful of you."

"Well, you don't want to insult the fair folk."

Spense grimaced. "It may be too late for that…"

His mother's eyes softened. "You'll find a solution, Spense. Use that brain of yours and figure it out."

"Yes, Mum." It always buoyed him that she had faith in him. Her assurance wasn't the only thing to lift his confidence, though. A young Fae needed him. So much of his learning had been experimental and playful, with little real consequence. But not now. This mattered.

"And in the meantime, get yourself washed up—you'll ruin the whole point of my generous gift if you bring it to her smelling and looking like a sweat-covered pine tree."

Spense laughed. "You want me to get this stacked for you first?" He gestured at the haphazard array of timber and kindling.

"No. It's fine. I'll get one of the kitchen boys to do it. Go. Be hospitable."

"Thanks, Mum." Spense leaned over and landed a quick peck on his mother's cheek. He left the kitchen yard to follow her instructions, wishing he had better news for Dewy. For now, he could look out for her well-being. One small challenge. But one he could meet, thanks to Mum.

Chapter 24

Dewy bolted from the lounge. And promptly slid off, landing with an un-faerie-like thud onto the floor. The dark images of the nightmare still swirled in her head. Her water failing. A forest, feral and frayed. A cold, mirthless laugh.

A door slammed.

Someone spoke soothing words into her ears, touched her arms and her hair. Dewy peered at the shadow-free face in front of her, speaking to her and warming her trembling arms with his hands.

"Spense?"

"Dewy, are you all right? What happened?"

She shook her head. "I don't know...I fell off the chair?"

"You're shaking." Spense's forehead creased with worry, and something funny and wrinkly happened to his chin when he frowned.

"Oh..." Dewy took a deep breath. She tasted the dust motes in the air, and little bits of mossy earth. The coal fire smelled of lingering smoke. Beyond that, she sensed water. Cool and clean, springing up from the earth. She drew it in, pointed one shaking hand, and opened it, releasing a small drink to the roots of the trees. The remaining air in her throat rushed out in a stuttering whoosh.

"D-dream," she said. "Nightmare."

Spense sat back, releasing her arm. "Must have been some nightmare."

She nodded. "It was…awful." Dewy bowed her head, shuddering as the images replayed, the pressing darkness, the tightening in her chest, and that cold laugh. Her eyes felt hot and watery.

"Here," Spense whispered as he opened his arms, allowing her to fall in. Dewy tucked her head and rested it on his chest. He wore a different tunic. It was a thick, fine linen, a costly fabric by human standards, but well-worn. Spense's arms slowly closed around her, his hands stiff and fluttering as he patted her hair.

Dewy listened to Spense's heartbeat through his shirt, steady but a bit faster than she would have expected. She breathed in his clean soap scent, his damp, curling hair, letting his presence clear away the remnants of the dream.

Another scent reached her. It was warm and yeasty.

Dewy withdrew from Spense and turned her face to the new aroma. A full basket sat near the open door, dropped when he rushed in. "What is that?"

"What?" Spense followed her gaze to the forgotten basket. "Oh…right. I brought you something to eat…in case you hadn't gotten around to foraging. Hospitality and all. That's a Fae thing, right?"

Dewy turned her face back to Spense. "That's very kind of you."

His neck and cheeks turned a delightful shade of pink. "My mum made the bread—but don't worry—the rest is all uncooked."

"Thank you." She was surprised to find the thought of food appealing. She couldn't recall her last meal, other than the tea Spense prepared for her earlier.

He scrambled over to the door where he snatched the basket. He brought it back and sat down, placing the food between them. He pulled a linen cloth from the basket and smoothed it onto the floor, arranging the foodstuffs in front of her. "Maybe if you eat something, you'll feel better."

Dewy reached for an apple, and raised it to her teeth, taking a tiny nibble. It was crisp and juicy, with just a hint of tang. It watered her dry mouth. Spense pulled a fat round object from the basket and tore a chunk off. It was the thing emitting the inviting fragrance. He held out the torn piece. Dewy lifted her chin and glanced sideways at Spense's proffered item. "What is it?" she whispered.

Spense crinkled his forehead. "You're kidding, right?" He waved the wheaty object around. "It's bread."

Dewy had heard of bread—the thing made from pulverized grains. She hadn't expected it to smell so good. He continued to extend his arm. "Here. Maybe…just try a piece?"

Dewy touched one finger to the bread. It was still warm. The edges were rough, but the inner portion, where Spense tore it, looked soft. She took the small piece from his hand and brought it close to her face. She glanced back at Spense. Something like a smile caused the corners of his lips to lift, and his eyes were wide, expectant.

She took a bite. The outer portion of the bread crunched under her teeth, and she ripped the soft middle. It melted in her mouth, releasing the ripe wheat taste she expected, and other more subtle flavors, milk and oats. She closed her eyes, letting the soft, savory experience take her whole focus.

"Do you like it?"

"Mmm…"

"Is that a yes?" Spense laughed.

She nodded. "I never knew…"

"I told you—my mum's bread is the best."

"Hmm." Dewy crinkled her forehead, tilting her head to get a better look at Spense. "I've never had this before. I wouldn't know."

"You'll have to trust me, then." He shrugged, broke off a piece himself, and started chewing.

"I do. It's just that…" How was she to phrase this? Yes. She did trust him. She *had* to trust him. She had no choice. Dewy huffed. "I could be eating cow dung, and when you tell me it is wonderful, what if I believe you?"

"Oh." Spense's face fell.

Dewy frowned. She'd upset him.

"I wouldn't make you do that," he said.

"I *believe* you." She met his gaze and held.

"But you don't trust your own belief?"

"How can I?" She shook her head.

"What about this?" Spense scooted closer, and leaned in. "What if I say…that you should make your own opinion…not just about this bread, but anything that comes up? Would that help?"

"Maybe," she hedged.

"Dewy." Spense took on a serious expression. "I would like to respectfully request that you sample this bread, and…determine if it is to your liking."

Dewy eyed the remaining chunk in her hand. She took a tentative bite, closed her eyes, and sighed. It was still delicious.

They continued the rest of the meal in relative quiet. Dewy glanced at Spense over the top of an apple she raised to her mouth, considering her feelings. She felt gratitude, as was appropriate for a generous show of hospitality, but could she trust it? How was she to know if this gesture was truly up to Fae standards? Or did she just perceive it as kind and generous because of this Claiming business? Dewy dropped her hands to her lap, apple and all.

Spense looked at her askance, a bit of cheese halfway to his mouth. "I'm almost afraid to ask."

"I just—"

Dewy cocked her head. There was something past the grove—making a terrible sound.

"Yes?" Spense prodded.

She held up a hand. "Wait."

The noise grew louder. A keening shriek rose from beyond the trees. From the far side of the River Selden and the bridge Spense had tried to Claim. It was almost as if—she jerked her gaze up to meet Spense's. "We have to go. Now."

"What? Why?" Spense scrambled from his place on the floor.

Dewy was already at the door. She turned back only long enough to say, "Your people are in danger."

Chapter 25

Flora pulled the brush down Buttercup's flank in quick, brisk movements. The normally stoic horse kept sidestepping away from her. "What's going on with you, today, Butter? You are in as bad a mood as me—and that's saying something. Someone leave thistle in your hay?"

The golden mare stamped her feet to the side again and snorted.

"Well now, that's not so ladylike," Flora chided. "If you and I are going to be left alone on Market Day, with naught but each other and Old Moss for company, you might try being civil."

She laid her hand flat on the side of Buttercup's face to calm her. With most of the horses, that was all it took, but the mare pulled away and whinnied. Her eyes were wide and roaming. "Butter...?"

But then she heard it. A feral shriek broke the quiet of her family's farm. Followed by another. And another, cascading into an unceasing wail.

The voices came from the forest, along with the thunder of feet marching through the trees, headed *her* way. And with those pounding feet and wails came another growling engine of sound.

Flora grabbed hold of Buttercup's reins with one hand and threw open her stall with the other. She lunged for a nearby stepstool, launched herself one-legged, and landed squarely on Buttercup's bare back—no time for a saddle. The mare lurched forward, galloping through the barn. Flora knocked another stall open as they bolted past with the brush still in her hand, freeing Moss, their mottled gray gelding.

As soon as they cleared the barn doors, Flora drove the crazed horses into the woods behind the barn. She would have to loop the farm, and her equestrian friends wouldn't like the thorny underbrush, but it was a clear route to the main road. Flora pulled her knees in tight to Buttercup and whooped, urging the already sprinting horse faster.

Were the Fae attacking Telridge? Why now? Faeries had maintained a cool peace with their human neighbors for centuries. With some obvious exceptions, of course, but those incidents were generally mischievous and held no malevolence.

Flora felt heat on her back. She risked a glance behind her and got her answer—a roaring forest fire. The shrieking may have come from the Fae, but the fires and loud marching shredding the undergrowth in the forest belonged to men. Humans bearing a crimson and gold standard. Soldiers from Verden.

Flora tucked her face in tight to Buttercup as she raced to the Castle of Telridge.

Chapter 26

Staccato rapping sounded against the door to Lord Ferrous's study. "Enter," he said, turning from the window, where he watched an uncanny haze settle over the distant forest.

A small unit of five soldiers—Knights—crowded into his study. All of their faces shared the same neutral expression and schooled features, even the usually jovial Sir Gervais and the charming Lady Xendra, Dirk's most-trusted lieutenants and friends. Close observation revealed the subtle tells, the clenched jaws, the elevated heartbeats pulsing at their necks, the reddened ears where some of that rapidly flowing blood had settled. Ferrous frowned. "What's happened?"

"My Lord." Dirk jutted his chin forward, an officer reporting to his king, not a son speaking to his father. "Aggressive movement in the forests, coming from the Northeast."

"Near the White Rock Mountains?"

"Yes, My Lord, but moving this way. They are striking at any in their path. Two outlying farm holdings have already been taken."

"Taken?"

"Fire, My Lord. We scouted for survivors but found none."

Ferrous ground his teeth and stared hard at his son. "How many?"

"My scouts estimate between ten and fifteen companies—judging by the devastation. Their forces are not organized in the usual manner, My Lord."

Ferrous nodded. No, they wouldn't be—not if faeries were involved. The Fae had no need to follow human military protocol. They had elemental magic.

"Sound the evacuation alarms immediately. I want our people on *this* side of the river. And behind stone walls if possible." What could a farmer and his family do against an army with the power of fifteen hundred? He would sacrifice crops if he had to, but there was no replacing his countrymen.

"Yes, My Lord. And our soldiers?"

"Prepare for battle, Commander. I want all your regulars to their stations immediately, and as for your Knights…let's see if we can't leave a few surprises for this horde."

The ghost of a smile flashed across Dirk's face. "Yes, My Lord. Right away."

"Go to it, then. May Grace follow you."

"And you, My Lord." Dirk nodded a quick bow, then pivoted on one foot and ushered his Knights out of the study. Their boots clomped in quick time. Ferrous released a shuddering breath and lowered his hand to his massive desk, leaning into the broad, steady oak. Faeries. Attacking his people. And why? Because he and King Lumine were no longer capable of negotiating through words. Words led to anger, to hard memories, and that led to violence. Ferrous cursed the reckless inevitability of it.

But he had no time to brood. Not a moment after the soldiers made their precision-timed exit, a petite shadow dusted his threshold. Ferrous angled his head around the corner and straightened at Cait's approach. He forgot that he'd summoned her some time ago to go over the weekly menu, which would be quite trivial in light of Dirk's news.

The tiny woman bowed her head. "My Lord. You asked for me. How may I serve?" She raised her gaze to meet his.

"Yes. Of course." He hesitated. Sometimes the kingly phrasing for such things as impending war eluded him.

She narrowed her eyes. "If it is not too bold, you seem…concerned."

It baffled Ferrous that Cait could read him. He'd practiced containing his emotions for decades, to the point where he sometimes barely felt them himself. And yet Cait understood his tells. Perhaps it was why they had become close after Iris died.

He squared his shoulders. There was no regal way to say this. "Actually, you may concern *yourself* with corralling the kitchen staff. We will be sealing the castle and making ready to receive refugees from the outlying villages and farms."

Her eyes widened. "Y-yes, My Lord."

"And send in my valet, if you see him."

"Of course—what should I tell him?"

"Tell him to bring my armored vest and sword."

Cait blanched. "Y-your armor? Are we under attack, My Lord?"

A screeching sound rang through the forest, still far in the distance, but loud and grating enough to pull their attention to the open windows. A roiling haze descended upon the forest, expanding and drifting in an unnatural fashion. Lord Ferrous trusted Dirk's scouts to accurately report what they'd seen, but hundreds of faerie warriors could hide in that mist. Who knew what type of force the people of Telridge would face?

He met Cait's expectant gaze. Her unanswered question still hung in the air. "So, it would seem."

Chapter 27

Spense cringed away from the pitched keening coming from the forest.

The shrieking doubled as Dewy wrenched open the door and bolted into the grove. The once-calm forest shivered with activity. Furred and feathered creatures fled their nests and warrens, scurrying from the piercing wails.

Dewy ran into it.

He scrambled after her, launching himself into the woods, over bramble hedges, skirting saplings while Dewy flew through the trees with ease. It seemed as if the branches parted for her but slammed back into place as he tried to reach her.

The keening grew louder and sharper. "What is it?" Spense panted from several strides behind Dewy.

She glanced sideways, slowing enough for him to take in her stricken expression. "The war cry of the Winter Fae."

Spense winced as a particularly high-pitched warble whistled through the trees. It drilled straight through his ears and into his skull. He clapped his hands to the sides of his head, trying to stay upright.

Dewy halted. She crouched and laid a flat palm to the ground. "I hear something," she mouthed.

Spense nodded vigorously and gestured to the forest.

"No!" she mouthed at him, waving her arms. "Something else. Come. Now."

She grabbed his hand away from his ear, and pulled him into the forest, over fallen logs and into the shadows. In moments, he lost sight of the track leading away from his grandfather's home. The canopy grew thicker as they darted through undergrowth and around boulders. A sliver of sunlight illuminated Dewy's path along a stream. They followed it for no more than two hundred heartbeats and then Dewy crossed the stream in a couple of splashy steps. Spense slogged after her as they began to gain in elevation. The stream marked the lowest point of a broad ravine, and they crawled up the far side.

Dewy was as nimble as a mountain lion, leaping to rocks and low tree limbs, whipping herself up the hill. Spense was more like a three-legged geriatric mountain goat. But he hoofed it up the tangled hillside and remained close to the faerie.

Near the top of the ravine, Dewy ran low alongside a grouping of boulders, and planted herself on the downhill side. Spense fell next to her and tried to control his breathing. She peered around the craggy stone, and Spense realized they'd reached the new market road.

Dewy squinted far down the wide path. Spense could make out shadows but nothing more. A couple of pebbles jumped along the edge of the roadway in time with a regular beat Spense could not quite hear but could feel. He looked at Dewy. "Horses?" He mimed holding reins and galloping.

She nodded and held up two slim, freckled fingers.

He crouched lower, concentrating on the dancing pebbles and the throbbing ground. He strained his gaze until an image began to form out of the shadows, barely lit with a penumbra of setting sunlight, but moving quickly. As Spense distinguished two distinct forms, Dewy launched herself into the roadway.

Chapter 28

Dewy landed in a crouch on the neat gravel path and put a hand to the ground. The other hand she held palm out toward Spense in warning—lest the sweet human who'd introduced her to bread—think of following her. Whatever this thundering, warring threat was, she would wreak destruction upon it, and she didn't want Spense getting in the way when she was trying to protect him.

Dewy closed her eyes and felt for the rhythm of the roadway, the spring waters running far beneath it. The waters echoed a greeting up through the strata of rock and soil. The underground spring was young, a playful pup. But she needed the destructive wolf that lived inside it.

She focused, calling forth the waters with her mind and will. When she sensed the spring's burbling acquiescence, she threw her arms out toward the pounding horses. Rushing water burst forth, carrying along rocks, mud, and other road debris, and the spring became a silty leviathan intent upon its quarry.

Over the faerie war cries and the crashing water, a horse screamed. Its hooves pounded into waves of water that had not been there only moments before. The horse reared, and little water stars fell around it and its rider, catching and refracting the last bits of sunlight. The rider flew off, a dull human dress billowing around a small female form just before body and skirts splashed into the frothy waters.

Oh no.

"Dewy!" Spense shrieked.

Dewy whipped her gaze to Spense and back to the girl. The girl had landed in a heap of misdirected linen and leather right into the path of the second panicky horse. Dewy whisked one hand to the water, and it split at the point where the girl sprawled, leaving a patch of dry earth and two mounting walls of water on either side. The horses caromed off the walls of water, Terrified, they hurled past the girl, missing her prone form by no more than a hand span each, kicking up arcs of sand and water.

What have I done?

Dewy held out two open palms. The water wall collapsed and eddied around her. She laid one hand in the swirling pool. *Easy girl. Time to go home now.* The spring swished at her ankles, and broke into sleepy rivulets, retreating into the earth.

She turned to the girl, watching as the human pushed herself up from the muddy road. She had long, honey brown hair tied into a messy plait and wide brown eyes to match. Her linen clothes were splattered with dirty spray. The girl couldn't have seen many more summers than Dewy herself. Dewy felt tiny rivulets streaking down her face to join those she so foolishly called forth. She met Spense's gaze as he peered over the stone wall.

His expression was filled with horror, and he scrambled down into the mud-filled road, quickly gathering the reins of the circling stamping horses. The beasts lowered their heads at Spense's calming words and touch, whinnying as he led them to their bedraggled owner.

As they passed, the golden mare shook her head and stamped.

Dewy looked into its soft brown eyes and accepted her reprimand. "I am so terribly sorry about that," she whispered. The mare snorted and cantered on to nuzzle her master.

Chapter 29

Spense approached the girl, leading the still-skittish horses. The pair—a buttery yellow mare and a patchy gray gelding—were rounded with muscle. Working animals. Their manes and tails were trimmed and clean. Both were well-fed and cared for. "Are you all right?"

She shied away from him. "Who are you?"

"I am Spense." He held out a hand to help the girl up. She eyed it but did not take his hand. "I...work at the castle. Is that where you were headed?"

The girl nodded. He leaned forward with his still out-stretched hand. The girl yielded her hand to his. Small but calloused. Spense tightened his grasp and yanked her up. "Who's that?" The girl nodded toward Dewy. "Did she do...this?"

Dewy's breath hitched. When Spense looked her way, she shook her head slightly. "She is...a friend."

The groomed roadway had become a muddy pit. The quaking farm girl was sopping and bruised. *Sweet Spring.* He'd never seen such a display of elemental power. But he felt—somewhere deep in his belly—that Dewy hadn't meant to harm the girl or her equestrian companions. Dewy wore contrition for her mistake on her tear-stained cheeks and by a singular haggard sob. It wasn't something that could be faked—no faerie trick. Spense felt no fear in turning his back to her as he helped the girl.

He wanted to comfort Dewy, put his arms around her freckled shoulders, as she allowed him to do back in his grandfather's cabin, to relieve the burden of distress.

But the human farm girl who stood dripping before him seemed the more urgent matter. "What happened to you?"

The girl had ridden the mare as if she were a seasoned horseman, and as fast as a Fae racer. Like a warrior. Not a farmer. She turned her wide brown gaze to Spense when she answered. "There were hundreds— setting the farms on fire. I was trying to get to the castle."

Spense nodded, trying to keep his voice soothing and calm. The girl was as jumpy as her horses. "Us, too. We heard the faerie war cries."

"Not just faerie."

Spense's forehead came together. "Who?"

"I saw banners." The girl choked on her words. "From Verden."

"Verden?" Spense repeated.

The girl nodded.

"No." He shook his head. "No. It's not possible."

"I know what I saw." The girl gripped the corn-silk mane of her horse, as if she could draw strength from the beast. "There is no mistaking The Crimson and Gold."

"Indeed, there's not." Spense knew the pride the Verdenians took in their flag, their insistence upon bearing overlarge representations of the colors wherever they travelled, including minor diplomatic events with neighboring countries. Verden had a well-earned reputation as an arrogant and pompous nation. But enemies? Allying with the Winter faeries *against* Telridge?

Spense lifted his head as he sensed Dewy

108

approaching, her light floral scent wafting into his presence. When he met her gaze, he saw the same fear mirrored there that he felt. "We have to warn them."

"Yes," Dewy murmured. She looked away from him, shy with regret, and stepped up to the girl. "I am very sorry about…before. I thought you were one of them."

The girl's hands relaxed, smoothing along her horse's strong neck. "It's all right. Just a little water…and dirt…rocks…bruises." The girl looked sidelong into the faerie's contrite face. "I didn't know your kind could *do* that."

Dewy's eyes shuttered. "Not all can. I should *not* have."

"But you—you're *with him*, right?"

Spense never realized how many interpretations two little words could have. "Yes," he blurted. "Yes. She is. With me, I mean."

"And you're from the castle?"

Spense nodded. "We were headed that way. We can go with you if you like."

The girl whistled through her teeth. "I wouldn't mind having *her* as a friend."

A corner of Spense's mouth twitched up. Indeed. Dewy made a very good friend, and a terrifying foe.

"I don't suppose you could spare one of your fine horses?"

The girl lifted her chin towards the gray mottled gelding whose reins Spense still held loosely in his hands. "His name is Moss. This here is Buttercup. And I'm Flora."

"Many thanks, Flora."

As the three mounted the stocky farm animals,

Spense tried not to think too hard about his *friend's* slender arms wrapped around his middle. He tried not to notice her sweet lilac and water lily fragrance. He valiantly attempted to ignore the warm breath that tickled his ear.

The wind that lent them speed helped to whisk away such distractions. And then there were the faerie war cries that grew more piercing, accompanied by the thumping crash of human—Verdenian—soldiers as they drew closer. The two armies joined together in a chilling and unexpected alliance as they marched on Telridge, a threatening arc stretching from the North and East, and catching anyone in its path. Those were pretty motivating, too.

Chapter 30

Ferrous felt the tremor of hundreds of boots echoing in pounding discord with the shrieking war cries. He strained his ears listening.

Human boots. Faeries didn't make that kind of noise.

As soon as his valet buckled his armor secure, Ferrous was out the door of his study and marching across the castle grounds to climb the high, protective interior towers of Telridge Castle. From there, he was pleased to see that Dirk performed his role admirably. Guards were stationed at extra points on the crenellated wall. A small but seasoned force formed a bulwark of defense on both sides of the gates. Young boys ran along the walls supplying archers with ammunition, quivers of traditional arrows, tar-covered, and several special incendiary projectiles. He prayed they would not need to use them. The incendiaries were an invention of Spense's. Often the consequence of deploying one was as damaging to the bowman as to his intended target.

Out of the haze, a mass of writhing, screaming beings emerged, feral and wild. Ferrous could feel the tension rise as soldiers took sight of the attackers, but they held fast. Dirk had trained them well.

Ferrous squinted through the haze at the oncoming threat. Winter faeries waved burning torches of blue flame. Nowhere did he see humans among their number, but he still felt their boots pounding the earth, tremors rising up through the stone.

Ferrous reversed course and headed back down the interior stairs. When he reached the bottom, he knelt in the castle courtyard and placed one hand on the ground. He closed his eyes and listened.

The clattering of soldiers and servants preparing for battle moved to the background. Wails of the wild faeries faded, and Ferrous felt the earth absorb scores of marching feet, charging hooves, and something slow and rolling. Coming from the North.

He opened his eyes and scanned his people. Soldiers, courtiers, merchants, farmers and servants. All looking past the East Gate to the crazed faerie warriors.

"Dirk!" Ferrous shouted. He scanned the courtyard full of armed citizens, and the soldiers on the walls, but could not spot his son. "Where is your Commander?" He yelled to a nearby officer sporting a crested helmet.

The officer responded, "My Lord, I believe he is positioned on the ramparts above the East Gate. Shall I summon him for you?"

"Yes. Wait—no. There's not time." Ferrous eyed the insignia on the man's uniform. That, in combination with the helmet told him the man's rank. "Assemble a company of soldiers and archers on the North wall, Captain. And as many armed townsfolk as you can muster."

"The North Wall, My Lord? But won't that deplete our forces from the East…?"

"The East Gate is the diversion. We are being attacked from the North."

The captain's face lost color.

Ferrous clapped the soldier on his armored shoulder

and leaned in. "Make haste, soldier."

The captain erected a quick salute and turned to assemble troops, barking orders as he bolted to the North side of the castle keep. Ferrous quickened his own stride in search of his first-born.

Dirk stood on the East wall, receiving confirmations and updates from his lieutenants. He held out a hand, cutting off an officer's report when he spotted Ferrous moving towards him.

"My Lord?" Dirk strode briskly to his father. "Why are you up here? I assure you we have the situation with these wild faeries in hand—"

"Son!" Ferrous barked. More quietly he said, "I wish that were true."

Dirk blanched. "What do you mean?"

"We are not being attacked by Fae—just distracted by them."

"My Lord, I wouldn't call *this* a distraction." Dirk waved his arm towards the oncoming horde as their flickering blue orbs wove closer, and shrill cries grew louder.

"You must trust me."

Dirk lifted his skeptical chin, but remained silent as Ferrous spoke, explaining what he could sense through the earth.

"We are being attacked on two fronts?" Dirk let out a gusty curse.

"Indeed."

"By whom?" Dirk swiveled his head from the oncoming assault back to meet his father's gaze.

"I imagine we will soon find out. Come with me."

Ferrous and Dirk made their way through soldiers and archers around to the wooded side of the castle. Dirk spoke encouragements to the enlisted men and brief explanations to his officers, who in turn, issued orders of their own. As if a new gear had been selected in a well-oiled engine, men began to shift their positions, hurrying to opposite and perpendicular sides of the castle's defenses, leaving only two tithes of the archers behind on the East.

They rounded the Northeast towers and were bucked nearly to their knees by a distant explosion. Ferrous braced a hand against the wall. "It's starting."

Dirk shot from his knees and peered through an arrow slit. He swiveled to face his father, a menacing grin on his face. "Little brother's trinkets actually worked this time."

Ferrous joined Dirk at the narrow viewpoint, commandeering an eyepiece from a nearby logistics officer. He focused the scope and understood his son's reaction. A furlong past the River Selden, a crater had been gouged out of the earth, and dozens of faerie warriors were strewn upon the ground, most unmoving, but a few, farthest from the blast, writhed in agony.

"Wicked Winter! Spense created that?"

"It was his idea to fill the powder kegs with a mixture of iron filings. Heinous shards for ordinary men. Deadly to faeries." Dirk pushed back from the arrow slit. "You see, Father, sometimes I do listen—when Spense proves useful anyway."

Ferrous brought the scope back to his eye and scanned the destruction his sons had wrought together. Bits of debris fell to the earth and into the forest. Clods of dirt and rock splashed into the river, causing the banks to shudder and lap.

He surrendered the scope back to the logistics

officer, shaking his head. He'd seen the substance his people were pulling from his mines, and the brief sparks small amounts of it could create. But the destructive power unleashed when piles of the stuff were amassed together…he wasn't sure this was such a great discovery. But to protect his people, he would use whatever he could.

Chapter 31

Dewy clung to the fabric around Spense's middle, straining as he leaned over the gray horse. The animal—Moss—trampled the soil beneath its feet, reacting to the fear and anger roiling in waves from the two human riders. Dewy's heart thumped a wild fear-filled beating against Spense's back. She squeezed tighter and Spense's clean pine and soap scent bombarded her nostrils. That sharp scent of him both steadied her and left her disoriented.

The wailing Winter faeries kept up their fearful chorus. The wild warrior voices shrilled louder as she and Spense merged closer to their trajectory. Dewy feared she knew their aim, but why would King Lumine attack Telridge?

The roadway hugged an ancient stream that fed the river surrounding the castle—the one the humans called Selden. Dewy whispered to the venerable stream, introducing him to the young underground spring she raised earlier as it lapped and splashed in the wake of the horses. Gravelly murmurs echoed along the old stream's banks, calling to heel the irreverent youngster. The stream forged its path thousands of years ago, leading melt water to the River Selden beyond, smoothing stones, clearing away silt, and providing spawning grounds for trout. It was home and guardian to the mountains and forest.

And that forest was under attack—by a people who swore to live as one with the natural world. The stream hissed its frustration at the betrayal, spitting up sprays of sharp snowmelt. Dewy hummed in bleak sympathy, begging for all that the stream knew, could feel from the waters that provided its source and from those it joined with in the river beyond.

Ropey tendrils of water curled in response to her request. Dewy's eyes grew damp as the old stream shared its frantic news. Her thudding heart grew tight, breaking as the stream burbled in grief. Above ground springs and tiny cricks boiled and died deep in the forest. Mere babes succumbing to fierce blue flame. Downstream, the River Selden raged as it felt the faerie attackers approach its own waters.

Dewy closed her eyes, heard the cry of the river and let its wild anger fuel her own. She gripped Spense's tunic tighter with her left hand but slid her right arm away from the safety of his body and lifted it palm up to the waters of the forest. She closed her fist, against the injustice and betrayal.

The old stream surged beside them. The young spring joined in, offering itself in a crashing display. Leagues beyond, the river responded, yielding its ferocity to Dewy, as a soldier obeyed its general.

Dewy leaned in to Spense, yelling into his ear. "Faerie warriors are getting closer—they're heading to the castle!"

He half turned and cried. "I know!"

"I can help—get me to the River Selden!"

Spense glanced at the rising stream waters and nodded woodenly. He wheeled his horse off the main road, following a narrow road that curved south. He bent farther over the gray gelding and urged it to give more speed. Dewy gasped as they pounded along the roadway, away from the raging warriors and their direct line to the human castle. But she'd no time for panic. They rode to the brackish waters at the mouth of the river, bristling on the southeast side of the castle. She needed to gather her own troops, and ready them for battle.

Chapter 32

Dirk gritted his teeth as the massive hordes spread out upon his threshold. *His* castle. It would not become *theirs*. No matter how much they threatened with their magic—their shrieking and their blue flame.

"My Lord?" An officer approached.

"Report, Lieutenant."

"Something is happening to the river, sir. I am not sure if it came from the blast, but I think the river is receding, sir."

Dirk peered through a nearby arrow slit. The river was already at half its normal height.

"Sir, did we do *that*?"

"No," Dirk spoke through a tight jaw. "That isn't us."

His soldiers held their positions, ready for battle. His officers maintained near-perfect order amongst the ranks, but he could feel apprehension rising. His rose, too, as the River Selden pull away from the banks, leaving muddy walls exposed. If it continued, their foes could splash across the easy barrier to flank and surround the castle walls.

Dirk had no interest in defending against a siege.

"Ready the trebuchets!" he bellowed to his officers, and heard the command repeated down the line. "Archers! Ready! Hold steady! These faerie scum made the wrong choice when they decided to attack our castle and our people today! Let's show them what happens when you go up against Telridge!"

His soldiers answered in growling hollers and screams—nearly as feral as the faeries themselves. But that was what they needed to find their anger and to use it. Anger was an effective means to tamp down fear. Dirk ran down the column straightening lines, clamping soldiers on their shoulder plates. His encouragements and corrections played in a symphony with resounding calls for Telridge.

A trebuchet projectile was released, and Dirk braced himself against the wall as its destructive boom shook the castle. A moment later, he squinted through an arrow slit to find the crater Spense's explosive machine created. Dozens of faerie warriors lay sprawled, dead and dying, but more were ready to take their place.

Dirk muttered a curse and continued on to reconnoiter with his Knights. His father had taken command of the North Gate, while Dirk stayed to manage the battle with the faeries. Dirk lurched up one of the East towers.

His two best Knights—Sir Gervais and Lady Xendra to most, Gerry and X to him—waited his command. He breached the top of the stairs as another trebuchet launch shook the castle. *Wicked Winter.* Spense's toys were damn effective, but a little wearying on the nerves. Gerry and X met him with precision salutes.

"Ready?"

"Yessir."

Dirk met the steel-eyed gazes of his best soldiers, his closest friends. The time for teasing and joking was over. And they were ready to work. "Let 'em have it, then."

In choreographed union, both soldiers turned to retrieve incendiary arrows. In the space of three heartbeats, they let them fly. Dirk looked out over the stone wall and watched the high curves of the arrows' paths. It appeared that both shots did little more than excoriate already brown patches of earth on the far side of the waning river.

But appearances can be deceiving.

Dirk could barely make out the flickering flames licking their way along narrow corridors in the fields beyond the river. He lost track of the little sparks completely as they reached the edge of the faerie line— and their true targets.

Seconds later, earth erupted, and red flame rushed forth—extinguishing all that unnatural blue and the lives of a hundred enemy warriors.

Dirk nodded. "Well done."

Gerry and X accepted his thanks. He could see the ghost of a grin on Gerry's face. Dirk didn't blame him. Of all of the Telridge marksmen, Dirk knew only two archers who could have made those shots. And they were standing on this tower.

"You know your orders."

"Yessir."

"Then, hop on over to the next tower—let's give these bastards another opportunity to appreciate your exemplary skills."

Gerry's grin was nearly visible by this point. "Yessir."

Dirk clapped them both on the shoulder and turned away to rejoin his main archers. Two more trebuchets were released in his brief sprint. For all the damage his forces inflicted, still more faeries poured into the gaps.

And they were pushing forward.

Down the enemy surged over the banks of the river and into the shallow waters below. The Selden was Telridge's greatest barrier. Hundreds defeated it as if it wasn't even there. At the moment, it wasn't.

Dirk cursed. "Ready Archers!"

"Ready!"

"Hold…hold…" Dirk scrutinized the wild masses, stomping blasphemously across the wide riverbed and filling the channel like it was nothing more than a muddy swamp. Even if Spense's attempt to Claim the bridge had been successful, in the end, it was moot. The first of the shrieking faeries reached the opposite bank. "Now! Fire at will!"

Telridge rained down iron-tipped arrows on their foes. Potentially fatal if imbedded, but a poisonous graze was dangerous, too. Faerie warriors collapsed under the onslaught. His archers continued to release their arrows. More faeries fell. But still more came, filling the riverbed, pushing, pushing, forward.

Dirk tightened his jaw, grinding his teeth. His archers would never take them all. They would run out of arrows well before they ran out of targets. He would have to ready his forces for close combat. That was when it got bloody.

Another pair of explosions rocked the trampled meadows beyond the river, cleaving a set of wounds in what had become the faeries' rear guard. But it was not enough. Nowhere near enough.

He had to think of something else. They were spending all of Spense's incendiary machines. And would soon run out. Dirk bit down on these hard realizations—there was no use in him despairing. His job was to command, and to fight, and fight he would.

"Ready steel!"

His order was bellowed down the line followed by the sweet swish of metal swords zipping from their scabbards and the pounding of spears on stone.

"Sir! Look—sir! The river!"

Dirk peered through a break in the crenellations. The faerie warriors were frenzied, surging up the dry banks of the river. Some reached the near side. A few were taken by arrows. But many more slid back into the muddy channel, climbing over and on top of their faerie brethren.

Whatever held the waters back…was now failing. The River Selden was returning, and it looked like it wanted vengeance. Dirk choked on a curse, a sob, a prayer.

"Riders!" A scout from the Southeast tower shouted. Dirk whipped his head to where the young soldier pointed. Grabbing a scope, he lurched to the battlement and peered through.

Dirk let loose the curse. And snorted, "Spense."

He roared. His brother sat astride a speckled gray horse—definitely not from the castle stables—alongside a buttery yellow horse. Two females were with him.

One of them leapt from the horse and ran to the river's edge. She waved her skinny arms, as if she were conducting a musical performance. Something loud and crashing.

It looked like the little freckled faerie Spense ran off with. He'd seen her with Spense on the bridge—only this morning—appearing small and meek. But in front of the River Selden, she was a water wraith, a fierce god in miniature, and she commanded the waters—all of the river and more—to exact her justice.

Scores of Winter faeries crashed into the writhing waters. Violent and thrashing. And in a few terrible moments, over.

Dirk's army erupted in celebration. Shouts of "Telridge!" echoed along the walls.

Dirk shook his head and grinned. "You lucky little bastard."

Chapter 33

The faeries' icy, blue orbs of light were extinguished by the frothing river. Golden orange fire burned on the far side of the river—wreaking destruction upon the faerie warriors and pushing stragglers back into the forest.

Spense watched, open-mouthed at the mayhem. Dewy stood a hand-span away, her arms raised in quiet command, as calm as a stone in a stream. She *was* the rock. The waters had bent their will to hers. The winds created by fire and waves swirled around her still, small form, blowing her copper hair and cobwebby dress, but her body was rooted.

He started to speak. "De—"

Dewy whipped her head to face him. Her intense gaze choked the rest of her name from his lips and he couldn't look away. But then she blinked. The hard burning in her eyes blew away with the wind. Her arms dropped to her sides. Spense rushed to her as she began to sway. He caught her as her eyes shuttered and knelt down alongside her on the grassy banks of the river she commanded only moments before. Its waters calmed, finding its regular current. Little sprays lapped near Dewy's prone form while Spense held her. She did not stir.

"Is she alive?" Flora whispered.

Spense placed two fingers upon Dewy's neck. He

could feel the twittering of her heartbeat, fast but strong. He nodded to Flora. "Just exhausted. I think."

"I've never seen anything like that."

"Nor I." Spense looked around at the chaos Dewy's magic left behind. The muddy banks, the trampled marshland and meadows, and the dead. Hundreds. Blue-clad faeries and goblins lay strewn alongside the river or floated in its current. Spense moved his gaze back upon the tiny sleeping Fae in his arms. Her bird-like shoulder blades pressed against his chest. Her gossamer, stringy hair draped across his arm and onto the ground. Such a fragile creature did all *this*.

And he was grateful. She committed this horror on behalf of him and his people, when she very easily could have been amongst the warriors on the other side. Spense pulled her closer.

He met Flora's stare. She held the twitchy horses' reins. "I need to get her to safety…inside the castle…"

Flora startled. "Can I help?"

Spense nodded. "Take a horse and ride across the bridge to the main gate—on the southern side. Ask for Commander Dirk Ferrous. Tell him what you saw in the forest. And ask for healers."

"The Commander? You mean, the Prince? Why would he listen to me?"

Spense shifted Dewy into a cradled position and rose from the ground. "Tell him that you're with me. He's…my brother."

Stammering, Flora said, "Y-yes, sir. I mean—My Lord." She stumbled through a clumsy curtsy and turned to launch herself onto Buttercup.

"Not a lord," Spense muttered, but Buttercup was already pulling long strides away.

Chapter 34

Dirk uttered the command to redistribute troops and archers, providing support to the North Gate, and to fortify all other walls. He gave the soldiers on the East Gate their moment of victory, but no more than a moment. This battle was only half over. An enemy still marched on his castle.

A messenger came hurtling through the lines, his young face pink and chest heaving. "Report," Dirk barked.

"Yes, sir. There's a farm girl, sir, at the South Gate. Asking for you."

"What would I want with a farm girl?"

"She rode in with Master Spense, sir. Says the faerie is hurt. She also said she had information from the forest, but she'll only speak to you."

Dirk exhaled sharply through his nose. His little brother was full of surprises. "Come with me."

He took the stone steps down from the wall two at a time. Reaching the bottom, he found a captain. "Find some healers and meet me at the South Gate."

"Yes, sir."

Dirk strode through the ranks of assembled soldiers. Cheers increased as he passed officers, foot soldiers, and archers. "As you were," he grumbled.

By the time he reached the South Gate, the healers he'd ordered rushed to meet him. A brown-haired farm girl stood inside the portcullis but hadn't been let past the gate into the keep. Her hands fisted into the mane of a yellow mare. Despite the soldiers blocking her entrance, she held her head high, and met his gaze when he broke through the crowd.

"Make way," Dirk said to the nearest guard. The command echoed and soldiers repositioned until Dirk had an unimpeded path to the girl.

"M-My Lord." The girl bowed her head.

"You have a message for me."

She lifted her round brown eyes. "Yes, Commander. I rode with y-your brother from the forest. There was a faerie. She *did* something to the river. She's hurt or maybe just exhausted."

Dirk looked around the enclosed space, past the partially open port, and back to the girl. "Why aren't they with you, now?"

"He—Lord Spense—sent me on ahead. To get help."

A few muffled coughs escaped from his soldiers. "Quiet," Dirk snapped at the soldiers. To the girl, he said softly, "Spense is *not* a lord."

"Oh." The girl wrinkled her brow.

"Where is he now?"

Her face cleared. "Still by the river. He had the faerie, so it would be slow-going for him…"

Dirk nodded. He knew the precise location where Spense and his faerie had controlled the River Selden. "Healers—extraction team to the river."

He scanned his crowd of soldiers. "I need a half cohort of archers. Volunteers?"

Seven men and three women stepped forward—all marksmen.

"Good." He nodded. "On your way."

The crowd of rescuers hurried under the portcullis. The bowmen flanking them each had an arrow nocked and ready before the group passed under the stone archway.

One of his captains approached. "Archers, sir?"

Dirk looked at his officer. "Least amount of iron." The captain narrowed his eyes. "She's a faerie."

"Oh. Yes, sir."

Dirk shook his head, and stomped closer to the farm girl, still waiting with her horse. He signaled a nearby groomsman. "Your horse looks like she requires attention—you were riding hard?"

"Yes, My Lord. From our farm. I heard the wails and got away as fast as I could."

Dirk reached for the reins of the lathered mare. He handed them off to the groomsman. The beast was sweating and puffing out its breath but was otherwise in good health. Muscled and brushed clean. "We'll take care of her..." Dirk looked at the girl.

"Buttercup, sir."

"Buttercup. Of course." He patted the golden horse as she trotted past, nudging his groomsman's hand for another bit of the hard sugar cubes the man kept in his pocket. "And you?"

"I'm called Flora, My Lord," the girl mumbled. Her face was open and rose-cheeked, as healthy as her horse.

"Flora, you came from a farm? In the forest?"

"Yes, My Lord." Flora's eyes were bright and clear, urgent. "I saw the faeries and the fire, but I also saw human soldiers coming from the north, joining up with the faeries."

"Could you identify them?"

"Yes, sir. They were from Verden. I saw their banners. There is no mistaking the Crimson and Gold."

Dirk blanched, not daring to believe it. "No. There is not," he muttered.

Flora nodded. Her wide-eyed gaze met his. He knew that look, the pleading for assurances of safety. The expectation that he—at least someone who held his position of authority—could offer protection.

Not that she appeared to need it. Her windswept hair, her dusty work clothes, and the way her mare frothed showed evidence enough that she was a sound rider. She escaped the blazing forest ahead of hundreds of professional faerie soldiers. There were small scrapes on her knuckles and a minor cut on her face, but no more.

Dirk cleared his throat. "Thank you for...the information." He half-lifted his hand to the whip-cut on her face. "You can see to the cut in the infirmary..."

She touched her face with small, work-roughened fingers. "It's nothing, My Lord. Just a branch."

"Still...you never know when there may be some sort of infection..."

Flora creased her forehead. It had the effect of making her round, brown eyes, rounder—and browner.

"Thank you, My Lord. I'll see to it." The girl nodded a half-curtsy.

"Very good." He tapped the side of his leg with his thumb.

"My Lord, I wonder if..." She hesitated.

"Yes?"

"My family was at Market today. I just wonder if they might be here still?"

"We evacuated all Market patrons and vendors to the commons inside the keep."

"Might I…"

He gestured to a nearby officer. "Please escort the *lady* to the commons to look for…" Dirk turned back to face Flora.

"My Aunt Lily and Uncle Mason, sir. And cousin Rook." Another half-curtsy. "They were selling wool today."

"Right. Lieutenant?"

"Of course, sir. Right this way, *My Lady*." Flora picked up her linen skirts and hastened after the young officer toward the commons.

A small commotion diverted Dirk's attention. The healers returned, carrying a small figure on a pallet. The archers followed bringing a gray horse with them. The portcullis clanged as iron gears lowered the grate.

Spense ran alongside the faerie. His knees were muddy, tunic coated with road dust. His hair was a wild mass, matching his eyes. Dirk knew Spense's expressions of anger, frustration, mischief, and fear. This was something else.

The faerie lay senseless on the pallet. "Spense." Dirk laid a hand on his little brother's shoulder. Spense looked up, the panic clearing as he met Dirk's gaze. "Take her to the infirmary."

Spense nodded. A simple task. A thing he could do, to keep his hands moving, to clear his mind of the frantic, wild, spiraling thoughts that could so easily leave him lost and spluttering. "Thank you, Dirk."

"And Spense, make sure they take good care of her. We all owe her our lives."

Chapter 35

Spense tripped through the arched corridors of the castle, following as near as he could to Dewy on her stretcher. Healers and surgeons alike buzzed around the infirmary—a hive of orders shouting, wounded moaning. As soon as the healers laid Dewy out among the injured in the infirmary, they were off to recover their next patient.

Spense grabbed a clean cloth and basin from one of the healer's stations and knelt down by Dewy's side. Her face was flushed, making the freckles blend together in a speckled rosy patch. He placed the cool cloth on her forehead, smoothing away her hair with shaky fingers.

"You look like you need attention, yourself."

Spense didn't turn. "I'll be fine."

"Don't lie to your mother."

Spense swiveled his head. Cait's hands were fisted on her hips at the edges of a stained healer's apron.

"What are you doing here, Mum?"

"What do you think?" Cait edged Spense from Dewy's side, taking the cloth, rinsing it, and wringing it out in the basin. She washed Dewy's face and arms with gentle but efficient motions. The faerie let out a soft breath. Her pulse fluttered in her neck, light but strong.

"Careful, Mum. You won't be able to touch her skin...the Claiming spell..."

"Are you still here, then?" Cait asked. "Go on. Get

on with you. Find yourself a fresh tunic, and at the very least, wash your face. Let me tend to her."

Spense stammered out a response, more guttural than actual words.

Cait met his gaze and laid a hand on his forearm. "She'll be well looked after until you return. I'll make sure others understand…her restrictions."

"Th-thank you."

"Be off, then."

Spense huffed out a reluctant, chalk-dry laugh, and held up his hands, backing away. He turned into the corridor and had not taken more than a few uncertain steps when the castle trembled, bringing Spense to his already unsteady knees.

He waited for the shaking to stop and then pushed off the stone floor and made his way through the covered passageways. He hazarded no more than a glance at the stairwell that would lead him to his quarters. Instead, Spense wound through halls and common spaces, where hundreds of villagers took shelter. He squared his shoulders and marched past them, picking up speed as he joined with the dozens of soldiers mobilizing to the North Gate.

Chapter 36

Ferrous glanced out over the multitudes of soldiers approaching to reinforce the North Gate. He blanched when he saw a windswept mop of mud-colored hair weaving in and out of the disciplined ranks.

He turned and swept down the stone steps, meeting his younger son halfway. "Spense—what are you doing here?"

"I can help!"

"You shouldn't be h—"

Ferrous was cut off by a loud boom, followed by trembling granite. He crouched over Spense as flakes of stone debris showered them.

"What was that?" Ferrous shouted to the nearest officer.

"Verden, sir. War machines," the officer said and handed over his eye-glass. Ferrous took the proffered item and pulled himself up the stairs to peer through an arrow slit. Red and gold clad soldiers propelled their lines through vine-covered lands. They dragged wheeled towers with ropes attached to oxen. More men pushed the towers from behind.

One of the towers shook as it launched a goat-sized boulder at the north-side wall. Another rainstorm of dust and pebbles hit the men as the boulder broke apart on the wall. But the wall held.

Ferrous counted the Verdenian armored towers—

mobile catapults—and the wagons of ammunition trailing behind. The walls of the keep wouldn't hold forever. And fire wouldn't work against those steel plates.

"Sir!"

Ferrous whirled his head. He'd nearly forgotten that Spense was still with him. "Sir," Spense repeated. "I have an idea."

Ferrous was about to protest, but he recognized the glint in Spense's eye. It meant his mind was at work, which could be providential—or disastrous. He frowned and asked, "What do you have in mind?"

Spense nodded toward the vineyards that Verden's war machines were crushing. "Remember last year's carrot harvest?"

Chapter 37

It should have worked last harvest. It was *supposed* to work, the simple concoction to add a few more minerals to the soil and promote growth. It was *not* supposed to turn vegetables into giant, iron-hard monstrosities. Lord Ferrous had rolled his eyes and directed Spense to dispose of the potion, like every other disaster he'd created in the lab.

But Spense hadn't gotten around to it. And the potion had been sitting in a dusty corner of the basement and fermenting for months. The evidence was clear when he pulled the burlap off of the two vats, causing the three soldiers assigned to help him stagger back from the smell.

Together they carried the cauldrons up one level and across the courtyard, two people to a pot, and then carted them around the outer walls of the castle keep on the western side. They ran hunched over through the orchards until they reached the northwest boundary, where the trees gave way to the rows of orderly vines. Row upon row, each plant reaching for the next, all connected in one leafy entity.

Spense signaled one of the soldiers. The soldier grimaced at his brothers-in-arms but stepped up beside Spense at the pot. Together, they shuffled it across open space between the orchards and vineyards to the nearest vine, staying low. Using the vines as thin cover, Spense and the soldier tipped the cauldron. The potent mixture pooled onto the soil surrounding the grape plants. They dragged the large pot to the next and the next, until they emptied it all. The remaining two soldiers maneuvered their pot and repeated the action down the rows until they, too, emptied their cauldron. In total, Spense's thrown-together team poured the potion on only eighteen rows of vine, a small fraction, but they were the rows where Verden's soldiers were headed next, expecting to crush the green leaves and ripe fruit like confetti.

Spense gestured again to the soldiers, but they didn't require his instruction. They all ran stooped back into the trees, leaving the heavy cauldrons behind. He heard the first creaking of growing vines as he stumbled through the orchard and lifted his lips into a small smile. Grabbing a tree trunk, Spense ricocheted himself around to look.

The vines groaned and stretched, taking on a silvery sheen as they grew. Each plant reached to the next and the next, a metallic virus, infecting every leaf and hanging cluster of fruit. His failure of a potion worked its way through the vineyard, racing in neat lines to Verden's soldiers and war machines.

The spreading infection slowed as it approached the machines.

"Sweet Spring, come on…" Spense muttered, praying the potion hadn't yet run its course.

As if they heard his plea, the vines twisted and snaked around the first of the catapult towers, reaching up to cover the machines like garden lattices. Branches thickened and squeezed the metal and wood contraption as they wound up and around. Until—

The first tower erupted in a shower of splinters and

iron fragments. The Verdenians manning the machine leaped off into the roiling vines below. Their screams cut off as they hit the tangled earth. Spense watched open-mouthed as the next tower came down. And the next.

Verden soldiers pushed the towers at the end of the line forward, trying to escape the deadly vines, but the winding plants formed a trip line. Instead of rolling over tender leaves and fruit, the remaining towers toppled forward, crashing to the ground.

Spense's three companions snorted beside him in surprise. He could make out distant cheers from the castle's battlements. His mouth formed a full grin, as the vines continued to do battle and Verden soldiers ran yelling from the field.

And the plants grew and grew, up and over their kill, making leafy mounds across the fields. Tiny silver grapes expanded to the size of plums, popping from the vines and shooting out over their massacre. Spense's hands slackened beside him, stupefied at the terrible destruction his over-ripe potion caused.

"Get down!" one of the soldiers yelled.

Spense swiveled his head to the soldier. "Wh—"

Something thudded against his temple, knocking him to the ground and aborting his question. Spense's lids became heavy. There was sky above him and orchard leaves. Round, fruity projectiles made sinusoidal arcs overhead.

And then black closed in.

Chapter 38

Spense hovered near the window of his small chamber, looking out toward the destroyed fields and vineyards, the broken detritus of Verdenian war machines, now littering the ruined fields and scorched patches where his inventions left blackened scars. His head throbbed and his vision was still spotty.

"I'm pleased to see you about, son."

Spense startled—it seemed his hearing was affected as well, as he hadn't heard his father enter. He turned from the window and nodded a quick bow. "Thank you, My Lord."

His father scrutinized his face, the bandages, the dark circles. Spense knew he was a mess. He'd woken in the healers' rooms, surrounded by Telridgian soldiers and townsfolk alike, been scrubbed and bandaged and sent off as soon as he was fully conscious, in order to clear space for more patients.

He wasn't sure that he wanted to be. Waking and seeing the aftermath of battle felt like more than he could stomach. And yet here he stood, alongside so many others, taking another breath and another. They'd won. This was what victory looked like.

"Something on your mind?"

Spense met his father's gaze. "I'm not so sure I feel…pleased, sir."

"Ah." Ferrous closed the door softly and crossed the

small space.

Spense turned away from his father's scrutiny, back toward the window, and dragged a sleeve across his damp upper cheek.

Ferrous waited as Spense composed himself and said, "The first battle you witness…it stays with you. I wish I could offer you words of comfort, boy. There are none. It never gets easier."

Spense shuttered his eyes. "Then—how do you do it?"

Ferrous looked down at his scarred hands. Hands that Spense knew had once been covered in blood. "You work—with everything you have—to make sure that there are as few as possible in the future."

"So what happened this time?"

"I failed." His father lowered himself to Spense's narrow bed. He opened his hands, offering his palms up. "The words I'd meant to hold off this type of aggression, seem to have had the opposite effect."

"I don't understand."

"I've angered the Winter faeries—King Lumine, in particular."

"That doesn't explain Verden."

"King Tempra is an opportunist—always has been—and a chance to take advantage when Telridge is weakened. That's a temptation he'd not be likely to pass up."

"So, this—" Spense waved out his window at the broken lands, bloodied and blemished. "It's not over."

He met Spense's gaze, and Spense knew that in this moment, their frowns matched, and their brows drew together with the same concern. "No. It's not."

Chapter 39

"Enter," Ferrous said.

Dirk pushed through the door of his study. There were fresh scars on his son's hands. "Sir." Dirk nodded a salute. "It was a rout, My Lord. They've fled into the hills and White Rocks. I've already begun assembling a campaign."

Ferrous narrowed his eyes. "You've done well, Dirk."

"Thank you, sir. If I may…"

Ferrous waved his older son to continue.

Dirk looked as if he'd swallowed something rancid. "I realize that more than military strategy may be needed…in some circumstances."

"Magnanimous of you," Ferrous said. "Nice to see you recognizing the value in the magical arts."

Dirk released a huff of air.

"But of course, there is more than just magic available to us as a resource."

"I don't follow, My Lord."

Ferrous rose from his desk to his window, where he also had a view of the devastated fields Spense gazed upon earlier. He would give half his kingdom to ensure that his people were not made to suffer again as they had today. And he felt the loss of life for the poor foot soldier from Verden who maybe joined the army to better his station and care for his family. He thought of the silver-haired faeries drowned in the River Selden for doing no more than following the orders of their Fae lords. He wanted it to end.

"I was thinking of diplomacy."

"Indeed." Dirk broke from his military stance and rubbed his jaw. "What did you have in mind, My Lord?"

Ferrous heard the skepticism in his son's voice. It was about to grow exponentially.

"I was thinking that your younger brother has made a fortunate alliance with a faerie. Fae actually. Perhaps, it is time for his duties to expand."

"Spense? He's dead on his feet, more bruise than boy. You must be joking—and isn't he the reason we are in this conflict? With whatever happened with that faerie?"

Ferrous slowly closed his eyes, and carefully opened them, meeting his son's demanding gaze. He didn't want to be the cause of disappointment, but there was nothing for it. "No, son. Spense is not the reason we are in conflict. I am."

Dirk all but spluttered.

Ferrous waved to a chair facing his desk. "You better sit down."

Seated across from his scowling son, Ferrous saw the ruler he would one day become. He had passion—sometimes a temper—but he also had the patience that grew with responsibility. Dirk waited with a controlled forbearance, and Ferrous remembered the feeling of sitting before his old tutor, Professor Stone, as a young child when he spilled ink on his master's robes. And, as in that circumstance, he might as well get on with his confession as it served no one any good to delay.

"You know of our strained relationship with Lumine

and the Winter Fae." Dirk nodded. His scowl grew deeper. "He asked for aid…in something of a personal quest. I denied him. And have gravely insulted him in doing so."

"But what about Verden?"

"Your brother asked the same question." Ferrous waved dismissively. "You know the Verdenian king as well as I do."

"Tempra's a greedy bastard." Dirk snorted derisively.

"An opportunist. Yes. It would appear he did not deny the Winter King."

"This…personal quest…it's enough to go to war over?"

"For Lumine, it is. Today, I fear was just the beginning."

Dirk fell back in his chair, nonplussed. "I can't see how Spense is going to be of any help. He's not a soldier. And he's badly injured—I wouldn't send one of my Knights out in his condition, and they're trained for it."

"Never-the-less Spense *must* remove the Claiming and he will need faerie help to do it—this I am sure. I am hoping that he can convince Lady Radiant to be merciful and renew our alliance."

"You're putting a lot of weight on him." Dirk pointed an accusing finger. The feeling of reprimand returned, and Ferrous lifted the corner of his lip.

"Indeed, we all are."

Chapter 40

First, she noticed the sharp antiseptic smell, masking the coppery tang of blood and the rank odor of river dirt. Then she heard voices. Cool whispers and searing moans. Nothing in between.

Dewy opened her eyes. Colors swirled around her, attaching themselves to forms that grew into distinct objects. She rolled her head to the side. She was lying on a human bed, with knobby linens smushed under her head and spread over her body. A figure sat on a stool near her cot. His bandage-wrapped head was in his hands.

Spense.

Dewy let out a shuddering breath. Spense dropped his hands and looked up.

"You're awake."

"Where am I?" Dewy asked, her voice rasping and dry.

"You're in the healing rooms of the castle."

She pushed herself up with her hands and looked around at the long hall. Humans were stretched out on cots in neat rows. Bright morning light shone through windows high on the stone and timber walls.

"H-how do you feel?"

Dewy frowned. She felt…spent, as if she'd been squeezed and wrung and twisted until there was no life force left in her. No water.

"Tired," she said. "Have I been asleep long?"

Spense nodded. "About a day. Do you remember what happened?"

Dewy closed her eyes. The River. The faerie warriors. Her heart stuttered. She'd *killed* them.

"You saved us," Spense whispered.

"What happened...after?"

Spense started to speak, cleared his throat, swallowed, and started again. "The remaining faeries retreated, joined up with Verden, but...Telridge pushed them back."

Dewy tilted her head. He was keeping something from her. "What happened to you? Are you injured?"

He lifted his fingers to his temple and huffed a small, dry laugh. "My plan to help took on a life of its own," he said, shrugging. "I missed the retreat, but I heard that Dirk's forces chased stragglers into the woods all the way to the foothills of the White Rocks."

"Dirk?"

"He's...my brother." Spense's cheeks turned pinkish. "Half-brother. Commander of Telridge, under my father."

Oh. That sounded important. Dewy had no context for human social or governmental structures. It had never mattered to her, and didn't affect her daily life in The Vail, although her aunt tried to impress upon her the importance of understanding the politics of neighbors, allies and rivals alike.

"What happens now?" she asked.

Spense chewed on his lower lip and looked down at his hands. "My father has a job for me," he said and then looked up to meet her gaze. "And you, if you are willing."

Dewy felt her chest squeezing. It was uncomfortable but not constricting. "Are you asking or commanding? I can't tell."

Spense blanched. "I—"

"Sweet Spring! Why didn't you alert me that the dear girl was awake, Spense?" A petite woman carrying a basin full of supplies hustled over to Dewy's cot. The woman set the bin down and patted a cool cloth over Dewy's inflamed cheeks. Her movements were quick and firm. Her hands, efficient. Working hands.

"Mum—" Spense said.

Dewy looked closer at the tiny woman. She had brown hair and eyes, with the same warmth and openness as Spense's. Her skin was the color of mature acorns, a shade or two darker than Spense. *Mum?*

"Really, son." The woman sorted items from her bin and laid them out on Dewy's cot.

"Mum, wait." Spense laid his hand on his mother's to still her busy fingers, then turned to Dewy, his eyes wide and imploring. "I am *not* commanding you."

Dewy released a breath as the tightness in her chest relaxed. "Oh…"

"I should hope not!" Spense's mother pointed imperiously toward the exit. "Out with you. I have a patient to attend to."

Dewy looked back and forth between Spense and his mother. He shrugged and turned away. She felt a twinge in her belly as he drifted to the open doorway. Even if their conversation had been awkward, even if it hadn't quite gotten started, she liked having him present. He was solid and kind, someone she could lean into when the world was disorienting and new. When it was filled with cold stone and iron.

"There dear," the woman said as she renewed her ministrations. "You're flushed. This will help." The woman rose. "Let me get you spring water and maybe something to eat."

"Thank you. I don't suppose you have any...bread?"

The woman lifted the corners of her lips. "Of course." She turned to leave, but stopped herself and said, "You can call me Cait."

"Thank you...Cait." Dewy watched Spense's mother stride out the door. There was kindness in her—like Spense—but more purposeful. Dewy settled herself back onto the cot and pulled the linen sheet around her. In The Vail, she had attendants, but they didn't fuss over her, and they almost never smiled. This was a strange world that she had come to inhabit.

Chapter 41

Spense wandered into the courtyard, where scores of Telridgians were doing their part to recover from the attack. Villagers, farmers, and castle-dwellers raked debris and hauled away chunks of wood and stone, broken from carts, walls, or weakened support pillars. The remnant haze of smoke still hovered over everything, sharp and dry. The old huddled in groups comforting the young. Those who'd received injuries not severe enough for the healers' attention were tended to by castle workers.

Some folks glanced his way and nodded. Others looked at him askance. He understood their wariness. He'd used a spell to fight the Verdenians and invited a *Fae* to help him. Not Telridge's usual ally. He understood their biases. But he knew he would do it all over again.

"Spense."

He recognized Dirk's bark and looked up. His half-brother handed something to an officer and strode to meet him in the open courtyard.

"Dirk...umm, hi. My Lord." Spense scuffed his foot on the cobblestones, waiting for further accusations and reprimands from his brother.

"You are coming from the healing rooms?" Dirk asked instead.

"Uh...yeah." Spense gestured at his head, still

throbbing a day after he'd been knocked out by a giant iron grape.

"Have you spoken to...the faerie?"

Spense nodded. "She just woke up. My mum is attending her."

"And have you explained our plan?"

"There wasn't really time."

"We don't have the luxury of time. We need to execute this immediately. And *you*"—Dirk pointed at Spense's chest and scowled—"have to make it happen."

"I know, Dirk." Spense batted away Dirk's hand, and stepped toward his brother, his hands fisting at his sides. "I was there, remember? The attack? You weren't the only one fighting back. And maybe you don't remember, but that faerie in there saved us, so you think you can give her a little room?"

Spense didn't know where his anger was coming from. He didn't make a habit of challenging Dirk—that never ended well for him—but the events of the last days overwhelmed him. The Claiming, the attack, the faces of grief filling the castle, and Dewy—what was he supposed to do with *her*?

In the two days since she'd come into his life, he'd ruined hers. She was banished from her people and recuperating after defending his. He wasn't sure she would recover at all when she first collapsed. She used a tremendous amount of magic and Spense knew what that kind of drain could do to a person—even the highest of Fae. All because of his botched spell.

Dirk held up a placating hand, though his scowl deepened. "Do what you need to do. Heal up as best as you can." He grimaced and ducked his head, almost as if he regretted what he was asking, as if he cared.

"But...get her on board. You're leaving tomorrow after sunrise. My soldiers and I depart imminently. I expect the next time I see you will be at our camp." Dirk spun on his heel and clomped away.

Spense let out a breath he hadn't realized he'd been holding. The almost confrontation and the rare show of concern left him feeling deflated. He shook out his hands and crossed the courtyard, finding the steps that would lead him down, away from other people and their sadness and judgment and demands. When he reached his laboratory, it seemed smaller than it had only a few hours before. Quaint. Juvenile. The world could not be contained in his shelves of books. It was much bigger and more violent than the history texts implied. When the historians spoke of war, they never mentioned the blood stains that had to be washed out, the smells that would not blow away with the wind, or the destruction that ordinary people repaired—his people, Telridgians.

Spense shook out his hands again and pulled out supplies, ingredients for basic potions, his notebook. He would have to get a change of clothes from his quarters, maybe something for Dewy, too. What did faeries wear for travel? He grabbed his leather satchel and headed back up the stairs. He had work to do.

Chapter 42

Dewy watched Spense from Lord Ferrous's study window. His clean scent lingered around the floral, feminine curtains. The humans in the castle had been kind, inviting her into their personal spaces. Spense's mother—Cait—comforted Dewy in practical ways, bringing cool water and warm broth made from strained vegetables and herbs. Dewy marveled at the woman's determined proficiency, attending to patients in the healing rooms while keeping the kitchens running elsewhere. And she brought that delicious bread.

Lord Ferrous visited her and invited her to his study. While she found his manner brusque, he'd shown no disrespect, and even offered Fae-worthy hospitality. He honored her—an outsider—with his attentions. Before, she might have been considered a visiting dignitary, but banishment meant that she had no importance whatsoever. Yet Lord Ferrous behaved as if she were an honored guest.

Together, they watched the pink and golden light creeping over the horizon, lighting the faraway figure of Spense as he sat upon the bridge over the River Selden. Sunlight gilded Spense's brown hair copper. She could see his long fingers splayed out over the bridge's planks, youthfully awkward, and yet still elegant. She couldn't hear him but saw little puffs of chilled air escape his lips as he spoke the words of the spell to claim the bridge.

Properly this time.

Dewy studied Lord Ferrous as he stared out the wide window, scrutinizing the actions of his son. He bore little resemblance to Spense, not in his iron-colored hair and eyes, nor his large frame and powerful bearing, but right there—his chin when he frowned—that was just like Spense.

She returned her gaze to Spense. The sun was nearly up, and Spense had completed his spell. She could tell by the way his shoulders relaxed and tension rolled in waves off of his arms, out into the world, to dissipate and disappear, until Spense was a still being at one with the solid bridge. She recognized the sensation, felt it at her core, in her bones, that deep knowledge and understanding. The knowing without knowing. The feeling without words. Slowly, gently, he drew his hands from the wooden planks and laid them to rest on the tops of his knees. Two deep, cleansing full-belly breaths— she breathed along with him, as if she could taste the water-filled air out on that bridge.

Spense pushed himself from his seated position. He looked toward the distant study window and nodded. His father echoed the gesture before turning away from the window.

"What now?" Dewy whispered. She been asked to accompany Spense to the land of Summer—where she was no longer princess, but an exile and outcast. Useless as emissary or guide, as anything more than a human's companion. Perhaps they didn't realize how severe her demotion had been or what it meant.

Lord Ferrous fixed his steely gaze upon Dewy. "Now, my dear, you begin a journey, and I pray that Grace be with you both on your way."

"Upon us all," she murmured. And she grabbed on to that thin strand of hope, that reminder that Grace covered the world, even when she was alone and helpless and a stranger.

"Yes," he agreed. "Upon us all."

Chapter 43

Spense adjusted his pack as he and Dewy trekked along the market road. It would be more than half a day's walk before they reached Dirk's soldiers, if they cut through closed forest. He wasn't used to balancing a weapon with his full satchel. The bow and quiver were beginning to dig in on his left side.

Dewy skipped along beside him. She'd been given an extra set of human clothes along with other provisions in a soft linen pack, though she frowned in confusion when his mother first offered them.

And she'd agreed—without a direct command—to lead Spense to The Vail, where he was to plead for mercy and help in releasing Dewy, and act as emissary of Telridge. Ambassador. A titled position. And a huge responsibility.

Meanwhile, Dirk had an even larger task as he continued to defend Telridge with his military force. Spense tried to remember that when he felt daunted by his own, and his head pounded with his still-healing injury.

Spense fidgeted with his straps and rubbed his thumb over the pad of his first finger. There was a tiny button of dried blood where he'd pricked it. When he performed the Claiming spell on the bridge, he used blood instead of saliva and mixed a drop of his with his father's and Dirk's. It would strengthen the spell, and the best hope he could give his family and his people, if his attempt to reach The Vail and convince the Summer Fae to help failed.

But he couldn't fail. Not this time.

"Where are your thoughts?" Dewy smiled at Spense, her face lighting up like sunshine. "You look...crinkly."

Spense blew out an almost laugh. "I have a little on my mind. Maybe you hadn't noticed."

"Yes, I know. I do, but..."

He looked over at her bright, freckled face. Dewy didn't really do dejected—even after exhausting her magic and her body all for his sake, a human she was regrettably attached to. "What is it?"

She pulled the straps of her bag up and then let them go. "Is it not understood by humans that sadness doesn't lend itself well to...speed?"

"Pardon me?"

"Or are humans generally very slow walking?"

Spense thought that they'd been moving at a good clip. Maybe not by faerie standards.

"Oh! I know!"

Spense squinted as Dewy ran—flew—through the forest trails. She ducked in and out of trees. He cursed under his breath and doubled his pace, barely keeping sight of her lithe figure. For a moment she disappeared altogether and a heartbeat later reappeared by his side with a delicate flower pinched between her fingers.

"Sweet Spring!" he yelped.

She giggled.

When he restarted his heart, he asked, "What is that?"

She cocked her head at the little blue-purple-pink flower, considering. "A pea-lily, of course."

"Is it supposed to give me speed and endurance?"

"No, Spense." Dewy found the buttonhole of Spense's overcoat and tucked the tiny flower into it. "It's pretty." Satisfied with her work, she shook her head and laughed before bolting ahead again.

Spense started after her. She let him catch up to her. "How far to The Vail?"

"At *this* pace?" She blew out her breath with an unfaerie-like raspberry. "Who knows?"

Spense rolled his eyes. "You bring the dew to Telridge, right? How long does it normally take you to make it there and back every dawn?"

"Almost no time at all...but I am a faerie...and you are not."

Spense scowled. What she might have meant as a statement of fact came out sounding a lot like an insult. "Have you ever carried something back with you?"

"All the time."

"Really?" Spense brightened.

She stopped to face him. "I have brought back flowers, acorns, leaves—samples of my work." She laid a freckled hand on his chest. Spense felt his chest warming and heart beating faster. "I can't carry *you*."

"Uh...why not?"

She tilted her head and shrugged. "You're too big."

"Oh." He tried to imagine a magical solution but couldn't. "I guess it's just as well. We're meant to rendezvous with Dirk—"

Dewy clamped a hand over his mouth. She held one finger to her lips. Her eyes widened. Spense strained his ears but heard nothing. In the next second, he stood alone on the market road with nothing but the remnants of Dewy's floral scent left behind. *Wicked Winter. Not again.*

He bit his lip and strained his eyes to find her. He'd taken a fraction of a step when an arrow whistled past his left ear. Spense dropped to the ground, and scrambled to the banks of the road, scanning for any type of cover. He scurried crab-like to a fallen log but only made it halfway when a figure loomed before him, wearing crimson fighting leathers and pointing a sharp-looking sword at his neck. A Verdenian soldier.

Spense lifted his satchel up as protection, but the soldier batted it away with his sword. A few items fell out.

He looked up. The Verdenian's lips parted, showing his teeth. It wasn't a smile. "Dangerous woods, these days," the soldier said. Three of his companions emerged from the woods. One of them had a bow strung and ready.

Spense closed his eyes. He placed one hand on the ground, trying to steady his mind as it zigzagged through hundreds of unhelpful thoughts. Frustration at the spilled contents of his satchel. Worry for Dewy. His mind skipped to his work, and he remembered a spell he'd been working on days ago. It was so close to being right. Strange to imagine that he wouldn't get to perfect it because he'd been killed by Verdenian scouts in his own blooming country.

At least he would die with Dewy's sweet scent in his nostrils. It grew stronger as he imagined her sun-kissed face. Not a bad last thought, all things considered.

The arrow left the bowman's fingers, its wood whistling a last song.

And missed him completely.

Spense opened an eye. He saw sunshine. And *she*

was wrapped around the bowman pressing a carved hawthorn knife into the man's throat.

"Dangerous woods, indeed," Dewy hissed.

The lead soldier—the one with the sword still pointed at Spense's chest—laughed. "I think you're outnumbered, faerie."

Dewy narrowed her eyes and looked at Spense, calculating. "I think you have miscounted, soldier. I am no common faerie." To Spense, she mouthed the words, *Do something*.

He was a step ahead of her.

Spense squeezed his fingers around the cluster of lavender blossoms and single nightingale feather that had fallen from his satchel. He closed his eyes and whispered the words to the spell he'd been working on.

"Wuz going on?" the Verdenian soldier asked. The tip of his sword wavered.

Spense repeated the words. He heard a thump and then another.

"Hey…sshtop…thaaaat…"

Spense didn't stop. A third body fell and then a fourth. He opened his eyes, just as a freckled fifth began to sway. He lurched towards Dewy and grabbed her shoulders, keeping her upright.

"Dewy."

She blinked slowly, languorously.

"Dewy, stay awake."

Her eyes shot open. "What happened? What did you do?"

"Sleeping spell. I've been working on a lullaby for one of the miners' children. Colic." Spense shrugged. "I thought it was worth a try."

One of the scouts released a gusty snore.

Dewy laughed. "Seems to work."

"For now." Spense rubbed his jaw. "I haven't been able to get it to last through the night, yet."

"What should we do with them?" Dewy waved toward the slumbering soldiers.

Spense assessed. He knew he wouldn't be able to drag them all the way to Dirk's camp. "Help me tie them up?" Dewy used the knife to cut a vine, thanking it.

"Where did you get the blade?"

"Your mother." Dewy shook her head as if he'd missed something obvious.

Mum is just full of surprises.

They went to work wrapping vines around the soldiers' ankles and wrists, while divesting them of any weapons. She pursed her lips and considered the slumbering Verdenians.

"I think I can do one better." Dewy winked at Spense and laid her hands on the trunk of a nearby cedar. It creaked in response to her touch. The earth shuddered beneath their feet as roots pushed their way through, shedding clods of dirt and rocks.

Spense stepped back from the powerful cedar as it reformed its roots and hollowed out a portion of its trunk to create a cage around the soldiers. Dewy reached up to tickle low hanging bows. "Thank you, my friend," she whispered.

He stared wonderingly at Dewy. No common faerie, indeed.

"All tucked in now." She patted the trunk of the cedar.

Spense grimaced. "We...uh...we should get to Dirk."

Dewy gestured to the market road and grinned. "Lead the way."

Chapter 44

Dewy flitted through trees, dusting dry boughs with a few drops as she passed. Spense practiced a tiresome slogging he called "double-timing." She would hate to imagine what single-timing might be. He was all red and swollen, and little droplets trickled down his pink face. He pushed out air from his mouth in regular whooshes.

"Not...much...farther," he panted.

"Oh, no, not much. I have heard your brother's horses stamping for several minutes, now."

They reached the edge of the Telridgian camp and were halted by a pair of guards. Dewy shied away from their steel, peering around Spense as he bent over, his hands pressed to his knees. He sucked in mouthfuls of air.

"Sern...good to...see you," Spense said in between breaths.

"And you, Master Spense. We were told not to expect you until the afternoon," the older of the two soldiers said while signaling a quick two finger salute. The man was stout and gruff, salt and pepper in his dark hair and beard, but he treated Spense well and that warmed Dewy to him.

"We made good time," Spense said, straightening up.

The man—Sern—clapped him on the shoulder. "Ay, that you did!" He leaned to wink at Dewy. She took a step back.

Another soldier arrived. This one wore a helmet with ostentatious markings. Spense stiffened. "Sir Saylor." Spense nodded.

"Master Spense, the Commander has ordered you be brought to his presence immediately upon arrival." This soldier had none of Sern's friendly camaraderie. Dewy decided she didn't care for him, or his hat.

Spense nodded. "Lead the way, sir."

"Your companion—"

"Goes where I go." Spense traded glares with the soldier.

After a moment, Saylor shrugged. "I'll let the Commander sort it out. This way."

They wove through canvas tents pitched in neat rows. Dewy wondered at the structures. Humans were so insistent on sleeping under roofs they built themselves that they ignored the lovely canopy the tall cedars provided all around them—but she supposed she'd have to get used to it. Gone were her days of sleeping under the lacy bows of a cedar speckled with starlight.

Dewy clung to Spense as they walked, wrapping her hands around his elbow and forearm. Soldiers stood at attention as their party passed by. Sir Saylor nodded reciprocal salutes as he marched through their small groupings.

When they approached a larger canvas structure adorned with Telridgian flags, their party halted. A female guard holding a bow blocked their entrance.

"Lady Xendra," Saylor said. "Please inform His Lordship that his...brother has arrived."

The flaps at the front of the tent whipped open and a brutish-looking soldier stepped out. "Don't bother, X,

I heard him." He had the same color hair as Spense. His chin frowned in exactly the same way. And that ended the similarities. Where Spense was lean, his brother Dirk was heavy with muscle. His bearing said soldier and unapproachable, where Spense's said open and welcoming. Dewy shrunk back, leaning into Spense.

Dirk scanned the pair up and down. "So you made it."

Spense nodded.

"Come in then." Dirk held the flaps of the tent open. He glanced at Saylor who made as if to follow. "X, why don't you join us? Saylor can take watch."

Dewy followed Spense as he ducked in. Dirk stomped into the canvas-covered space behind them. The woman took up a guard position just inside the flaps. Dewy scanned the tent interior. Dirk had set up a table and chair, both simple and spare. In the corner was a human cot, blankets neatly folded on top of a small chest at the end. Several more camp chairs were folded and stacked against the near wall. A map was laid out in the middle of the table held down on each of the four corners with silvery metal weights. The utilitarian tent was far from Spense's cluttered, cozy house in the forest, even further from the twining elegance of The Vail.

Dirk positioned himself at the head of the table, leaning on his fists. "Report."

Spense and Dewy both looked at him blankly.

Dirk rolled his eyes. "Spense, that means...tell me something. What happened to you? How did you get here so fast?"

"Oh!" Spense let out a nervous laugh. "Right. Umm...all right...well, we ran most of the way—faeries are fast, in case you didn't know. And I should tell you we came across some Verdenian soldiers on the way—"

"You what?"

"Four scouts, I think."

"Where?"

Spense shifted to the table and looked at the map. "Not far—right about here." He pointed to a curving line with the words *Market Road* written in blocky script. Dewy frowned as she translated the human map into faerie. There might have been a few more natural landmarks if it were to have any real meaning. Spense glanced at Dewy to confirm.

She considered. "Tall, tall cedars and vines."

Dirk nodded. "I think I know the area. What happened?"

Spense fidgeted. "I put them to sleep with a spell, and we tied them up with vines."

Dirk stared silently for four heartbeats, while Dewy tried to interpret the silence. He broke it with a loud guffaw and reached over to clap Spense's shoulder with his oversized hand. "You always manage to surprise me, little brother."

The corners of Spense's mouth turned up.

"Hold on a moment." Dirk whipped around to the front of the table. "X, can you get Saylor in here?"

The guard nodded and opened the flaps of the tent. A moment later, the soldier Saylor—and his hat— entered. "Sir?"

Dirk scribbled a few lines on parchment while Saylor waited. *Scratch, scratch* went the pencil. Dewy marveled at Dirk's implementation of the delicate instrument in his large fist. He paused and considered his note. *Scratch.* He nodded and folded the paper. "Here you are, Saylor. Please deliver this to the Knights on watch. Tell them to prepare a brig."

"Right away, sir." Saylor saluted.

Dirk waved him off by returning the gesture. Once Saylor exited, he turned back to face Spense and Dewy. "So, we should celebrate your heroic defeat and brave capture of Verdenian soldiers! Join me for dinner?"

Dewy waited and watched Spense. His face morphed through several emotions, as if he couldn't decide how to feel about the invitation. She wondered if humans had the option to refuse offers of hospitality. For faerie-kind, unless one meant to create insult, invitations were never refused, especially among the noble Fae.

"Yes, of course," Spense said. "Thank you."

Dewy breathed a sigh of relief.

"Good." Dirk grinned. "We'll get you set up for the night, too—don't worry—nothing but Telridge's finest military lodgings!" He laughed.

Spense chuckled nervously. Dewy looked at the brothers sideways. She didn't get the joke. Must be a human thing.

Chapter 45

It was almost civil. Two brothers sitting down to a meal with a few close friends. Never mind that the friends were officers under Dirk's command and Spense's guest was magically required to keep his company.

Dewy chatted with Lady Xendra, remarking upon the many oddities of human behavior—apparently they didn't use tablecloths in The Vail—when the camp stewards brought in the meal. There were bowls and platters filled with simple fare. Potatoes and other root vegetables. Crusty bread, of course. A weak ale. All laid out on the long plank table.

And then Spense saw the venison.

Piles of sliced and steaming roast, carrying a wild, gamey fragrance. His mouth filled with water—but not in anticipation—in nauseated panic. He darted his gaze to Dewy. Her conversation with Lady Xendra came to a quick halt, and she launched herself back from the table, knocking her chair over in haste.

She blanched and pointed one accusing finger at the table. "That's...that's...murdered doe."

Before Spense could rise from his seat, Dewy tore through the tent flaps and was gone.

"What just happened?" Dirk looked at Spense. The Ferrous Frown emerged.

"You...uh...served meat."

"And?"

"She doesn't eat meat, Dirk. I don't think that any faeries do."

"You're joking."

Spense shook his head. "They're the caretakers of the forest. Its creatures are...their friends."

"Wicked Winter—how was I supposed to know that?" Dirk rolled his eyes and threw up his hands.

"Maybe I should go."

"Yes, fine. We'll...fix this." Dirk waved at the table. "Wait—what *do* they eat?"

Spense paused at the opening of the commander's tent. "My mum gave her raw fruits and vegetables, nuts, that type of thing. And she likes bread."

With a rueful nod, Dirk dismissed him.

The layout of the small camp was like a well-ordered maze—corridors of tented structures lined up in straight precision. Spense questioned the guards on duty and any other soldiers out for the evening. The sight of a faerie girl sprinting through camp didn't go unnoticed. They directed him to the area reserved for stables.

When he found her, she was whispering to a golden horse, stroking its nose and broad neck. The mare nuzzled into her, as she fed it a handful of oats.

"Thinking of starting a mutiny?" Spense asked.

She cut a glare over to him. "Possibly."

"That was a joke." Spense took a step closer and patted the horse's flank. "Don't worry—the horses are not in danger. I promise."

"You say that, but how can I be sure?"

"I guess you'll have to trust me." Spense held up a hand. "Not command. A choice."

Dewy peered at him—her grassy green eyes

narrowing and searching. "Thank you."

"Always."

She turned from the mare to the gelding in the next stall and murmured to it, working her way to each animal and the next, offering oats and calming whispers.

"I'm sorry...about earlier. I should've told them." Spense plucked a bit of straw from the mane of the golden mare and rolled it between his fingers.

"I suppose you can't be expected to think of *everything*."

Spense tilted his head. *Is she teasing me?* "Do you think you'd be willing to return to dinner? Dirk said he'd take care of the...well, you know..."

Dewy sighed, low and slow. "I suppose I must."

"No...I didn't mean...you don't *have* to."

"According to the customs of faeries, I should accept your brother's hospitality—barbaric and ignorant as it may be."

"That's...umm...thank you." Spense tossed the straw to the ground, made his way down the line to her, and offered his hand. "Shall we?"

Spense received more than a few questioning glances as he strolled through camp with a faerie on his arm. He wasn't used to the attention and didn't know how Dirk could stand it—all those eyes. It made his skin twitchy. When they returned to the command tent— Dewy clinging to his arm—Dirk's stewards had removed all evidence of their earlier meal, and even laid out a selection of raw vegetables and fruits—a rare commodity in an army camp. She nibbled the offerings but continued to cast accusing glances toward Dirk while he entertained his officers.

Dirk's officers—supposed Knights—made not-so-subtle comments to Spense regarding the possibilities of having Claimed a faerie. *You mean she'll obey any command you give her? That's convenient.* Nudge. Wink. He tried not to gag and prayed Dewy didn't hear or didn't comprehend their innuendos.

He thanked Grace when a voice outside the command tent interrupted the conversation, demanding audience with Dirk: "No. Don't put me off. Something's going on with the horses. The Commander needs to know."

Spense recognized the voice—not one of the gruff hands who'd worked in the castle stables for years. This was female. And young.

"Let her in, Saylor," Dirk said.

A young woman boldly pushed through the tent flaps. It was Flora—the farm girl they'd met in the forest. She was about to address Dirk and the seated officers when Dewy leaped up and ambushed the girl.

"I'm ever so thankful to see you—you've no idea what these brutal men can be like."

Flora gently took a step back from Dewy's enthusiastic presence. "Believe me—I know." She smiled. "They're not so bad, once you get used to them."

Dirk cleared his throat. "You had news, Flora?"

"Yes, My Lord." Flora turned to face him. "It's the horses, sir. They're behaving strangely."

"Strangely, how?"

"Unusually docile. Even the most spirited. I was worried they might've been drugged, but..." She gave Dewy a questioning glance.

"Oh no! I would never introduce poisons or potions into the bodies of my friends."

"Your...who?" Dirk rose from the table and turned

to Spense. "She was in the stables?"

Spense opened his mouth to confirm, his arms already rising to a shrug, when Dewy said, "I sang them each a lullaby—to soothe them—you know they're not quite comfortable away from their homes. Who among us are, really?"

His stomach tightened. *I did that*, Spense thought. He'd pulled Dewy from her home, her people. If she found comfort among the animals, maybe he should've let her stay there. Today, the beasts were in the officers' tent.

Dirk shook his head. "I...uh...I don't have time for this," he grumbled.

Spense couldn't quite blame his brother for his impatience. It wasn't like Dirk hadn't tried, but agreeing to house a faerie for one night, and offering a properly respectful display of diplomatic hospitality were very different things. He doubted there'd ever been an officer dinner quite like this one.

"Perhaps we should retire?" Spense asked.

"That'd probably be best," Dirk said. "You'll use the guest quarters for the night. Flora, I don't suppose you could show them the way?"

"I'd be happy to, My Lord." Flora bobbed a micro-curtsy.

"And then...meet me at the stables? It looks like I need to tuck in our cavalry unit, now that they've had their lullaby."

"Of course, My Lord."

If Spense wasn't mistaken, Flora wore the glint of a smile as she turned from the commander's tent. It was a nice surprise. Someone who didn't automatically bow and scrape to Dirk. And could put Dewy at ease.

Whatever motivated Flora to join the soldiers' camp, he was glad she was there.

Chapter 46

Spense stared at the tent.

The. Tent.

Singular.

He cleared his throat. Dinner had been a disaster. And now, *this*?

"You're sure this is what Dirk meant?"

"He said guest quarters." Flora shrugged. Her cheeks were tinged pink.

"You've got to be kidding me."

"So...I'll just leave you to it," Flora said, already sidling away.

"Have a lovely evening, Flora—thank you for your kindness," Dewy said.

"Sure. Well...bye." The farm-girl-turned-horse-handler—he'd have to ask Dirk how that came about later—bolted away in flash of streaming blonde-brown hair and back to her horses, where the magically induced sleepiness of horses was a problem easier to solve. At least, less awkward.

Spense glanced at Dewy. "So...umm...would you like to go in?"

Dewy rolled her grass-green eyes his direction. No. Of course not. What had Dirk been thinking?

The small pavilion was set back from other sleeping quarters. Spense squared his shoulders and pushed through the flaps and wished he hadn't. After having seen Dirk's spare tent, he knew that this was not standard issue. Who had they expected to host in their camp?

Instead of a simple cot—or preferably a pair of cots—there was a pillow-covered divan sprawling in the center of a room hung with rich, embroidered draperies. Lanterns were strung from the roof and let off a heady musk scent. The floor was covered in woven silk rugs. The quarters were nicer than his room in the castle—by far.

"Sweet Spring, "Spense muttered.

Dewy turned in place, examining the room with wide eyes. She drifted to the walls and fingered the swags of fine linen. "I confess you humans are a mystery to me."

"Me, too."

"I cannot comprehend how you live, choosing a strange diversity of sleeping and eating spaces. You create such interesting and varied constructions—when the natural world already provides all you need. It's as if...as if you *like* to work." Dewy's eyes brightened as she solved her puzzle. It was unnervingly distracting.

Spense closed his eyes. "Trust me—I had nothing to do with this."

"Hmm..."

He opened his eyes again, and Dewy put one finger to her carnation pink lips. She turned to him. "There is something wonderful about it—all this labor."

She lifted a section of embroidered drape.

"Look at these stitches. There must be thousands. Human hands created these flowers, here." She pointed out the winding roses bordering the drape and giggled. "It would be so much simpler to walk outside these walls and see far more perfect specimens, but no, that is not the human way!"

Spense blushed, hoping no one heard her, knowing what they might think if they had. He held up his hands. "If you are finished with your evaluation of our bizarre human ways, I'm going to get some rest. You can have the...bed."

He grabbed a pillow from the oversized lounge and pulled the extra blanket from the foot. He rolled the tufted quilt out on the floor and punched the pillow a bit more than was necessary.

Dewy glided to the divan and sat on the edge of it. She stroked a hand across the velvet surface of the coverlet. "That is lovely—just like pussy willows."

Spense kicked his boots off and stretched out on the floor. He laid his head on the plumped pillow and shut his eyes. Dewy was humming. "Are you going to sleep?" he asked.

"What a thought!" She laughed. "If only I could...I *am* quite tired."

She resumed her soft humming, and Spense squeezed his brows together. "So...why don't you?"

"Well...I can't."

What kind of faerie custom is this? Spense took the bait. He had to ask. "And why not?"

"Because...you *told* me not to."

He could almost hear the eye roll. Spense sat up and looked at her. Dewy's eyes were wide, insistent.

"What? No, I didn't—"

She leaned over and put one finger to his mouth. She enunciated her words. Carefully and clearly. "You ordered me to 'stay awake.' "

"But that was hours ago," Spense said around her finger. "I didn't mean forever."

"Did you ever rescind that command?"

"It wasn't a command."

She widened her eyes.

"Well, technically, I suppose, but I didn't mean it *that* way. I just didn't want you to fall asleep."

"Well done. It worked."

Spense put his head in his hands. "I'm so sorry." He dropped his hands and looked into her eyes. "Dewy, please...determine...your own sleeping requirements. Sleep when you need to or choose to, and...stay awake when you need to or would like to."

He watched her face and grimaced. "How was that?"

Dewy tilted her head to the side. "I think...yes...that will work."

She stretched her arms over head, releasing an elaborate yawn. "Yes...that will do nicely," she said as she collapsed onto the pillows and curled up like a cat. With one long arm, she pulled the coverlet up and over her body and closed her eyes. In seconds, her breathing slowed. Her lips parted, making a flattened *o* shape.

"Goodnight, Dewy," he whispered. "Sleep well."

He smiled. "And that *is* a command."

Chapter 47

Lady Radiant sniffed the air. It was filled with smoke. The forest was scorched and burnt throughout the human kingdom. There was blood in the air, too, and in the water. The iron stench of it filled her nostrils. She whirled her robes and stalked back from the cliffs to the neat cave entrance tucked into the hillside.

"My Lady." Her steward bowed his head as she passed.

"Thorn, I will need to assemble my court immediately. Please see to it that all nine members are notified." She strode through the torch-lit passages that wound down through the hill. Thorn followed her, just behind and to the right, as always.

"Of course, My Lady, but…"

Lady Radiant swiveled her gaze to Thorn. "But?"

He dropped his gaze, avoiding her direct look, the risk of confrontation. "Don't you mean eight, My Lady?"

"Yes." Her eyes shuttered. "Eight." Because Dew Drop would not attend—would never attend again. Because *she* had banished her.

But what choice did she have? A Claimed being of another kingdom—no matter whom—could not be a part of the Summer Court. It was not safe. For anyone. Lady Radiant chewed the inside of her mouth as she tried to convince herself.

Thorn hurried ahead of her, his pale green and gray

overcoat whipping behind him. Radiant took a more leisurely pace, pausing to peer through one of the many portholes in the hillside passageways. Her realm—forests and rivers—lay below, slumbering. A mist lay over the world, a cocoon wrapping The Vail in quiet. Beyond those woods, the mist turned to smoke, and the world trembled in grief and fear.

Lady Radiant reached up to touch the chain around her neck. There was a charm for each member of her court. She thought of her own grief as she toyed with the tiny silver water drop that she had not yet removed, the pendant that meant Dewy was alive and bright and spreading her joy in the world—now the human world. She thought of Lumine, the Lord of Winter, and how much heavier his own grief must be that his own daughter, Princess Snow, chose passing after her half-human lover passed—no longer wandering the stone castles and earthy farms of humans but gone to her final rest. What might he do to assuage that grief? What had he already done?

She arrived at the place of meeting in her royal chambers as the remaining members of her court assembled, drifting in through the aspens and cedars. Oak took his usual seat near the head of the table to her right. Lakefair settled herself on the left. The garden and forest faeries—Thistle, Shamrock, and Honeysuckle—found their places as well. Leaf, Cedar, and Rosehip followed after her and shuffled to seats. She hesitated to begin, eyeing the empty chair on her left.

Thorn closed the archway doors. He cleared his throat meaningfully after several moments of awkward silence. Lady Radiant looked up at her court's expectant faces.

"Thank you all for coming—Rosehip, why don't you move to the left side of the table—you can record our discussions just as well from there and I would prefer balance." She gestured to Dew Drop's empty seat.

"Oh—of course, My Lady." Rosehip vacated her place at the end and dashed to the new assignment, carrying her quill and parchment with her.

Thistle asked, "Are we not to expect Dewy back, then, My Lady?"

"Is she lost forever to the human world?" Her sister Shamrock supplied the follow-up question. No doubt gossip flowed rampantly throughout The Vail.

Lady Radiant shook her head. "I'm afraid so—as long as she is Claimed by the human, she cannot be a part of our Court—or enter our lands unaccompanied."

The Fae court members exchanged bewildered glances. Some muttered to themselves or to their near neighbors. Radiant held up a hand. "Be still."

They silenced at once.

"Thank you. Now." She smoothed her hands on the table before her. "We have more pressing matters to discuss."

She met each of their gazes around the table. Some showed fear, others determination. "I know you have seen the signs. The smoke and the blood."

Several nodded.

Lady Radiant took a calming breath. "War has come. We will do what we can to protect our borders, and to continue our duties, but you all know of the old wars. There was not a forest grove unharmed or a brook unsullied. We must prepare ourselves. Please tell all that you have seen in these past days, and we may use that knowledge to bolster our defense. Speak true, friends."

She waved at the court to begin.

They obliged with tales of dried creeks and burnt trees. Blood ran through the rivers and poisoned the waters for leagues. Smoke saturated the air, causing the local fauna to flee. They told her that their magic wavered. A trio of sapling sprites brought back news of the battle in the human kingdom of Telridge.

Telridge. Where Lumine searched for his heir. Where Dewy had been Claimed by a human.

Was it a coincidence that war had come to the same place? What had Lumine instigated? Lady Radiant imagined Dew Drop there. She touched her fingers to her necklace, to the round charm that represented Dewy— powerful Fae and delicate creature. The once future Heir of Summer. Her niece. What would become of her?

Lady Radiant thanked her court for their reports and excused them, holding her own rage and fear behind a mask of cool calm. When the last bowed a curtsy and Thorn closed the doors behind them, and it was only she and her trusted steward, her long-time friend, she let her face crumple. Along with her wounded heart.

Chapter 48

"You are not much like your brother, are you?"

Spense snorted. "Half-brother. And no."

Dewy condescended to keep to a human pace as they made their way into the foothills of the White Rock Mountains. Their route became steeper the farther they got from Telridge and Dirk's camp. The trees were taller and thinner with less underbrush. Coastal cedars gave way to spiny evergreens and aspens. They rose higher into the hills. Clinging mist seeped in between his layers of clothing, and he shivered.

"Except your chin," Dewy said.

"P-pardon me?" Spense asked with chattering teeth. The feature she alluded to had gone numb.

"Your chin," Dewy explained, taking long strides. She wasn't even winded. "It's shaped the same as your brother's, and you frown the same way, too."

"Oh."

What a thought—he had something in common with Dirk—the brother who'd wished him well as he set off from the camp. Spense returned the sentiments. No one was insulted or bruised in their interchange. Maybe they were maturing.

"But your size and the rest of your face, really— completely different. Take your ears, for example—"

"Can we not talk about my face, please?" Spense cringed. The chin was enough.

"Oh—what shall we talk about?"

Spense shivered again. "How about finding a place to camp for tonight. I think we've made good time."

Dewy looked around. "Yes, I'd say so. For a human. I think we're about halfway there. Hmm..." Dewy sauntered on. "I believe there is a cave nearby—you humans do like your roof coverings."

Spense was reminded of the roof they slept under the previous night and winced. He still didn't know why a military camp had a setup like *that*. Though Dirk whispered a brisk apology in the morning, muttering something about ambassadorial protocol.

It took him a while to fall asleep, and he'd watched Dewy. Not in a creepy way—just because she was there and she was calming. Everything else in the tent reminded him of what Dirk's officers thought was happening, and that...wasn't restful.

But Dewy was. Her face didn't change in her sleep. Most people's got softer. Hers was already soft.

And in the full light of day, she waltzed through the forest ahead of him, whipping in and around aspens and pines. Several paces on, she stopped abruptly and whirled her arms around. "And here you are, My Lord."

"Not a Lo—" He paused mid-step, caught in the vision of Dewy as her dress settled around her, her freckles dusted her cheeks under her dancing eyes. Spense shook his head. "S-sorry, what?"

Dewy pointed. They'd been skirting along a cliff for a while. There was a shallow indent in the rock overhang. Not much shelter, but enough of a windbreak for his shivers to calm down.

"Think we can risk a fire?" he asked.

Dewy surveyed the surrounding forest. "Better not

to. The trees could be offended. And the light would attract…well, perhaps it's best you don't know."

Spense frowned. Not a comforting thought.

"I might have a better idea," Dewy said. She approached the stone wall. Several fist-sized reddish-brown rocks lay strewn at the base.

"What can you do with these?" she asked.

Spense picked up two and knocked them together, contemplating. He whispered the incantation he used for coal. The red deepened. He picked up two more, then another pair and another, astonished his "cheap trick" might be something more.

Dewy gathered the red rocks into a pile. "Thought so. Come here." She beckoned him closer.

Spense took a couple of slow steps toward the pile. He felt the magnified heat even from a couple of strides away. Not a blast, like a fire or furnace, just a warmth.

"How did you know I would be able to do that?" he asked.

Dewy shrugged and settled on the ground near the red rocks, her back against the stone wall. "I've already seen you use elemental magic. But earth and fire—that's a valuable combination." She patted the flat dirt space next to her.

Spense obliged her invitation and lowered himself to the ground. He mulled over what Dewy said. It was nice to be thought of as valuable. He was so used to thinking of his elemental magic as a disappointment rather than a gift—even if his experiments did occasionally prove useful.

"So, you don't want to talk about…your face?" Dewy asked.

"What?"

"You've said your face is not a good conversational topic."

Spense chuckled. "Please, no."

"Then what shall we talk about?"

He turned his head to look at her profile while she watched the rocks, sorry that he'd been lost in his own musings. He'd likely violated some form of faerie hospitality. "You," he said.

"Me?" She flicked her eyes over to meet his.

Spense shrugged. "I don't know anything about you—other than that you're a water faerie and you're Fae from The Vail."

Dewy pressed her lips together.

"I'm not going to *make* you talk." He tried again. "I just…want to know. I mean, The Vail—do you miss it?"

"Yes," she whispered. "It's my home."

Spense hung his head. He pulled his knees up and rested his forearms on them. "And now you're stuck with me. I hope you get to go back there—once everything is over. I hope we can find a way to reverse this." He wiggled his index finger back and forth from himself to Dewy.

"Thank you."

"What is it like? The Vail?"

Dewy tilted her head. A gentle sadness came over her eyes. "There is order there, and discipline. Everything in its place. We faeries are the keepers of that balance. It's been getting harder to maintain it in recent years."

Spense cringed as he listened to Dewy's wistful remembrances. "Because of humans?"

"In part," she conceded.

"It sounds peaceful. All of that balance and order."

"It is. It's beautiful. The tallest trees you can imagine. No roofs, except what nature gives us herself." She winked at him. "And the most joyous songbirds. They were my favorite."

"I'd like to see them."

Dewy tilted her head. "You might get to. I'm not sure what accommodations Lady Radiant will grant you as an emissary of Telridge."

"What about you?"

"What about me?" She crinkled her forehead. It drew all of her freckles together in a new constellation.

"Well, you're...banished, so where will you go when we get there?"

The constellation grew tighter as if there was a gravitational pull coming from her worried eyes. Two moons in melancholy orbit. "I hadn't thought about it— I guess I can't stay in my quarters in the palace—because they aren't *my* quarters anymore."

"I'm sorry." He laid a hand in the middle of her back and blinked in surprise as she leaned into him.

"It's not your fault—wait, I guess it is." Dewy laughed, making her hair float out on her sharp exhalations. She gave him a watery smile and nudged him with her shoulder. "I suppose if I were to choose, you are not such a bad sort to be stuck with."

"That's generous of you—although it's probably just the Claiming spell talking."

"Probably."

He smiled, feeling rueful.

"And, since you are such a sad race, we *should* get some rest before you make your ambassadorial appearance."

"We should." Spense nodded. But neither moved

away, or pulled their sleeping rolls from their packs. Dewy leaned in a little closer, and Spense reflexively slid his arm to wrap around her shoulder. They sat in the quiet, watching the red rocks and their faint glow. Spense soaked in the warmth from the stones and from the small body pressed closely against him. He breathed in her lilac scent.

The moment felt good. And right.

And that was probably very dangerous.

Chapter 49

"You're not much like your brother, are you?"

Dirk was in the middle of brushing Lightning Storm's flank, but he paused when the girl spoke up. The stallion nickered. Dirk scowled at the horse caretaker— Flora, the farm girl he hired after the attack at the castle. "First, no. And second, that's a bold question from a stable hand."

She frowned back. "Sorry. My Lord." Flora hastened to perform a shallow curtsy.

Dirk tossed the horse brush into the waiting bucket and retrieved a shoe pick. He walked a hand down Lighting Storm's sleek front leg and gently bent it at the knee. His horse snorted and tossed his head, but otherwise succumbed to Dirk's attentions. He came to the stables because he had a problem to solve—he went to the sparring rings when he had other types of energy to burn. The stables were relaxing, the repetitive motions in brushing his horse, combing out its black mane and tail, patiently tending to an animal that could easily overpower him.

When he arrived, Flora had been feeding oats to the mounts. And now she was making conversation. All of the other stable hands knew well enough to leave him alone. He liked *that* system.

But she was new. He'd been impressed when she arrived with Spense and the faerie during the attack on

Telridge, and again when she volunteered to serve, to help his forces in any way she could. And he was curious. Anyone could see that he and Spense had little in common, so why say it?

"You had a point?" Dirk asked, leading the girl.

"Forgive me, of course my observations are inappropriate. I'm not used to dealing with nobility." The girl ducked around her own yellow horse, trailing a hand along its massive neck.

"Oh no, you started this. What were you going to say?" He leaned over the makeshift corral wall and pointed the pick at her.

"I just find it curious that you hide your...intelligence, when Spense—sorry, Master Spense? I can't keep up—Spense sort of flaunts his."

Dirk leaned back. "Excuse me?"

"Well, look at the way you handled the attack—the way your mind works—the strategies you came up with on the spot—but it's like you don't want anyone to know that you're smart. Like you're just all...muscle-y." She shrugged. "Spense's brain. That's what he's got, so it's all you notice."

Dirk's scowl deepened. He considered Flora's uninvited analysis. He was about to respond when—

"Do you smell something?" Flora's head lifted.

Dirk whipped around and returned to meet her gaze. "Smoke," they said together.

He dropped the shoe pick in the pail and rushed out of the stables. One of his sentries hurried toward him.

"Report," Dirk barked.

"Scouts have spotted blue flame, sir, headed this way."

Dirk scrambled up a nearby boulder and scanned the

far reaches of the tree line. A haze of sickly, blue smoke floated above the canopy about a league off. "Everyone to stations! Man the perimeter!" He hopped down and pointed to a nearby soldier. "Pass the word."

Dirk made haste to his command tent, grabbing armor, greaves, sword, and helmet once he got there. Lady Xendra and Sir Gervais pushed into the tent after him.

"We heard your orders," Gerry said. "Where do you want us?"

Dirk pulled his mail over his head and fitted his helmet. "Tree line. North and South checkpoints. Shoot anything that moves."

"Yessir. On our way."

Dirk whipped through the tent flaps after his marksmen, only to run into Flora. He grabbed her arm as she stumbled. "Wicked Winter, girl—what are you doing?"

"I can help."

He dropped her arm. "The best thing you can do is tend the horses and then get out of the way." He strode past her, but she ran to catch up.

"Hey," she said.

Dirk ignored her.

She ran in front of him and blocked his way. "Hey!"

"What?" he growled.

"I can shoot."

"How well?"

"My family has chickens and sheep. We haven't lost any to raccoons or foxes in three years." She held her chin up and met Dirk's gaze.

"Grab a bow from the arms man." Dirk nodded. "Let's see if you kill any foxes."

Chapter 50

Spense woke to a hazy light. His back was sore from being hunched over all night, and a warm, damp something pressed against his side. His arm had fallen asleep, and he tried to move it without disturbing the warm something. He was unsuccessful, and it—she—murmured in her sleep.

Dewy. The girl curled up against him in a lilac-infused coil. Spense whispered her name. Another murmur.

He nudged her and awkwardly patted her arm.

"Mmm?"

He leaned over to speak into her pink shell ear. It was pointed at the apex and dotted with freckles. "You're all sweaty."

"No," she groaned. "I most definitely am not."

"You're...damp. You sweat in your sleep." Spense nearly snorted.

"I do *not* sweat."

"What would you call it?"

She rolled her head and opened her luminous green grass eyes. "*I* would call it *dew.*"

Oh.

Spense leaned back into the cold rock lining the tiny cave. Dewy pushed away from him and unfolded, stretching her arms out to the sides. She shook a small spray of water droplets from her fingertips.

189

"Occupational complication." She shrugged.

"Occupation?"

"Well, of course, silly." She arced water his direction. "I'm a water faerie."

She looked at him as if that should mean something significant. He knew that she could manipulate water, and that other faeries worked with animals or plants, but—

"I'm not sure I know how it all works," he said.

"You didn't imagine that all faeries were the same, did you?"

Spense rubbed the back of his head. "No—I mean I knew you had different alignments—Light and Dark, Summer and Winter—and that *you* are Fae. You're a kind of nobility, right?"

Dewy rolled her eyes. "You see! This is what comes from decades—centuries—of almost no contact!" She plopped down beside him. "You humans don't understand anything at all."

He smiled. "Please, enlighten me."

Dewy sat up straighter. Her face went stiff. "As you wish," she whispered.

Spense reached for her arm. "No, Dewy. I didn't mean it like that—tell me or don't tell me anything at all about faeries. It's up to you."

She nodded.

"I was just…" He held out his hands, palms open. "I want to know you more about you. That's all. Truly."

She looked at him sideways, her mouth forming a small frown.

"So…you're a water faerie?" he asked, leading. "But you know about other elements, too." He waved at the still warm stones at their feet.

"I have some affinity to air as well." She cocked her head and gazed at him, scrutinizing. "Though I believe you have as much power as I, especially after your trick last night—you drew forth flame."

Huh. He hadn't thought…admittedly there was a lot he hadn't thought about.

"I'm tired of this conversation." She pushed herself up from the cave floor. "We should be going. Dawn has already come."

Spense squinted at the growing light that crept into the small cave. The rocks Spense had magicked and had stayed warm throughout their slumber were beginning to fade, and there was a chill in the air, wafting in from the forest beyond, heavy with morning fog.

He followed Dewy out of the cave. She stretched her fingers out wide, and contracted them, curling her arms in and around her belly. She glanced his direction and winked, again throwing her arms out wide, to the trees, to the hanging green moss, to the shrubs near the forest floor.

Droplets of water landed gently onto the green things all around. But as the spray reached the shrubs, they folded in upon themselves. The tree limbs drooped so that water rolled off, pooling beneath in tiny earthen valleys, away from the roots.

"That's…not right," Dewy frowned as dangling moss shrunk back from the flung water. She looked around the forest, bewildered.

"What's happening?" Spense asked.

"I don't know…something is wrong with this forest. I can pull in water from the air, but none of the plants will accept it. Look here." Dewy pointed to a cluster of shriveled ferns. There was moisture everywhere. Spense could feel it clinging to his skin. It was the perfect climate for the curling, lacy leaves, but they were brown and withered. Dewy bowed over the sad ferns, reaching with one hand as—

"Dewy, watch out!" Spense thrust himself in between the faerie and the fern as it reared back, resembling not so much a gentle and docile plant, but a feral predator. The fern whipped its lanky leaves and struck Spense across his back and outstretched arm, splaying like a cat-o-nine-tails.

Spense yelped and lurched forward collapsing on top of Dewy. He braced himself on his forearms, his face inches away from hers.

Her eyes grew wide as she looked past him up into the forest canopy. "Spense—we have to go. Now!"

He scrambled up, pulling Dewy with him. The forest rustled behind them. Dewy's face was stricken as she beheld whatever it was that moved with sinister intent. He darted a glance over his shoulder. The trees waved their limbs with no wind, a swirling, stretching maelstrom, reaching to brandish their new foe.

Spense grabbed Dewy's shoulders and whirled her around. "Go, go!"

They darted through trees that bowed over them, groaning. Dewy found a path between the angry greenery and skipped through switching grasses. Spense followed, panting and aching from the whip stings the fern had given him. But he ran on. And on.

They sprinted to the tree line, and the air grew cold and biting; the ground rocky. Never had Spense been so grateful to be out on an exposed, windy ridgeline.

"Wh-what happened?" Spense asked. He slowed to a quick walk and blew into his frigid, shaking hands.

"I-I don't know," Dewy said, keeping a brisk determined pace. "Just a few more yards and we'll be safe on the ridge."

The wind whistled through cottage-sized boulders, reminding them of its own threats. Diamond drops of icy rain fell on his face. He bowed his head and pressed forward. The wind swirled, blowing one direction and the opposite, tearing at their dew-damp clothes. Dewy ducked between boulders and Spense fought to keep up.

A great whooshing came from behind him, causing Spense to stumble into Dewy and forcing her to jog sideways around one of the huge rocks. He lurched, catching a glimpse of the menacing forest as the last row of brittle pines hurled spiny projectiles toward him. He cried out as dozens of green spears struck his back, his neck, his legs, and his arms. The force of the blow drove him to the hard ground, where he lay panting and shaking from pain, unable to move.

Chapter 51

After swiping a bow and a quiver full of arrows from the dumbfounded quartermaster who shrugged when she said she'd been sent on Dirk's orders, Flora ran to the boulders near the south end of the camp and scrambled up. Lady Xendra wedged in near the top, using a bulbous collection of rocks as a makeshift blind. Flora scooted in beside her.

"What are you doing here, girl?"

"Catching foxes," Flora said through clenched teeth.

The Knight lifted one corner of her mouth a fraction. "We don't need to capture. Go for the kill."

Flora nodded.

Soldiers rushed into even lines, shoulder to shoulder and shield to shield, stretching across the camp border. They made a wall of steel, spears poking through concave sections of their shields no larger than an orange. Archers scaled surrounding trees and boulders, readying themselves as blue-gray smoke rolled closer to their camp.

The puffs of smoke rose higher and reached out tendrils, seeking but not burning. Flora couldn't locate the fire from which the smoke came, just thicker curls of blue and gray. Her nose and throat itched, and her eyes began to water. Lady Xendra motioned for her to raise her thin scarf around her nose and mouth.

The haze reached her fellow archers in the trees and

the smoke cloud enveloped them. She squinted through the haze. She heard coughing and then branches crashing, followed by a thump. Then another. And another.

Flora spun to Lady Xendra, whose eyes were wide and imploring. They scrambled away from the encroaching smoke, around the boulders, gaining elevation. The Knight pushed her toward the ridge near the edge of camp.

The smoke was thinner, and they spotted the faerie attackers. A horde of blue and amethyst skinned goblins approached. Nothing like the ethereal Fae. Nothing like Dewy with her sun-kissed hair and freckled face, or little Petal, who could almost pass for human. The goblins' faces were covered in slit masks, and they wore spiked helmets so that nothing of their faces, save for their large round eyes, could be seen.

Three gangly faeries led them—and she wondered if they were noble Fae. Each wore a dark robe embroidered with strange symbols and carried a pouch. One of the faerie enchanters reached into his pouch and withdrew what looked like a ball of dense smoke. He blew on the smoke and whispered to it reverently. It drifted away from him, growing and expanding toward the Telridgian soldiers and their not-so-impenetrable line.

Lady Xendra pointed. Flora nodded. Those were their targets.

Flora lifted her borrowed bow and sighted down the arrow. The man or the pouch? She hesitated.

Lady Xendra's released arrow whistled and found its mark. Into the heart of the faerie. He stumbled, clutching his chest. The man dropped the bag of noxious smoke, but it kept billowing out in swirls. Flora fired at the sack. Her strike was true, causing the pouch to burst open. More smoke blasted out.

Lady Xendra swore colorfully. "That won't work!"

"What do we do?" Flora asked.

"I don't know. We've got to contain it."

Flora secured her scarf around her mouth and nose, and they inched along the ridge, all the while keeping sight of the rising clouds. Micro-drifts of blue dust, like ash, sailed past. The cloud was made up of tiny particles. It wasn't smoke.

Flora pulled her flint stones from her pocket. She crouched down and sparked the flint until she lit a small twig.

"What are you doing?" hissed Lady Xendra. "You'll draw their attention."

"Just wait."

Flora tossed the modified punk stick into the bits of drift. It missed most of the scattered smoke particles. But zapped and fizzed twice before falling to the earth, lighting those particles for a brief moment.

"It's flammable," Lady Xendra said.

"Yeah." Flora slid her gaze to the Knight. "I've got an idea."

They skirted back down the boulders, making their way into camp proper, where several fires burned for heat and cooking. Flora darted into the healers' tent. "I need linens!" An alarmed healer pointed to a clean, stacked pile on a table in the corner. Next to that was a bin of dry rags used for washing. *Even better.* She grabbed the bin and an oil lantern and bolted back outside.

Lady Xendra looked over the supplies. She nodded.

"This way."

Flora sprinted behind her, sliding to a stop next to a cook fire. Lady Xendra yanked the top off the lantern and spilled its contents over the bin of rags. They each grabbed one and wrapped it around the point of their arrows. Together they dipped them into the fire.

"Aim high."

Flora took a moment to sight and let the flaming arrow fly. Into the densest part of the smoke. It burned through the particles, creating a comet of clean air, sizzling and sparking. Lady Xendra's flew in a near parallel arc, with the same results. One corner of the Knight's mouth lifted.

"Again."

They punched holes in the smoke. One after another after another.

But it wasn't enough. She could hear the coughs of soldiers, mixed with the clashing of metal as the goblins charged, barely visible through the sickening fog until they were upon the line of defenders.

"We need to get higher," Flora said.

"You ever play lances?"

Flora lifted her eyebrows. "Yeah."

"Catcher?"

"Always." In the game, it was the only way to get her cousin Rook out. He was too fast at dodging the sticks.

"Good. Climb that boulder." Lady Xendra jutted with her chin. "I'll send the arrows to you."

Flora scrambled up, getting just high enough to make out the two remaining faerie enchanters with their bulging pouches. They hung back from the battle, spewing their magic. As Flora glanced down, Lady

Xendra drove an arrow vertically up to her, its point aflame. Flora reached out with a fist and caught it, positioned the arrow and released, all in the space of two panting breaths.

It flew into the cloud, toward the faeries, sizzling blue particles as it went, but missed the enchanter and his sack. "Another." Flora spoke between clenched teeth.

An arrow sailed up. "We're getting low on rags. Make it count!"

Flora sighted. Took another breath. Found her mark through the haze and the clashing weapons. And let go.

This time it hit.

The enchanter's pouch burst like fireworks. Sparks zinging out, cutting clear lines through the haze in every direction.

"Yes," she said, whooshing out all of the air in her lungs. "Another!"

Up came the arrow. Flora spied the last faerie enchanter, even farther back from the melee. And hit. Another explosion of sparking particles. The faerie fell to the ground, his robes on fire. He batted and rolled, clearing more air as he traveled.

"Get him?" Xendra yelled.

"Yeah." Flora fell back into the rocks.

A moment later, Xendra appeared beside her. "We're not finished yet."

Right. Flora pulled herself up, taking an arrow from the quiver.

"Go for the blue guys. Try not to hit ours."

They fired into the goblins. And prayed their arrows found their marks.

Chapter 52

As Flora and Xendra cleared the air, the real skirmish began. The full force of the dark faerie line advanced upon the Telridgians. But the helter-skelter goblins were no match for the well-organized humans. The soldiers roared as metal clashed with metal. When a faerie soldier fell, those around him immediately filled the vacancy. But their numbers couldn't match Telridgian efficiency and discipline. Many more goblins went down than humans.

Lord Dirk bellowed orders. A surge of goblins rushed the far end of the Telridge line, causing it to buckle in several places at once. Dirk rushed in, and beat back goblin after goblin, his sword singing as he swung. He struck, pivoted, swung again. He and his sword were a choreography of fluid dance, as if the weapon and shield were extensions of his limbs. Dirk battled multiple goblins at a time, while his soldiers re-formed the line. Flora watched, breath baited, from the safety of her protected position.

Dirk was busy engaging two goblins, when a third charged, his eyes gleaming and spear raised. Flora aimed, fired. The goblin leaped and her arrow pierced the goblin's throat. Blood sprayed as the goblin fell. Dirk finished his other attackers in two swift motions and then whirled his head to find his savior.

Flora locked her gaze with him for a moment. He

jerked his head in a nod and pushed back into the fray.

The battle proceeded into a full rout after that. Faerie soldiers were pushed back and back. She drew the last of her arrows and fired, not sure what may or may not have reached the forces below. When they were out of arrows, Flora followed Lady Xendra back down into the camp.

Cheers of victory sounded from soldiers all around her.

Flora watched the few remaining goblins flee into the woods. Her heart thudded a staccato beat in her head. She felt her hands shaking, her blood zinging through her limbs.

"Are you hurt?"

Flora staggered, catching short, rapid breaths. Lord Dirk towered before her, concern etched across his face.

"No. But...that's strange..." She rotated her shaking hand, dropping the bow.

Dirk grabbed her hand, squeezed. "You're fine." He met her gaze and told her again. Three times. She jerked her chin in a tiny nod.

"It's just the rush of battle." He let her hand fall. "Don't worry—you're normal."

"Oh." She examined her hand again. Her pulse was steadying, finding a regular beat.

"You saved my life, you know."

"All in a day's work, My Lord." She shrugged and raised her face to look at him. Bloody and dirty, but flushed and healthy. Had she done that? Saved him? She killed that goblin. It was different than hunting turkeys or shooting foxes. "That was...not what I thought a battle would be...it was awful, and also easier than I expected."

Dirk furrowed his brow. His chin wrinkled.

"You're right." His eyes narrowed. "Too easy."

Dirk swiveled his head, eyes searching the recovering camp and surrounding forest. He paused.

She followed his gaze until her own alighted on the fresh smoke rising up. From the direction of Telridge Castle.

"Oh, no," she said, breathless.

"Diversion." Dirk spat. He turned and began belting orders to his men and women in arms.

Chapter 53

"Spense!" Dewy screamed.

He staggered to one knee and lifted a hand to her. "No, stay there."

She froze. Tight bands wove around her legs and arms, pinning her in place. Dewy pushed against them in frustration and terror as he crawled, bleeding, to the meager protection of the boulder. With each struggled step, the spines in his exposed flesh dug in and twisted, drawing blood that beaded and rolled down his back and legs. He cast a glassy-eyed glance to the ground as it splattered.

Dewy squirmed and twisted in place by the protective boulder. Rings of heat and pain grew tighter as she fought—to help him. It felt like ages but was probably no more than a few moments before Spense reached Dewy and collapsed on the ground at her feet.

She crashed onto her knees near him, hands stretching and fluttering uselessly, just out of reach. *WhatdoIdo?WhatdoIdo?* Her words spilled out, frantic and nonsensical.

His breath sounded strangled and heavy and he coughed into the dusty, rocky ground.

"Dewy..."

"I can't help unless you release me," she pleaded. Hot, stringing tears tracked down her face. "Spense, please."

"What?" he wheezed. "Oh. Sorry. I release you."

The bands dissipated as if they'd never been there, and she scrabbled on the gritty shale to his side. She grasped his wrist, his neck, his face. "Hold still," she whispered.

"Won't go far," he choked, coughing again at his terrible joke.

It wasn't funny. Dewy didn't laugh. Not as she surveyed the dozens and dozens of lances piercing his skin. "This might…hurt a bit."

She twisted and pulled a sharp, sticky spine embedded in his neck. He moaned as the pine spear gave way. A trickle of blood took its place.

"Oh no…"

"Just pull them. it's all right," Spense grunted. "We need to get them out."

He gritted his teeth, waiting for the next, waiting for her to get on with it. There was no choice. She laid a firm hand on the base of his head and yanked. Dewy was faster with the next one until all four were out. And Spense's blood leaked onto the rocks in sprays and drops. She tasted the mineral tang in the dry air.

"You need a bandage…the blood."

"We need to keep going."

She closed her eyes, steadied her breathing and then grabbed ahold of his arm and stretched it out. She took his hand in hers, while he bled and shook, and moved to the pine spears in his arms and back. They were not embedded as deeply and came out more quickly. She lost count somewhere around thirty-two.

Dewy murmured to him encouraging, nothing, meaningless words. But his eyelids drooped and head fell heavy on her lap. She cried out, prayed.

"Stay with me, Spense…please, oh please…help me, help me, help me…someone, please…"

His eyelids fluttered, full lips moved. "I think you should go…"

"No, Spense. Don't give me an order."

"I'm so sorry…for everything…" he wheezed.

"Don't. Just don't." She sobbed, pressing her hands to either side of his face and bowing over him. "We're getting you out of here. You're going to be fine."

She gave the orders now. And sweet spring, he'd obey. She pulled spines from his legs. One after the other, until there was nothing left but rivulets of blood soaking through his pants and into his boots. It stuck, freezing to his back and legs.

"A-all right, D-Dewy. W-we'll do it your way." He shivered and shook with each breath.

She moved to his right side, hoisting his least injured arm and wrapped it across her shoulders. She forced him to a near standing position and urged him forward. He managed a shuffling step, and another, but collapsed to his knees with the third.

The wind tore at them from all directions. Clouds darkened.

"Whoozer?" Spense's head lolled, his gaze roving to their path ahead.

Dewy's head whipped up. She saw figures approaching in the mountain fog. Spindly, familiar. "Grace be with us…thank you."

"My Lady." Thorn, her aunt's steward, clad in his usual green and gray, tipped his head. He was accompanied by two faerie sentinels, Leaf and Cedar— both on her aunt's council. "You look like you could use some assistance."

She nodded, tried to smile. Fresh tears watered her cheeks and chin and dripped onto Spense's wounded shoulder.

The three faeries moved in. Their frowns and significant glances told her all she needed to know, as if the blood peppering the landscape wasn't enough.

"We can take him to The Vail—to the healers there. But you..." Thorn didn't need to say more.

"I understand. Just help him...please."

Dewy stood aside as Thorn lifted Spense, and Leaf and Cedar took up flanking positions.

Together, they descended, finally at faerie speed. The wind lost its bite, replaced by the gentle, welcome whispering in the trees, the echo of birdsong that told her she was entering the Summer lands.

And as they brought him into the palace at the very heart of Summer, Dewy leaned over and stroked a trembling hand down Spense's dirtied face. "You made it, Spense."

"W-where—" His words were no more than puffs of labored breath.

"The Vail."

Chapter 54

Spense woke to birds singing. Actual bird song.

He lay in a cushion of feather-soft, combed linen and down pillows. Ferns danced in his periphery, and cedar boughs bent over him. The forest canopy arced high above, creating a cathedral-like ceiling.

He blinked a few times, letting his vision clear, trying to make sense of the dappled sunlight. His last memories were of Dewy, sobbing, hiccupping, agreeing to something. Strong hands and arms like tree branches had lifted him and carried him through the labyrinth of boulders. Wind whipped past. A swirl of colors—mostly grays and blacks—spiraled past him. That was when he closed his eyes against the maelstrom of images.

Now, a dusty ray shone through the cedars down and down onto…Dewy.

She sat near his bed, her hands twisted in her lap. Her sun-kissed freckles drew together as he tilted his head to look at her better. Her face was wan, and faint shadows had settled beneath her eyes.

"Hi," he croaked.

Dewy opened her mouth and then closed it.

"Am I dead?"

Dewy furrowed her brows and shook her head.

"That's good to know." He found some solid surface buried beneath the down and pushed up with his hands. Everything ached. He felt the remnants of his many,

many wounds in the form of stinging all over his limbs, his back, and his neck. He breathed in deep and let it out. Nice to know that still worked.

"Why do I smell like...tea?"

Dewy gestured to his bandages. "The healers put a salve of chamomile and honey on your wounds." Her voice was scratchy. Tear-worn.

Spense reached out a wavering hand until he reached hers. She wrapped her fingers around his and squeezed. "Thank you," he said, "For whatever you did or who you called. To bring me here."

Dewy nodded. Spense pivoted, twisting his mid-section despite the stinging, so that he could reach with his other hand and wipe the single tear away from her face with his thumb.

"Have you slept?"

She shook her head, leaning into his cupped hand. He stilled for a moment, thinking through how to phrase his words, and what his invitation might imply. "There is plenty of room...in this pretty comfy bed...if you'd like to. Sleep, that is."

He waited a breath, and another, while she considered. When she pushed off from the stool, he scooted sideways. They nestled back into the downy cushions, she resting her head on his shoulder and one thin hand on his chest. As Spense smoothed tentative fingers around her shoulder and down her hair, something grew tight in his chest, and he didn't think it had anything to do with his injuries.

Chapter 55

She slept. And when she woke, he was still there. Still holding her. His fingers had woven into her tangled hair. The weight of exhaustion and worry pressing on her while the healers worked on Spense had lifted. At least a little.

"Feeling better?" Spense asked. His voice was soft and clear, not the sound of someone just waking up. She cracked her tear and sleep-crusted eyelids and looked up at him.

"I think so."

"Ready to face the world?"

"Hmm…" She pushed herself up and away from Spense. "The world, sure…but first, we should probably go see my aunt."

"Your aunt? Is she a water faerie, like you…or a healer?"

Dewy hesitated. This was why she'd resisted sharing much about herself when he'd asked. Once he understood, it would change how he saw her. It always did. "My aunt is Lady Radiant, Queen of Summer."

Spense's mouth dropped open in surprise. "You said you were Fae…I didn't realize you were *Fae* Fae."

"Well, that's a new way of describing our nobility."

Dewy swiveled around to find Thorn stepping through the arched entry of the healing space. His arms were folded over his chest, and his chin was elevated.

Spense scrambled from the downy bed, bending into something that might be called a bow.

Dewy cringed. "Thorn, may I officially present Master Spense...of Telridge."

Thorn sucked in a breath and let it out slowly. "Thank you, Dew Drop. Though I fear I must remind you that it is no longer a responsibility of yours to introduce visitors to The Vail."

Dewy opened her mouth and clamped it shut again.

The steward held up a hand. "My Lady welcomes you here as the Telridge ambassador's companion, but please try to remember that it is now your *only* place here."

If Dewy wasn't mistaken, she heard a slight tremor in Thorn's usually unshakeable voice at the proclamation. Dewy nodded.

"Master Spense." Thorn angled his body to the still off-kilter and unkempt Spense. "When you are refreshed, would you please join Lady Radiant in the reception room? Your companion is welcome to accompany you."

"Uh...of course, Sir Thorn." Spense stumbled into another half-bow.

Dewy bit her lip hard enough to draw tears.

"My Lady understands that you have been grievously injured. Take your time." Thorn nodded and left them, slipping as smooth as a shadow into the corridor, while both Spense and Dewy remained in semi-stunned, wholly awkward half curtsies.

Dewy let out a shaky breath. And another. In the next, Spense stood before her, lifting his hands to cup her shoulders, his fingers grazing her skin.

"Are you all right?"

She nodded, trying to hold back a sob.

"I guess this answers the question of whether or not you get your old room."

She hiccupped, laughed, choked.

"Dewy...I am so sorry...I can't say it enough. I've taken everything from you." His hands squeezed her shoulders. "We are going to fix this—I promise you."

She lifted her hand to his imploring face. "You haven't taken everything."

His heartbeat stuttered, and started up again, at a faster pace. He dropped his hands and stepped away from her.

"We...we should go see your aunt."

"Yes, we should." She scanned the room and then pointed to his folded clothes. "But I think you should do so dressed."

Spense took a couple of halting steps and picked up his tunic, neat, cleaned, and mended. "Fairies certainly know their arts." He smoothed his fingers over the fabric. Each tear had been re-woven, not merely sewn together. "Is there...?" His gaze circled the healing chamber.

"Oh! There is a bathing area through that arch." Dewy gestured at the curving aspens on the far side of the chamber and blushed.

"Thanks." Spense nodded and stepped through, taking his laundered pile with him.

"Sweet Spring, there's a pool in here...do you think I could—"

"Yes, of course—it's a healing bath."

She heard a soft rustle as he removed the linen shift, followed by small splashes. "Oh, that's heaven," Spense groaned.

She blushed again and cleared her throat, turning her gaze away from the arch. It didn't provide much of a screen.

"We should really be quick," Dewy called out. "My aunt doesn't care to be kept waiting." This, she knew from habitual experience—no matter Thorn's polite, elegant words. She tapped her fingers against her thigh, trying not to imagine the actions accompanying each splash.

"Not to worry. I'm almost finished—just wanted to get 'tea hour' off of me." That statement presented itself with a whole new set of images. Dewy raised her eyes to the canopy.

When she heard his padding feet come through the archway, she lowered her gaze toward him, and he lifted his tunic over his head. Her eyes widened at the brief glimpse of bare stomach and chest. Lean, but muscular. Not wiry. Maybe he had more in common with his older brother than he let on.

"Dewy, did you hear me?"

"Sorry?"

"Have you seen my boots?"

"Oh…uh…yes!"

He arched an eyebrow and ran his fingers through damp hair.

"Over here." She scampered to the articles in question, snuggled beneath the molded stool where his clothes were laid out. She bent to retrieve them and held up the freshly shined boots—one in each hand—as if she were presenting a prize.

"Thanks." He took them from her and pulled them on.

His cocked his head. "You sure you're all right?"

"Fine." She knew her response was too chipper.

"Hmm…" Spense held her gaze, brows drawn as he worked through his buttons. When finished, he held his hands out to the side palms up. "Am I presentable?"

Chapter 56

Cleaned and pressed, with a Telridge overcoat, Spense could pass for an actual ambassador. It was disorienting, like finding a favorite flowery weed was a rare specimen, prized for its powers. She preferred Spense in his usual rougher garb—clothes for working, trekking, and doing magic. She didn't know what to make of this refined, handsome version.

"You'll do." Dewy smiled tightly. "Let's go."

She led him out of the healing chambers, only to come face to face with Thorn. Again.

"Oh!" Dewy stopped so abruptly that Spense nearly collided with her. He put a hand on her shoulder to steady himself. Thorn arched one eyebrow at the familiar contact.

"Thorn. I didn't expect you," Dewy said.

"Clearly." Without the slightest hint of expression, the steward managed to make Dewy feel like a misbehaving child.

She released a nervous laugh. "Did you imagine that we couldn't find our way to My Lady's reception room? I have not been gone so long."

"On the contrary." Thorn lifted his lips into a regretful smile. "It feels as if you have been absent only a moment and forever all at the same time."

Dewy frowned.

"At My Lady's request, I am to serve as the Telridge

Ambassador's escort," Thorn explained. "Not because you, Dew Drop, are unfamiliar with The Vail, but because all foreign ambassadors—and their companions—require accompaniment in our fair city."

Dewy nodded. Spense wordlessly offered his arm. She threaded her hand into the crook of his elbow.

"Shall we?"

Thorn led them as they merged into the wide, winding corridor and along The Vail's main arterial. The sprawling palace-city evolved organically like a plant, with new shoots growing onto existing branches. There were no sharp edges or trapped air. When a chamber was no longer of use, the trees harboring the palace merely grew back over the space until a time when it was needed again. But no matter how far out a passageway stretched, they all led back into the main vein, like tributaries feeding into a river.

They nodded in polite reverence to the few other fairies and Fae making their own way along the path for their own reasons. All met Spense's and Thorn's gaze but averted their eyes from Dewy.

She understood why. It didn't hurt any less.

After the fourth such occurrence, Spense lifted his unoccupied arm and gave her hand a comforting squeeze.

Dewy was relieved when they left public spaces and condemning glances and entered into the presence of her aunt and queen. She should have known the judgment she felt was just beginning. As if any of this had been her fault. She did not choose to be Claimed by a human.

Though she *had* cried out to whoever might hear her—to the forest itself—to *help* a human. And said human had not issued any sort of command when she did so. She hadn't been compelled. She could have let him suffer. And possibly been free of the spell. Instead, she helped him.

Perhaps she deserved condemnation.

"My Lady." Dewy knelt low and tucked her head. Spense mimicked her actions, a half moment behind.

"Thank you for coming," Lady Radiant said.

"I owe you thanks, Lady Radiant." Spense spoke with a clear resonant voice. "If it were not for the services of your healers, I might never have made it off that ridge."

She rose from her floral throne, floating up like a feather on the breeze, and glided toward their party. "We faeries endeavor to respond to cries of need from the wilderness. We heard yours." She turned to face Dewy. "And Dew Drop's."

"Again, thank you."

Lady Radiant tilted her head to the side. Dewy recognized the look of scrutiny, having been on the receiving end many times. She rarely came out of that look with anything like approval. Her queen narrowed her eyes as she peered at Spense.

"Am I to be the recipient of more thanks from Telridge, Ambassador?"

Spense returned the Queen's stare, clear-eyed and sure. "That is my hope, Your Majesty."

"What more could you ask of me? You have stolen my niece. And we have healed you. Were we not to have done so, Dew Drop might now be free of you."

Dewy winced. She'd been thinking the same thing only moments before, and yet the words came out much harsher from her aunt. She heard everything Radiant hadn't said as well as what she had. Niece. Not Princess.

Not Heir. It was not only Dewy who was imprisoned by the Claiming. Radiant would never be free of the regency. Her temporary rule would last forever.

Spense cleared his throat. "You are right to censure me, and me alone, for that transgression. I can only assure you that it was not done intentionally, and I seek a cure, even now. But right now—"

"Now, it would be inconvenient, as you have more pressing needs?" Lady Radiant asked sharply.

"As you say, My Lady, Telridge *has* been attacked." Spense nodded. "And we do seek aid. But…"

"And I wonder when it will *not* be convenient to have a Fae enthralled to you, human?"

"Again, you have my sincere apologies. And if you can provide any assistance in helping me to release…Lady Dew Drop, I would gladly welcome it. Punish me any way you see fit, but please do not take it out on the people of Telridge when they come to you in need."

Dewy glanced back and forth between Queen Radiant and Ambassador Spense, hardly recognizing her aunt or her friend underneath their courtly masks. Spense used his words well, turning Radiant's own against her. The queen knew it, but she didn't like it. Her mouth tightened as she continued her analysis.

"Tell me about yourself, Master Spense."

"There is not much to tell, My Lady. I am an apprentice mage under Lord Ferrous—"

"Who is your father?"

"I am illegitimate, but yes, My Lady."

Dewy scanned the room for Thorn, who hung back near the entrance of the chamber, his face as impassive as ever. His network of informants knew their business.

"That explains your present position. Tell me of your mother."

"She is the Head Cook of Telridge, My Lady."

"Indeed. And from where do *her* people hale?"

"I've known no relations other than my grandfather. He was an orchardist. His cottage is not far from the castle of Telridge."

"Humble beginnings."

"Yes, My Lady."

"And there is no record of lineage?"

"My grandfather was a learned man, but just a grower of fruit. He kept ledgers of his crops, but none of family."

"This Master Orchard…did he have a given name?"

"Of course, Lady. My grandfather was called Clove. My mother is Cait. I never knew my grandmother. She was not spoken of by my grandfather, and my mother honors his practice." Radiant's face softened for a moment. Dewy did not think Spense noticed, but she was sure Thorn had. They were both well-versed in recognizing the flickers of feeling their queen revealed, and occasionally even what those insights meant. Whatever it might've been, Lady Radiant dismissed it in the space of a heartbeat, turning away from the party and returning to her camellia-covered chair.

"Forgive me, My Lady—why is my family history important? I come to plead for mercy for myself and for Telridge. That is all."

"I will consider your case. You may leave me now, Master Spense."

"Thank you, My Lady." Spense bowed his way from the chamber. Thorn waited to resume his escort duties.

"A moment, Dew Drop."

"Of course, My Lady." She knelt, waiting as Spense and Thorn made their exit. It was the first word Radiant had spoken to her. During the exchange with Spense, she could have been a nameless Telridgian, an insignificant companion or servant of the ambassador.

Dewy felt the whisper of her queen's hand along her face. But of course, she could not touch her. Dewy raised her tear-filled eyes to meet Radiant's equally watery expression.

"It is quite a mess you've found yourself in, Dewy dear."

"It really is."

"And yet…"

"Yes, My Lady?"

"He is not so brutish, this human of yours."

"Not at all, My Lady." Dewy shook her head.

"You care for him?"

Dewy paused. "I think so. If it weren't for the Claiming, I might be sure…"

"You cried out in the wilderness. On his behalf. When he could not command it."

"Yes." She bowed her head and knew what Lady Radiant was getting at. There was something happening that could not be explained by the misapplication of a spell. Spense might have command over her actions when he chose, but he did not control her heart. She blushed. Thorn all but found them in bed together.

"Though I would not choose it for you, your path includes this human. Perhaps Grace will show us the reason in time."

Dewy murmured the words of prayer in response.

"Grace be with *you*, daughter."

Dewy recognized the dismissal. She rose to make

her exit, but as she reached the arch, Radiant cleared her throat.

"Dewy, for what it's worth, I miss you."

She nodded and reached her hand to one of the towering aspens for support, but did not dare turn around. Tears threatened to burst forth, but she swallowed them back.

In the corridor, she was met by two faerie guards. She bowed her head as they formed her escort. Fae did not need such attention. But exiles did. She was now a stranger in her own home, and Radiant, despite her gentle words, made sure she knew it.

Chapter 57

He should have known. Despite the undeniable hospitality of the Fae, Spense's stay in The Vail was going to be short. He was, after all, a criminal of the vilest atrocity.

Thorn, his official escort, led him out of the queen's reception hall and down one of the many meandering corridors. How they managed to keep them all straight was beyond him. He would have to ask Dewy later.

Instead of taking him back to the healing chamber, Thorn ushered him through a curtain of hanging vines, through a door with an actual lock—one of the only he'd seen in The Vail—and into what looked like a private study and laboratory. It was both cleaner and more chaotic than Spense's own makeshift lab in Telridge. Blown glass vials of varying substances rested on curving shelves and bunches of dried herbs hung from delicate hooks. The furnishings—worktable, stools, and shelves—reminded him of those in his grandfather's cottage. No tree had been sawn or nailed but was shaped by water and wind. Natural curves dictated how each piece might come to serve its master.

Like everything in The Vail, this utilitarian space was both simple and elegant. Lady Radiant was glorious in her bronze beauty, smooth and calm like a large body of water, her power humming underneath the surface. Thorn barely twitched a muscle when his dark face changed expressions and glided through rooms, more wraith than being. His dusky green and gray clothing that blended with the treed atmosphere didn't help. And the warm-skinned Fae they encountered in the corridors all drifted along, silent and refined, as if clean fire burned through them, pure and glowing.

Spense tried to imagine Dewy here, but he couldn't. She belonged in the carefree chaos of nature, singing with birds and dancing amongst trees. She sparkled and laughed. She didn't glide in refined silence. He caught himself wondering if leaving this quiet, calm, beautiful world wasn't all that terrible for her. Spense shuddered and dismissed the selfish thought.

"Please sit, Master Spense. The queen will be with you presently." Thorn gestured to one of the curved seats. Spense sank into the chair, just as Lady Radiant entered, causing him to bolt back upright.

"Lady Radiant," he said, bowing.

She waved him off. "Enough of that. Please, sit."

Spense lowered himself in the chair, watchful of the queen. "Have you made a decision so soon?"

"When one's mind is decided there is no reason to forestall."

Spense frowned. It was too quick—which meant she'd determined her course before even meeting with him. The reception was merely a pretense to confirm her beliefs—or prejudices. He took a slow breath and waited.

"Thorn, have you the items I requested?"

"Of course, My Lady." Thorn reached into his tunic and produced two rolls of parchment.

Lady Radiant accepted them and placed the two scrolls on the table. She unrolled one of them, pressing it open with her long, golden fingers. "This document will grant you passage into the lands of the Winter—or what you humans incorrectly call the Dark faeries." The queen whisked a feathered pen across the parchment in swirling scrolls.

"Am I to go to…the Silver Horn, My Lady?"

"I am pleased that you at *least* know the name of the Winter Court's dwelling. Yes."

Spense wasn't sure what to react to first, the queen's obvious condescension or the realization that she was offering a form of assistance, perhaps diplomatic if not military. Or maybe that was better.

"Ambassador, your plight lies with Lumine, the ruler of Winter. It is to him you must appeal. This—" She tapped the parchment with the feathered end of the quill. "—will grant you passage into the Silver Horn, and an audience.

She waved the second parchment, already rolled and sealed with the mark of the Light—Spense corrected himself, *Summer*—Court.

"With this you may bring Lumine to your cause."

"Th-thank you, Lady." Spense fell back in the chair.

"Hmm…you may re-think that thanks. Lumine can have some rather strong opinions—about humans in particular. There is no guarantee that he will consider your appeal, at all."

Spense wasn't encouraged by the queen's remarks, even while she lent her support. She lifted one corner of her mouth. "I do not envy you the task before you…but like my niece, I believe this path has been set for you. Only you can walk it."

"But…as you said, I am a human, and not a particularly important one."

"I believe we shall soon see who you really are." She

leveled a focused gaze at him.

Faeries were known for their cryptic statements—in every story ever told about them. To be on the receiving end of one made him appreciate the tales.

"All is prepared, My Lady." Thorn slipped into the chamber, depositing Spense's belongings onto the ground near the entrance.

Spense shifted in his seat. He wasn't aware that Thorn ever left. He looked closer at his bags, plump with supplies. "What—now?"

"The journey is long—for a human—and as I said before, when one's decision has been made, I see no cause for delay. You have rested and healed. And here you have the final requirement, a competent guide." Radiant rose from her worktable. "Dew Drop, you know how I feel about lurking in doorways."

Dewy peered through the arch. Her freckled face was pink and blotchy, but her eyes were bright and clear. "Are we to leave so soon, My Lady?"

Radiant softened. "I think we both know it would be best."

Dewy nodded. He analyzed her face, wondering where she'd been, and what her last conversation with the queen entailed, if this was her reaction. Spense wanted to rush to her side and brush away the tears that threatened to fall, but he held himself back at the slight shake of her head. There would be time and space for that later, out of the presence of so many faerie ears and discerning looks.

Radiant approached Spense, handing him the two scrolls. "Guard these carefully, Master Spense."

"Of course, My Lady." He accepted the documents—flimsy pieces of parchment that may be his only protection in the faerie realms. "Thank you."

She tilted her head. "I will grant you one more courtesy and send a message to your home. I imagine Lord Ferrous will want to know that you have achieved your first task."

"Again, thank you."

"I hope to see you both again, in the days to come. May Grace guide your path."

"And yours," they whispered.

Chapter 58

"Can I assume you have the other item I requested?" Radiant arched an eyebrow to her steward.

Thorn closed her study door behind him and secured the latch. She waited as he strode across her study and placed a small vial on her worktable. "The results were most interesting, My Lady."

Radiant reached forward and swirled the tiny glass of glistening red liquid. She rolled the vial between her fingers, letting its contents catch the waning rays of light. "Thank you, Thorn. I appreciate the insight. As I expected?"

"Indeed, My Lady."

She set the vial down and looked closer at her steward—and her spy.

"Do you think we can trust him?"

Thorn leaned against a young tree that grew like a pillar in her study, holding up the feathery green canopy. She often hung items from its branches, but today its arms were bare, leaving plenty of room for her steward. He folded his arms over his chest. "Are you actually asking me that?"

Radiant blew out a puff of irritated air and rolled her eyes. "I suppose not."

"You'd never have let Dewy go with him if you didn't find some bit of his character redeemable." Thorn's words were measured and calm, as if he were approaching a spooked deer in the forest. It grated.

"Stop handling me."

He held up his hands in surrender. "I'm stating the obvious."

"I know what you're doing."

"And that is?"

"You're giving me time and space to come to peace about this whole blooming situation, to reason it out, and pray to Grace for the best, most honorable outcome, to not let my fears and worries control my decisions, but..." She leaned her elbows on her desk and rubbed her hands over her face.

"But...you want to throw something...perhaps at this human's head?"

"I want to blow something up!" Her hands dropped to her desk surface with a smack.

Thorns eyebrows lifted.

Radiant waved him off and she fell back into her chair. "I'm not going to incinerate the boy. Calm down. Imagine the diplomatic crisis that would create."

She could've sworn there was a twitch of a smile nearing the corners of Thorn's mouth. He strode toward her, placed both hands on her desk and leaned in. "How may I serve you, My Queen?"

Radiant reached forward and placed one hand on his. "As you always have. Put your spies and scouts to work and listen. Find out what you can."

"Anything specific?"

"Does it compromise my royal integrity if I ask you to keep track of my niece?"

Thorn met her gaze. "Considering that she is the Heir of Summer, I'd say no. This court has a vested and specific interest."

Radiant withdrew her hand, and Thorn returned to standing fully upright before her, as if shifting back into a more comfortable and familiar stance.

"I exiled her," Radiant reminded him.

"I don't recall you naming a new Heir—I assume you don't intend to."

She pressed her fingers to her temples. "Is it folly, to hang on to this thread of hope, that Lumine—that frosty old king—could see past his prejudices and grief and actually help them? That we might get her back?"

"Hope is never folly, My Lady. Or misspent."

Her fingers drifted to her necklace, searching for the single water drop charm.

"In that case…just make sure you're discreet."

His head shook with a light chuckle. "Of course, My Lady. As always." He bowed before her and retreated, leaving her to her swirling, conflicted thoughts. She squeezed the little tear drop gem, and felt a corresponding tightening in her own chest.

Chapter 59

Dirk stood on the battlements atop Telridge castle, looking out toward the skirmish underway. His soldiers had been quick, and cavalry even faster. He'd have to thank Flora later for the fine care of Telridge's war horses. On top of saving his life from goblins.

His soldiers intercepted attacking Verdenians and battled their way to the gates of the castle, cutting a spear through the enemy forces. Once through, the Verdenians had numbers enough to reform their massive lines. But the element of surprise gave Dirk and his Telridgian Knights an advantage, and the rallying burst of momentum that the castle soldiers needed to continue their defense. Judging by the overwhelming numbers Verden had sent, they meant to lay siege, and Dirk's fighting forces would need their spirits reinforced every step along the way. Sieges were lost to battle weariness more than anything else, and Dirk needed that to happen outside the walls of Telridge rather than in.

He took some comfort that the Verdenians were human and tended to operate within the bounds of traditional warfare. He never knew what to expect from faeries.

Smoke rose from the fields below—from the launching of Telridgian munitions and from that same blue gray smoke the Dark faeries used in the earlier attack on the outpost. His enemy wasn't entirely human.

But he knew something about the noxious substance and directed his archers to maintain a barrage of flaming arrows as well as lit torches all along the castle walls, keeping the air clean and free of the particulates.

"Lord Dirk." Sir Gervais pointed into the distance.

Dirk looked in the direction the Knight indicated.

"What is that, sir? More of the faerie smoke? I still can't believe Verden has sided with the Winter faeries, sir."

"Nor I, Gerry." An amorphous cloud approached from the foothills of the White Rock Mountains. Dirk squinted as it grew closer. It moved against the wind, not with it, and he could make out flicks of orange and yellow as the shifting mass beat closer and closer. He shook his head. "But that's something else."

Dirk strode along the battlements to get nearer. Sir Gervais shadowed his path. A few of his soldiers gasped as he moved past them.

"Hold your fire!" he barked to archers who already swiveled into position towards the fluttering cloud.

"Sweet Spring," Dirk muttered as he was enveloped by a swarm of citrus-colored butterflies. "Little brother made it." He let his grin grow as his soldiers released a string of their own mutterings and laughs.

"Looks like Master Spense did his part," Sir Gervais mused at his side.

Dirk nodded. "Yeah—let's do ours."

Chapter 60

Ferrous smoothed out the feather light parchment on his desk and heard the predictable thuds of his oldest son's knocking.

"Enter."

Dirk burst through the doorway. "What does the little upstart say?"

Ferrous cocked an eyebrow. "This message is not from your brother—at least not directly."

"Then who?"

"Lady Radiant—of the Summer Court—sends her regards."

Dirk fell into the chair before Ferrous's desk. "Then he made it? To the Summer faeries? To The Vail?"

"It would seem so." Ferrous scanned the lines. Relief and dread both grew in equal measure. His *ambassador* had done his work and gained the support—though not in military terms—of the Summer Court. Spense continued on to the Silver Horn, to the domain of Winter, to plead his case for Telridge—with a scroll of passage written by none other than Lady Radiant herself.

But his *son* had been injured during the journey to The Vail. And though Spense was now healed, he headed into even further danger.

Ferrous frowned.

"Well?" Dirk prodded.

"Your little brother has earned the blessings of the

Summer Queen and walks boldly to face the leader of the Winter Court. He is taking on one front of this war alone. We are left to battle human foes—but if he is successful, *only* human foes."

Dirk lifted one corner of his mouth. "I guess I better get to work then. Can't have Spense confronting faerie warriors all by his lonesome only to come home to a castle overrun by power-hungry Verdenians."

"No, indeed." Ferrous matched Dirk's jovial expression, causing Dirk to escalate to a full laugh, which Ferrous echoed with interest. Their chuckles spent themselves in a few moments, as the weight of their present worries resumed their pressing, but it felt good to enjoy one small victory. They needed the short respite of levity, a brief but bright flicker of hope.

"Any thoughts as to how we are going to overcome this siege attempt?" Ferrous asked.

"A few," Dirk said.

His son was not known for being cryptic. Ferrous saw machinations at work, and he liked this side of Dirk—it was good to see the subtle game of strategy being worked out, alongside the straightforward battle skills. He wondered who was encouraging it, or if it naturally came about as he took more leadership in the kingdom.

"Tell me." Ferrous tented his fingers.

"I met this girl…"

"Really?" Ferrous couldn't hide his surprise. Not the first words he thought might come from Dirk's mouth.

"No, no. Not like that." He waved away his father's suppositions. "There's this farm girl—Flora—she fled to the castle during the first attack."

"The one who rode in with Spense?"

"Yeah—her. From what she's said, I think her family farm might be near where some of the old tunnels let out. If we can reach that farm, I think it could serve multiple purposes."

"Not all of the tunnels are stable. You'd have to be careful through the old mines, but go on."

"Verden fights as we do—by the same traditions."

"With the obvious exception of allying with Fae and utilizing faerie magic, I will have to agree with you," Ferrous conceded. He wondered where his son's mind was going.

"It occurred to me that the farm wouldn't be a bad place to set up a camp for staging ambushes as well as a good place to help fleeing refugees. And of course, if we can get out, we can also get in. A siege is a useful means of attack only when those under it begin to run out of supplies—food, clean water, weapons." He ticked the items off on his battle-scarred fingers.

Ferrous pushed back in his chair, considering. "I suppose Verden made the fateful mistake of attacking a country that made its fortunes in mining." He smirked at his son. "You would think that little detail might have occurred to them."

Dirk shrugged. "You'd think…but they're traditionalists."

"It may be very well for us that they did not, and that same tradition may be their downfall."

If only it could be so easy to outsmart Lumine's faerie army, Ferrous mused. But the Winter King was tricky and scheming at the best of times. Dirk and his forces were skilled, but he'd never gone up against a tactician like Lumine. So far, Grace had been with them, and a little luck, the uncanny and timely arrival of a Fae princess and a particularly useful farm girl. He prayed that it held. "Make sure the farm girl's family is well compensated for the trouble we're about to unload on them."

Dirk bolted from his chair and nodded a hasty salute. "Will do."

Chapter 61

Spense chuckled to himself as they made their way through the meandering forest trails leading from The Vail. A small cluster of monarchs flew before them, guiding their path. Dewy looked up sharply, and Spense tried to contain his laughter, but to no avail. It burst out of him in uncontrolled spurts.

"What?" She frowned at him, making her freckles squish together around her mouth.

He smiled. "It's nothing. I just can't help but picture Dirk being swarmed by butterflies." He waved at their companions and erupted in another round of giggles. Brawny, masculine giggles. Sniggers.

Dewy looked at the butterflies and smirked. A little giggle came from her mouth, too, before she covered it with her hand.

He shook his head. "I know I shouldn't be laughing—and I'm so appreciative of your aunt sending the message—but butterflies?"

She put her hands on her hips. Maybe going for intimidatingly annoyed? He wasn't sure, but it made him start laughing more. Dewy held up an accusatory finger. "I will have you know, human, that monarchs are considered to be one of nature's most treasured messengers. It is an honor to receive such a missive from the Queen of the Summer Court."

"Right, right, I know." Spense bent over and put his

hands on his knees, still shaking.

Dewy rolled her eyes. "But…I suppose…that they are not very Telridgian, are they?"

Spense tilted his head and grinned. "Not at all."

"Humans!" She sauntered over to a nearby boulder, where she flopped onto the rock in a not-so-noble-Fae manner. "Let me know when your convulsions are finished. I will rest here in the meantime."

It was Spense's turn to put his hands on his hips. "I thought faeries didn't need rest—just us weak humans."

"Well, you are not as slow as many of your kind. And I find myself actually wanting to be still for a moment. It has been a trying few days. That's not so unreasonable, is it?"

"No, of course not." Spense settled on the rock beside her. "That was thoughtless of me." His laughing spasms finally abated, and he turned to look closer at her face. She was pale. Still kissed with sunshine, but as if it shone through a misty cloud. "Maybe we should think about making camp?"

Dewy scanned the forest and trail ahead. "Perhaps. Dusk approaches."

Spense stood up, offering his hand, which Dewy accepted. "Let's see if we can make it a little farther. There must be a meadow or even a cave somewhere near." The truth was that as much as Spense was happy to be trekking through idyllic—non-predatory—forests and out of the stifling polite society of the Summer Fae, his body was still sore from the attacks of the malevolent woods, not to mention his own carelessness with the projectile fruit back in Telridge.

She wiggled her fingers at the butterflies. They flew to her hand, and she whispered to them. "Let's see what our fluttery friends can find." Dewy winked at him as she released the monarchs.

Chapter 62

Dewy held out her hands, full of fat, ripe blackberries. "You look like you could use some more. Eat."

"Now you're giving me commands?" The corners of Spense's mouth lifted, and he obliged by reaching for a couple of the sweet berries.

She watched as he popped them in his mouth. How many meals had she shared with Spense—this human— now? Enough they were comfortable, shared an ease between them, even a trust.

"It's lucky we found these," he said around a mouthful of the sweet fruit.

"Oh, I don't think luck had much to do with it. Monarchs are excellent guides."

He nodded, surveying the dry, animal-free cave. "Seems as if someone is looking out for us."

Dewy agreed. "Did you know blackberries are restorative?"

"I did, actually."

"Something you learned as a mage?"

Spense snorted. "No, my mum."

"Really? Your mother is well-versed for a maker of heated wheat."

He wiggled a finger at her. "You liked the bread, remember? And, also, my grandfather knew a thing or two about fruit."

"The orchardist with the faerie-like cottage." She remembered the feeling of coziness that she experienced in the curving home. She'd enjoyed the warm fire and candlelight of the place.

As if Spense could read her wistful thoughts, he stood and began rummaging for twigs and branches. He laid them out in a neat pyramid. "My mum doesn't just make bread, you know. Whenever I was forced to train with Dirk's soldiers, she made a blackberry tart for me."

"You, a soldier?"

Spense cupped his hands around his mouth whispering and blowing into the pile of twigs. A tiny flame caught. He looked up at her, smirking. "The trainings never ended well. I was not meant for physical battle."

Dewy had seen the lean muscle hiding beneath his layers of clothing. She wasn't sure she could entirely agree.

"Which is why my mum made me eat blackberries after—she never would have gotten any work out of me if I'd passed out after every session." He grinned and threw a couple of larger pieces of wood on the small pyre.

Dewy scooted closer, letting the glowing warmth fill her. For all of the energizing effects of the berries, she still felt sleepy and could happily curl up in the sweet comfort of the cave for a few hours...or days.

They watched the flames grow in silence. As necessary, Spense poked at the fire with a long stick. When he seemed satisfied that the fire would burn without his interference, he sat back, gazing across the flames at her.

He waited a few moments longer, and said, "Tell me

what happened in The Vail."

Dewy bolted upright and stared back, her anger growing with the leaping flames. "That is unkind, Spense."

"I know," he whispered. "Tell me."

"Why?" she said, breathless. Her chest began to clench uncomfortably.

"Because I don't think you would tell me honestly or at least not fully if I asked gently. You are hurt— maybe not in body, but in spirit—and that can be just as exhausting."

The bands around her ribs and lungs tightened and tears rolled down her face. "You have no right."

He nodded but did not release her.

She glared at him and let one hiccupping word free and then another. Anger and resentment that he was making her do this fueled her speech.

But she told him everything, how much it hurt to be banished, how she'd never felt like she fit in, how she pushed and pushed to break out of the dutiful mold Lady Radiant and the Court of Summer forced her into, and how it was still devastating to be exiled. The tightness in her chest released as she obeyed Spense's command.

Something else released while she was talking, and Dewy kept going. Tears rolled down her cheeks. Her nose ran. She'd never been more vulnerable, or soggy and messy. A thing lifted from the very center of her being, a weight laying on her soul, not gone but lessened as she gave part of it to Spense.

Dewy told him about her parents and how they'd died, how this banishment was only the last step in a painful dance of loss, how she'd been grieving them for years, and being taken out of her home seemed fitting.

When she came to the point of their deaths, he stopped her.

"You don't have to tell me this. You can—if you need to—but you don't have to. This isn't what I was asking for."

"I know that." She brushed her cheeks and lifted her lips in a watery smile. "My chest stopped hurting a while ago."

"I'm sorry for that." Spense pulled his knees to his chest and rested his chin on them. He kept his gaze and attention fixed on her, as if expecting her to make a sudden and risky move.

She returned his gaze. "Thank you for saying that. I understand why you did it."

"Is there more that you'd like to tell? Your choice, this time."

She thought about it for no more than a heartbeat. "They were killed—my parents—murdered in the forest. By humans."

Dewy waited for her words to settle on Spense. He frowned. "How?"

"They were playing a foolish and romantic game of make-believe. They were both gifted with shape-shifting, so they got the idea to go running through the forest as a doe and a buck." Dewy remembered the forms they took during night dances and how they tantalized the court, how they swooped around her as birds, tickled her cheeks as butterflies.

"How old were you?"

"It was the autumn when I was six years old." How she'd wanted to go with them for the romp through forest, to see the golden changes in colors, but her father chided her, winking when he said that time alone with her mother was a gift. He'd kissed her on the head and said they'd bring her next time.

"Autumn?" Spense's frown grew deeper.

Dewy nodded.

"Hunting season," he whispered. "Dewy...I'm...I don't know what to say."

She snorted. "You're sorry, of course. *Everyone* is sorry. But at the back of your mind, you're thinking that their folly led to their deaths."

"No." He tried to protest. "That wasn't..."

"It's true, isn't it?" The tears flowed from her eyes. "It's what everyone in The Vail has thought for years. My mother was too frivolous. She distracted my father from his princely duties. But do you know what else is true?"

She paused and sobbed.

"They loved each other. And they loved me. And all of that playfulness that is supposed to have been so terrible...it's what I cherish the most about them." Dewy let the jagged sobs and hiccups overtake her.

She heard a quiet scuffle and then felt Spense's warm arms slide around her. She leaned into his shoulder.

"And now it's happening all over again. With me. The same foolish mistakes."

Spense smoothed his hand along her back. "No, Dewy, this was *my* mistake."

"Don't you see?" She lifted her head. "I was only in the marsh that night because I was being punished for my irresponsible behavior. And even when I was out there, I wanted to swim in the river. They're right—the whole court. I am *just* like her." Dewy beat her fist on his chest for emphasis.

241

He let her.

"I'm too frivolous." Pound. "I am irresponsible." Pound. "I don't take my duties seriously." Pound. "I deserve whatever consequences come my way." Pound. "Just. Like. Them."

When her fists finally tired out, he took her hand, and held it. "They sound like they were wonderful parents. They loved you and each other with their whole hearts. Is it such a bad thing to be like them?"

Dewy had no words. How could Spense nudge the perspective with a few words and change everything? How she understood her parents and their deaths? How she saw herself?

She opened the hand he held and flattened it onto his chest. She felt his steady heartbeat, its tempo increasing the longer she held his stare. Her mouth parted and she released a small breath, as she released her burdens onto Spense—giving them to him so that he could reshape them and find the blessing and not the curse.

How was it possible that this human mage, of no apparent consequence according to him, could have unsettled her so and reordered her in such a way that she found comfort and wholeness? The Claiming could've broken her as her will bent to his. It should have. There was a reason it was considered dark magic. But instead, she felt a growing bond to him that had nothing to do with the spell and in it a sense of lightness. It was confusing and paradoxical. Like nothing she'd ever experienced—certainly not the giggling trysts with the wood faeries.

Dewy leaned in and licked her lips. She'd kissed many young faeries before, but it would mean something different if she did so here—if she kissed Spense. She held his gaze, watching as his eyes softened and drifted to her mouth.

She waited a breath. And another.

Spense jerked his chin up and away, as if something near the fire had caught his eye. His hands fell away from her, and despite the heat of the fire, she felt chilled.

"I...uh..." He stuttered and scrambled up. "You should think about getting some rest. I'll go find more berries. We'll need them. We've still got a long journey ahead of us. And you're exhausted."

Dewy followed his abrupt movements around the cave. He tossed her a blanket from his satchel, and lurched to the cave entrance, hesitating for a moment before darting outside. "I'll be back soon."

She considered his words. He hadn't quite directed her to rest but suggested that she might think about it. There was no tightening in her chest.

Dewy pulled the blanket around her—a work of fine craftsmanship from The Vail. She grabbed one of the supply packs and laid her head on it. She watched the fire as it consumed the remaining logs. She thought about rest. She thought about Spense and his awkward flight from her. She thought about what it meant and what it didn't mean. Disappointment. Frustration. She thought and thought.

When her eyes grew heavy, she closed them.

Chapter 63

Spense bolted from the cave into brisk mountain air. He stumbled into the forest and took deep, bracing breaths.

He didn't know what'd happened. Or might've happened.

He knew Dewy was hurting, and he knew she needed to confront those hurts, or they'd weigh on her. He wasn't sure how he knew. But he knew. And so he pushed. No, he commanded, which was perhaps cruel but also what she needed. That's what he told himself.

And when Dewy shared with him her worst hurts, and her face became pink and blotchy and she was a crying mess—her hair and freckles scrambled together in a pile of sogginess—it was instinct to go to her and hold her. To find the good and golden bits that shined through the mess. He felt it was his responsibility to give them back to her.

Spense wasn't expecting the next part. Her reaction. He was about as sure as he could get that Dewy wanted to kiss him. And he wanted to kiss her, too. Every sad, soggy bit.

But how could he? How could he know that her affections weren't an effect of the Claiming? And if that was the case, then he was the worst of souls, taking advantage of her in a vulnerable state.

Spense stomped into the forest and collapsed onto a

fallen log. He ran his fingers through his hair and hung his head. Quite the tangle he'd gotten himself into. And it kept getting worse.

But he had a mission, a job to do. And the next step was simple. Find berries for a weary Fae...princess. He realized with a start that princess was indeed Dewy's title. Her father had been destined to be the next King of Summer.

He snorted. *Wicked Winter!*

Around every turn, the situation became bleaker as Spense pieced the history together. Dewy's father had been the Crown Prince of Summer. But when he died, his sister had taken on that mantle. And at the passing of the last Summer King, Radiant became regent. Until her niece came of age. Dewy should be the next queen. Except that she'd been exiled. And it was his fault.

It was nothing short of a miracle The Vail hadn't declared war. Or his execution.

Spense pushed himself from the log and retraced their steps from earlier, muttering to himself the whole time. He managed to find the prickly blackberry bushes and began snapping berries off their stems and into a pouch.

He should've noticed when the woods grew quiet, but he was making so much noise himself that he didn't. Snap, flick, mutter, mutter.

Thud.

Spense's knees buckled underneath him, and his face fell forward into a mass of berry thorns. His choked wail came out garbled. Despite the thorns, he propelled himself over, angling to find his attacker.

Attackers.

Three blue-gray goblins lurked over him, grins

spreading their faces wide.

"What do we have here?"

"Looks like a tasty morsel."

"A bit lean for my tastes." The last speaker cocked his bulbous head in consideration.

"What a delightful specimen to have wandered so near our territory."

"Most humans aren't nearly so brave."

"Or so stupid."

"Agreed, brother."

Spense's gaze darted between the goblins as if he was watching some macabre game of lances. "Wait, wait!" he yelled and scrambled to a standing position. Spense held out a placating hand, while searching in his vest for the scrolls.

"He has a weapon!"

"Get him!"

They pounced. He landed with a crash back into the blackberry thorns.

"No!" Spense screamed as they flipped him over. "I have passage." But his face was held to the ground, making speech come out muffled.

"What was that?"

"I think he's trying to talk." The pressure lifted slightly.

Spense spat out dirt and leaves. "I have passage. A scroll. In my tunic." He coughed.

"Let him up." A cool male voice spoke.

At the command, the goblins released him. Spense wasted no time in scrambling upright. He found the source of the voice in the form of a towering faerie, with snow pale skin and hair nearly so—nothing like the warm brown and golden faces in the Summer Court. The faerie's diamond blue eyes were furrowed, his gaze hard.

"If you have passage, let's see it. It won't go well for you if you are bluffing."

"I believe you," Spense said. He removed the scroll he received from Lady Radiant and handed it over.

The faerie scanned it, his gaze racing over the royal words. "You serve as ambassador to the human kingdom of Telridge?"

Spense nodded. He tried to brush off leaves and dirt.

"And you seek audience with King Lumine?"

"Yes—to plead for mercy"—Spense spoke quickly—"for a cessation of conflict. Lady Radiant wrote that missive herself."

"So, I see." The faerie frowned. "Why would Lady Radiant seek to help you? You don't seem to be anyone of consequence."

Spense had no rebuttal. It was true. He was no one of consequence, except that he held a Fae princess enthralled. That didn't seem like the best detail to bring up.

After a moment's consideration, the male faerie sighed. "I suppose we are left to escort you." He didn't sound pleased. His goblin companions rubbed their hands together and grinned menacingly.

"I...uh...thank you for the courtesy," Spense said, trying to re-order his scrambled thoughts and make sense of this quick turn of events. "I don't mean to be rude, but are you sure they won't...eat me along the way?" He nodded to the goblin trio.

"Have the boys been playing tricks again?" A lilting female voice asked, followed by the faerie it belonged to.

Spense's heart skipped. Where she'd come from, he

had no idea. One moment, no indication that there was anyone else in the dark wood and in the next there she was before him. The blue-haired, female faerie was as lean as the male and as pale. The goblins tittered.

Spense looked at their faces and then back to the female. "You mean they were…joking when they said I looked like a 'tasty morsel'?"

"Hah!" The female barked a laugh. "They do like to have their fun—and quite frankly you humans are far too gullible." She mussed the head of the nearest goblin. "Really Tun, you're too much."

The goblin—Tun—shrugged and smiled guiltily. It didn't do much to allay Spense's concerns.

"You can call him Frost." She indicated to her silently intimidating companion. "And me, Misty."

"You'd give me your names?" Spense asked.

"Not our true names. Just what you can call us."

Spense thought these names suited them each well and wondered what their true names might be. These seemed too perfect.

"It looks like we're your new companions—at least if you want to see Lumine."

"He can't be allowed to know the way to the Horn." Frost slid his eyes to the female faerie. His words were sharp and clipped.

"True." Misty pursed her lips. "Well, there's nothing for it. We'll just have to blindfold him." She whipped out a midnight blue scarf.

Spense groaned. His shoulders fell as he succumbed to the faerie precaution. Once the scarf was snug, he felt his arms being gripped by rough, bony hands. Goblins, he presumed.

"Better get going," Misty said.

They urged him forward and tittered as his foot hit a root. He gritted his teeth. It was going to be a long road to The Silver Horn.

And Dewy would have no idea where he'd gone.

Chapter 64

Dirk jerked his head up. Lady Xendra slid through the farmhouse's kitchen door and latched it behind her.

"Report?"

"Camp is secure, My Lord. Perimeter monitored by four-point watch."

"Good. Scouts?"

"Yes, My Lord. I've sent scouts in multiple trajectories. They should be arriving back here soon."

Dirk nodded again. He looked down at the map he'd laid out on Flora's large kitchen worktable. She helped him fill in unique land features on the sparse map he'd procured, providing a more detailed understanding of the land surrounding them.

In addition, Flora aided his team by creating a sort of barracks in the horse stalls—the barn was largely unharmed after the attack and even had fresh hay, which they used for makeshift bedding. The fencing around the animal pens was trampled, which meant livestock roamed free or wandered in the forest. Dirk sent a few men to check the immediate area. They managed to return with a small flock of sheep.

Flora opened her family's cottage as their officer quarters and command center, while assisting the cook with meals. Dirk wondered if the girl ever slept. As she'd given up her own bed, he was guessing not. Her family was settled in nicely at an inn in the city, paid for from the Telridgian Royal coffers. He'd personally tipped the caretaker extra to ensure they were well tended to.

Dirk caught Flora's eye as she flew by for the third time in as many minutes. "Do you need something, My Lord?"

He lifted a corner of his mouth in quiet amusement at her delayed application of his title. He knew Flora was unaccustomed to courtly manners. Why would she be? Who needs it on a farm in the woods? With her hair tied in a messy knot and her simple sturdy clothing, Flora was a far cry from the decorated members of court, or the city girls who plaited their curls up in ribbons and flowers.

"Sir?" Flora asked again.

"I...uh...yes, actually." Dirk cleared his throat and extinguished the image of Flora with a crown of flowers in her honey-brown hair. He pointed to a cliff marked on the map. "I was wondering if you could tell me a little more about this outcropping here."

"Of course, My Lord." She set down the jug she'd been carrying and turned to lean over the table alongside Dirk. She gave off the aroma of baking bread. He noted the dusting of flour on her apron and the smudge of it on her cheek.

"This one, My Lord?" She asked, confirming the area in question.

He nodded.

"Are you thinking of a lookout position?"

"Perhaps."

"Should work for that. My uncle Mason often starts from that point before a game hunt—gives him an admirable view of the surrounding land and an indication of where to find his quarry."

This comment presented him with a whole new set

of images. "Do you hunt?"

"Sometimes." She shrugged. "I don't mind it. Usually, there's too much work to be done, though, and I leave it to my uncle and cousin."

That picture fit better with what little Dirk had learned of the farm girl. Much more so than the imagined garland.

"Anything else, sir?"

"No. Thank you. I'm sorry to have kept you—I know you've been busy tending to a house full of Knights."

"It's no trouble, My Lord." Flora bobbed a half curtsy, picked up her jug, and darted back through the kitchen.

Before he resumed his concentration back on the map, he caught Lady Xendra staring at him, one eyebrow arched.

"What?" he growled.

She shook her head. "Nothing, My Lord."

Sir Gervais saved him from trying to decipher what Lady Xendra's look implied when he entered the kitchen headquarters. A bloodied scout followed close behind.

"What's happened?" Dirk asked.

Sir Gervais led the scout forward. "Found him rushing back to camp. Tell the Commander what you told me."

The scout nodded. "A full company of Verdenians approach from here." He pointed to a spot on the map.

"Did you engage? Why are you injured?"

"That's my own fault, Sir. Got caught in a hunting trap on the way back."

Dirk shook his head. Though relieved the scout hadn't been seen, this type of error still cost them. And he was one man down. "Go see about your wounds."

The scout bowed his way out.

Dirk sat back, hissing through his teeth. He looked at his two most skilled Knights—and closest friends. "Think we can take a hundred Verdenian soldiers?"

"Yessir." Lady Xendra and Sir Gervais answered in near unison.

He smirked. It wasn't overconfidence. Though they had only a quarter in number of the Verdenians, they were the best Telridgian Knights. They knew their trade. He tapped the edge of the wooden chair with his finger.

"Gerry, think you can track down our host?"

Sir Gervais frowned in confusion.

"Flora—the girl whose family owns this farm?" Dirk clarified.

"Of course, My Lord." Sir Gervais ducked out through the kitchens.

"If I may be so bold, My Lord, what are you thinking?" Lady Xendra asked.

"I am thinking that we need a hunter who knows these woods."

Lady Xendra nodded. "Catching foxes."

"Something like that." Dirk pushed up from the table. "Filling the time while we wait for Spense to save us all."

"Do you think he can?" Lady Xendra tilted her head.

Dirk snorted. "If I have learned anything about my little brother, it is that he never does what is expected. I have no idea if he can make a difference. Doesn't mean I don't hope for it. While he's out being an enigma, I'll do my own blooming job."

Chapter 65

She must have slept for a long time. The fire had burned down to a few dusty coals, casting the cave in a dim orange glow. Much less cozy than Spense's cottage in the woods. Dewy pushed up from her pile of blankets and stretched her arms overhead. She was stiff from the cramped ball she'd slept in. Her eyes felt dry and crusty. Little salt tracks reminded her of the state she'd been in...how long had it been? Judging by the remnants of the fire, hours.

Perhaps Spense was right to push her, though she'd resisted him at first. There were things that needed to be said and feelings that needed to be felt. And he managed to position himself in the right place to take on all of those words and feelings that came pouring out of her. Dewy rubbed at her eyes.

Where *was* Spense?

She glanced around the cave, but there was no sign that he ever returned from berry picking. His pack lay undisturbed near the entrance, next to his bow.

Some supplies had fallen out and lay strewn on the ground near the last of the berries. She nibbled while repacking. One of the pouches was missing. She shrugged and stuffed the apples and sachets of nuts into the top of Spense's satchel. He'd want to be ready to continue on to the Silver Horn as soon as he was back.

Dewy looked around, wondering what else she

could do. She lifted the blanket from the ground and shook it out, refolding it and placing it inside the pack. She kicked dirt over the coals, smothering them.

When all was in order, Dewy peered out of the cave entrance. The sun had long since set. Stars sparkled in an inky sky. They must be close to the Winter Fae territory. The cold nights of Winter always made for the clearest skies.

She scooped up the pack, shouldering it with ease, and reached for Spense's bow. She wrapped her hands around it, feeling the smooth, worn wood. She plucked the taut string. Dewy held it for a moment. She'd committed her own acts of violence, but she couldn't bear this particular human weapon. She set it back down amongst the stones.

Dewy closed her eyes, breathed in the night air, and listened to the sounds of the forest. She blinked her eyes open.

Her feet retraced the path he'd trod, and she skirted saplings and underbrush until she made her way back to the overgrown blackberry bushes.

But Spense wasn't there. She located a row of thorny bushes, but no human male. It looked as if some wild animal had gotten caught in them. Whole sections were flattened, leaves torn, fat berries on the ground. She cocked her head. And something else.

Dewy crouched to get a better look. A piece of faerie-made cloth glowed in the moonlight. She picked it up. It was the missing pouch, and it was half-full of berries.

She extended her senses. Water flowed throughout the trees, shrubs and bushes, life in forest animals and insects, but she couldn't feel Spense. His was a warm presence. Since the Claiming, she felt him like a tug in her mid-section, pulling her to him. But it was faint now, barely a tingle.

A burst of fluttering orange and gold descended upon her. Dewy nearly fell over as a small swarm of monarchs swooped toward her.

She gasped. "Oh! It's you—what happened here?"

The butterflies darted to the smashed branches of the blackberry bush, to the ground where the berries were strewn, and then back to her. She lowered her hand and grasped a pinch of dirt. She raised her fingers, and smelled blood. A few drops. But sure as the night was clear, it belonged to Spense.

Dewy's hands began to shake as cold overtook her, and she re-examined the evidence around her. The trampled bushes, the discarded pouch.

"What happened?" Dewy cried. "Where *is* he?"

The monarchs swarmed her and zoomed off into the forest. A moment later, they returned, fluttering urgently, as if to lead her. She nodded in understanding. Spense had been attacked, and taken, but he was alive. She could find him.

"Take me to him, friends."

Chapter 66

Spense had a new understanding of humiliation.
Blind trekking with a goblin entourage. Worse than
anything his brother had ever done to him. His faerie
escorts didn't worry themselves overmuch about his
feelings, though. They trekked on and on. Without
stopping.

Dewy had estimated several nights of making camp.
But these faeries didn't believe in rest. Mostly they were
frustrated that they had to move at something nearing
human speed, which lagged more and more as they went
on. At some point in the journey, the goblins began
kicking him and yanking on his arms to propel him
forward. The conversation was limited to prodding and
threats, so that wasn't much incentive, either.

When it occurred to her, the female faerie—Misty—
offered him water or a small bite of food. Once or twice
they let him see to his needs and collapse for a few
minutes of respite.

By the time the party reached the Silver Horn, the
goblins were all but dragging him. Misty whisked his
blindfold off in what he was sure was meant as a
dramatic flourish. Spense squinted through his too tired
and stinging eyes, but he couldn't muster the enthusiasm
she was hoping for.

"Well, human, you're now looking at a sight few of
your kind will ever gaze upon." Misty waved her arms at

the blurry, silvery structure behind her and the dark cliffs it was built into.

Spense's eyes were watering too much to make out the actual form of it, but he nodded in acknowledgement regardless.

"Enough theatrics. Let's deliver him to Lumine and be done with it," Frost said.

Spense agreed with the terse faerie male. The idea of being *inside* of anything held great appeal. He was sorely tired of all the wonders that nature provided—especially since it'd been so long since he'd seen any of them. He *felt* the biting cold, and tripped on jagged rocks, sensed the surface of the earth, stony, damp, and sometimes muddy, but he witnessed no great vistas or towering forests. Dewy might be disappointed in him. He didn't care. He just wanted to collapse in a heap at the first opportunity.

But that wasn't to be. They were barely through the great foyer of the Silver Horn when a booming voice echoed down.

"What have you brought to these halls? Who desecrates my court?"

All five of Spense's new companions bowed as a tall Fae male clad in swirling indigo and quicksilver robes strode before them. He was as pale as the other Winter faeries, moon-white skin and flinty, granite-colored eyes. Spense swayed on his feet while the scents of edelweiss and clean snow swirled past him. After days and days in the forest, the odors he brought with him would be a desecration, indeed.

"We found him near the borders of the Winter territory, Your Majesty," Frost explained. "He has a note of passage from Lady Radiant, and another sealed message to deliver to you."

Lumine—who else could it be—stepped closer to examine Spense.

"Who are you?" he hissed.

Spense lifted his head, squinting up at the king before him. He licked his wind-chapped lips. "Spense of Telridge."

"You're human." It sounded like a foul accusation coming from Lumine's lips.

"Yes." His voice was raspy. "I'm an ambassador. I had hoped to arrive in a…more presentable manner but your court values expediency."

Lumine snorted. "You certainly speak like a human politician. Ambassador you are, then." He turned his attention to Frost. "You said he bears scrolls with Radiant's seal. Let's see them then."

Frost relinquished the two rolled parchments. Lumine scanned the first and thrust it back into Spense's hands. He cracked the seal of the second and read the letter. His mouth tightened as his gaze zig-zagged across the queen's curling words. When he was finished, he re-rolled the document, and slid it into his wide sleeves.

"Bring him to the Receiving Chambers before moonrise. It seems we have *diplomacy* to conduct." Lumine whirled away, heading back in the direction he'd come.

"Yes, Your Majesty."

"And for Winter's sake, get him cleaned up and fed. We are Fae and there are hospitality protocols—even for humans." Lumine barked his orders before disappearing down a long corridor.

Misty whistled. "That actually went better than I thought it would. Have to wonder what your precious letter says."

That was going *better*? Spense cringed and tried not to think too hard about what *worse* might have been. He processed Lumine's words as the goblins got hold of his arms again. "Wait—'we are Fae'?" he asked.

Frost eyed him but did not respond.

"Ah—you noticed that?" Misty elbowed him and winked.

He stared at her open-mouthed and wide-eyed.

"What? You thought you were being seen to by ordinary, common faeries? You'd think that you'd recognize nobility." She performed a little skipping flourish.

"Let's go," Frost said, striding towards one of the many corridors that led off from the massive open space like spokes of a wagon wheel. In fact, the whole foyer resembled a half-wheel, with large wood beams overhead, linking together massive wood columns— they must have used whole trees for them—that were arranged in a semi-circle around a central stone fireplace.

The warmth of the fire and the escape from the constant chill of the wind brought sensation back to Spense's near-frozen fingertips. Just when he thought he couldn't keep awake for another moment, the stinging bite of his thawing hands brought him to a new excruciating level of consciousness.

The goblins goaded him through a labyrinth of corridors, keeping close to Frost and his clipped steps.

"Thought you'd take him to the kitchens?" Misty asked.

"I think it will suit best," Frost said.

They pushed him into a cooking and workspace much like that of his grandfather's cottage in design, but with grossly oversized proportions. A goblin, the one they called Tun, plunked him down at a nearby table.

"Cook, are you about?" Misty called.

A rotund, pink-cheeked faerie emerged from the larder, toting nets of onions and apples. "Back from your rounds so soon, Misty dear? I thought Lumine sent you out for the full loop."

"We caught His Majesty a prize." Misty patted Spense on the head. He slunk down on the kitchen bench.

"That you did!" Cook peered closely at Spense. "Is he...human?"

"Sure is." Spense could hear the proud grin in Misty's voice. "From Telridge."

Frost cleared his throat. "We've been asked to provide...hospitality." The word sounded distasteful.

"Well, of course you should." Cook chastised Frost while completing her inspection. "Frost, don't you know that you have to feed and water humans? And give them time to rest—this soul looks like no more than a bag of bones."

Spense winced. He'd been called worse, but the appellation still stung. So much for his attempts to appear ambassadorial. He supposed that hope was dashed when three goblins tackled him and shoved him into a blackberry bush.

Cook leaned over and pinched Spense's chin in her plump fingers. "What are you called, child?"

"Spense," he rasped.

She tutted. "Sit tight. Cook will fetch you a bowl of venison stew I have simmering. That'll perk you up, no doubt."

Spense frowned. "You eat meat?"

"What, don't you?"

"No…I do. I just thought faeries didn't."

Cook bustled around the massive kitchen with surprising speed. "You'll be thinking of the Summer Court," she said while ladling stew into bowls. "Quite prim about only eating nuts and berries. That's all well and good if you live in summertime weather year-round. We need warmth in these parts. And that comes from eating real food. What's more, deer can't survive here long. No creature can last in these Winter forests. Starvation is a slow, cruel death. We are doing them a kindness. And they us." She proselytized as she laid out a mug of water, a spoon and a bowl brimming with carrots, potatoes, onions, and chunks of aromatic venison before everyone—Fae, goblin, and human alike. "Eat up. You'll feel better soon. All of you."

Spense did as he was told, guzzling the spring water, sharp with minerals and slurping the spicy broth. He sighed as warmth slid into his belly. He felt sure Dewy wouldn't approve of this either, were she here. The mercy argument seemed thin. Truth be told, he was glad Dewy wasn't with him and not just because of her gastronomic sensitivities. He took a small comfort in knowing she was safe in the territory of Summer.

Spense managed half a dozen mouthfuls of the stew, chewing the tender meat with enthusiasm, and another full mug of the astringent spring water before the heat of the kitchen and the food itself did their work and he began to doze at the table.

Chapter 67

He bolted upright as a bracing bucket of water hit him. Spense yelled something garbled and shoved back from the table. His legs tangled on the wide wood bench, and he fell unceremoniously to the stone floor of the kitchen. Laughter echoed around him.

Spense gave up and released his dripping head onto the stone. "I suppose it's comical when a human falls into exhausted sleep."

Misty towered over him, peering down and grinning. "Well, that, and Lumine asked us to clean you up. He did *not* specify how." She shrugged and smacked a pile of Winter-ready clothing on the table.

Spense groaned and rolled to his knees. "If you point me to a privy, or at least a curtain, I'll change my clothes."

She jerked her thumb over her shoulder. "That way. Be quick about it."

Once outfitted in a simple tunic and fur-lined overcoat and boots—practical workers' clothes—Spense emerged from the small changing room to find that his companions had reduced in number. Frost and Misty remained.

"Where did—"

"Where did the goblins go?" Misty finished his question. "They're not really partial to Receiving Chambers business."

The pair of Fae marched him through twisting stone and timber hallways until they reached a pair of thick closed doors. His mind was still fuzzy with exhaustion and he was sure he'd never find his way again. The doors swung open as if on silent hinges as they approached, revealing yet another massive space. It had high, vaulted ceilings painted in a deep midnight blue and speckled with twinkling stars. Or perhaps he was looking at the night sky in Winter. It could be either, given his sleep-addled state.

The two far walls were made up of expansive crystalline glass, allowing a sweeping view of the forest and mountains surrounding the Silver Horn. The landscape was tinged with the faint blue glow of moonlight, giving the snow-dusted peaks a jewel-like appearance.

Spense took several faltering steps in wonder. Misty nudged him. "Close your mouth and kneel."

Spense obliged.

"King Lumine," Frost and Misty murmured together.

"Rise."

Spense peeked through strands of his still drying hair, wondering if the command applied to him. Lumine sat on a throne made of fully grown fir trees. Their branches wove together to form a wide seat. His elbows rested lightly on a pair of thick, branch armrests. In one hand, Lumine loosely held the scroll from Lady Radiant.

"Do you know what this says, Ambassador?" Lumine asked, waving the scroll.

Spense pushed to his feet. "I do not, Your Majesty. As you saw, it was sealed."

Lumine tapped the end of the parchment with his

fingers. "Interesting." He rose from the throne and stepped forward. "The Lady of The Vail suggested some uses for you, Master Spense."

Spense frowned. "Uses? I don't know what that letter says. I come here only to plead mercy for the people of Telridge."

"Mercy? Is that what Lord Ferrous showed to *me*?" Lumine leaned in close.

Spense could feel his icy breath.

"I don't understand. I don't know what you speak of." Spense shook his head. "Indeed, Lord Ferrous knows not why the people of the Silver Horn would join with Verden in attacking Telridge. I have come to settle any grievances or misunderstandings."

"But how can you when you haven't been given all of the information? Or any of it! I'm expected to believe this nonsense? This falsehood?" Lumine straightened to his full height. "Or perhaps you are a fool, Ambassador, and have been manipulated first by your Lord who keeps his correspondence from you, and second by Summer's queen, who serves you to me, like a mysterious delicacy on a platter." Lumine's sneer distorted his face. "And despite what Radiant's missive suggests, I have no *use* for fools."

"But what…My Lord—"

"Enough! Take him away." Lumine waved his hand and turned from Spense.

"Where to, My King?" Frost asked.

Lumine pondered. "For now, guest chambers. In the western wing. We'll see how long his tongue remains tied."

Spense's mind raced, trying to understand what had transpired and not to speculate what "guest chambers" was a euphemism for.

Not that it mattered. Spense had failed. Again. And he didn't even understand what had gone wrong.

He might as well be in a prison cell.

Spense hung his head as Frost led him out of the Receiving Chambers and the end of his diplomatic career.

Chapter 68

Flora ran stooped through the grasses of the grazing land. Dirk kept close behind her. She could hear his even, regular breaths. Her uncle built a blind for hunting out of a pile of large stones. She dove behind them. Dirk hit the ground a half-second later. She hoped it would work as well for hunting enemy soldiers.

The sweet scent of the grass filled her nose, and she drew it in. This meadow was supposed to be a safe place, but like her home, it had been tarnished by the stink of battle.

Dirk eyed her with concern. "You sure you're up for this? It's not the same as deer or foxes."

"I know. I'm good."

He resisted whatever comment he was considering making and instead hefted a large sack filled with dozens of her uncle's traps. Gingerly, he pulled out one and another. These traps would offer a little more than the usual snap.

"Disperse as many in the field as you can. Don't create any type of pattern. And Flora—" Dirk grabbed her arm. "Be careful."

"Of course, My Lord." Flora was taken aback by the tender words and Dirk's insistent look, but she shook off her surprise and launched herself into the tall grass. A few yards out, she placed one of the traps, attaching the packet of dark powder as they had practiced. A few more yards and she found a home for another.

When she'd placed all of the crude, explosive traps throughout the field, Flora made her way back to the stone enclosure. Dirk readied another set—these were for throwing. He glanced at her as she settled beside him.

"Well done," Dirk said. "Now, stay low and out of sight. We don't want to give Verden an opportunity. And be careful. These devices will just as easily tear off one of your limbs as one of your enemies."

Flora nodded. She could have lived without that last visual.

Dirk picked up his bow and sighted through a crevice designed for that purpose. He was still. Waiting. Flora peered through another gap, just as a line of Verdenian soldiers marched onto the field. Dirk let his arrow fly.

It sailed unseen through the grass and found its mark in the farthest of the traps. Snapping it just as the soldiers crossed through the tall weeds.

Flora closed her eyes against the shower of earth that rained from the explosion, but she felt its shudders and heard the crash, along with the screams of men.

The first trap set off the next and the next, like a game of tiles. As Verdenians fled one, they were led into the path of another.

Flora breathed in short pants, waiting for the screams to end. They didn't.

Telridgians added to the noise with their own shouts of triumph, but they were cut short as a second wave of enemy soldiers poured in from the east. They'd been waiting in the tree cover, to ambush, and launched themselves at the cheering, distracted Telridgians.

Dirk swore. He grabbed hold of Flora's shoulders.

"Give me a minute, then throw these into the thickest groups of Verdenians." He pointed at the pile of waiting explosives. "Try not to hit us."

Before she could respond, Dirk bolted into the field of oncoming warriors, barking out orders at his own soldiers. He surged forward like a berserker of old myth, yelling and brandishing his sword.

He took out three Verdenians with swift smooth strikes before they could react. Hacking at chest, neck, and tendons with a cool rhythm. One, two, three. One, two, three. Each fell, and Dirk moved toward the next in the line.

But Flora could see that the Telridgians were greatly outnumbered, and no match for the oncoming force, despite their famed skill. She scrambled behind the stone protection and fumbled for the first of the explosive traps. She counted to three, leaned around the stone, and threw. It fell short of the Verdenians' formation, exploding in a spray of dirt. The nearest soldiers were hit with debris and distracted.

Flora grabbed the next and threw again. This time she hit the mass of men, resulting in a score of flailing limbs and bleeding faces. She ducked back behind the stone, breathing hard. She shut her eyes for the briefest of moments, gritted her teeth, and threw again. Another hit.

Their combined attacks rallied the Telridgian Knights, who reformed their line and pushed against their enemy. From behind, a volley of arrows fell on the Verdenians, causing more to fall. The crumpling of their formation led to chaos. The Knights took advantage of it and surged forward like a spear point driven through the heart of the enemy.

She could barely distinguish friend from foe through the screams and clangs of metal. Debris flew and men fell in graceless thuds.

Flora looked for an opening for another explosive, but she couldn't throw any more traps without risking hurting her own people.

And so she watched, trembling. She saw a Knight fall. He'd helped her with dishes this morning. Another, who'd asked her for a cup of tea late last night.

Dirk fought on, sometimes taking on two or three assailants at once, mixing sword-play with bar-room punches. She breathed a choked sigh of relief with each block or thrust. When two Verdenians ambushed Dirk, Flora bit back a scream. He threw the first off, but the man staggered back into the uneven fight. Dirk batted the second's sword away, but it left him open on the left side. The first Verdenian drove his sword down. At the last moment, Dirk swiveled, saving his mid-section but sacrificing his thigh.

Flora screamed. Dirk roared in pain, but still managed to keep fighting, slashing at his attacker from the ground.

She scouted the field, selected her target—a narrow band of earth at the edge of the Verdenian line—and hurled the last of her uncle's hunting traps into the melee of crimson-clad soldiers. It hit the ground with a snap, followed by a concussive slam. Men were thrown into the air. The one who brandished his weapon over Dirk only a moment before lay sprawled and bleeding on the ground as a rain of dirt pelted his prone form.

It was enough. Telridgians plowed through the remaining survivors, pushing them back from the perimeter of the farm.

Dirk elbow crawled his way through the dirt, dragging his wounded leg behind. Flora lurched towards him and grabbed both arms, yanking him to his good leg. He leaned heavily on her. And he wasn't a small man. But she took a step and then another and another until they reached the safety of the stone blind. Both collapsed, breathing hard and sweating.

Flora checked the battle. Archers pinpointed those still fighting, while Telridge pushed back, an even line of steel and will. Soon Verdenians began fleeing into the woods. She tipped her head back against a stone and got her first real look at Dirk's wounded leg. What she saw wasn't good.

"We have to get you out of here—can you keep going?" Flora asked.

Dirk nodded. He started to push himself back up, but his limbs were shaking. Flora scrambled underneath his arm and grabbed hold of his waist. Together they eased him into a semi-standing position.

"Just a few steps. You can do this." She gritted her teeth, urging Dirk forward through the grasses and into the trees surrounding the farm.

"You. Should. Run." Dirk bit out.

"Not without you, My Lord."

They hobble-stepped through the trees. Dirk's breaths grew faster, but he stayed with her.

"See that up ahead? That outbuilding? Get to it— that's all. Almost there."

They struggled the last few steps and fell against the farm's storeroom wall. Flora kept one hand on Dirk as she wrested the door open. She all but pushed him through the entry and down the stairs into the dry cellar below. She knew her ministrations weren't doing any good for his bleeding leg. She'd worry about that later.

She barred the storeroom door with farm tools, locking them both in and then found old linens and a cask of liquor. Flora rushed back to Dirk, kneeling on the dirt beside him. "I have to clean it. This might hurt."

"Just do it," he hissed.

Flora tore open the hole in Dirk's breeches to get access to the wound and poured the liquor onto it. The amber liquid washed away the worst of the blood and dirt.

He gritted his teeth and squeezed his eyes shut.

Flora used his inattention to clean and wrap the cut, aiming for speed over precision. It was long but not too deep.

"That went well." He joked, but his words were underscored with pain.

"You're an idiot—My Lord—no man could take on that many single-handed."

Dirk clenched his jaw. "Had to."

Maybe he was right. It was his role, his responsibility. How many more of the Knights might've been lost had he not jumped into the fray and risked himself?

But the cost. It would always be too high. She felt anger brewing up, along with a whole range of other emotions she didn't care to identify. "You do know that you're injured?" Flora waited a beat. "Right?"

Dirk shook his head. "It's not important."

And that was the truth, wasn't it? One man, even a skilled commander like Dirk could be injured. The Telridgian military force would battle on. They had to.

But at the end of today, there still one less Knight to help her with dishes, and one less Crown

Prince walking. Flora slid down the wall next to Dirk.

His head fell back and eyes closed. He wouldn't see the tears that ran freely down her face as she imagined every friend who had fallen and every enemy she killed herself who was someone else's friend.

She prayed for Grace. She prayed for Spense, that he would reach allies, so that maybe tomorrow she wouldn't have another day like this. Her prayers felt hollow.

Chapter 68

There are some places that Summer monarchs are not meant to survive—like the lands of Winter. The butterflies had been her companions for most of a day when the thin air grew too cold and they were forced to turn back. They left Dewy with fluttery kisses and breathed their farewells as she made a cloak of the blanket from her pack and plunged into menacing forests.

She turned to the water to be her guide. Even in Winter, with so much of it frozen, it spoke to her, barely. She inhaled the faint moisture from the air and listened to its muted song. What had the mist and clouds witnessed?

Through whispers and swells, they told her a story of a young man, blindfolded and bound, the goblins and Fae who held him, and where they'd taken him. She saw a foggy picture of him as he struggled through Winter territory, heckled by goblins. Tears formed in her eyes. Spense was humiliated and hurt, but he was alive. She thanked the water and fled—at full faerie speed—toward the Silver Horn.

She whipped through spiny forests and craggy mountain passes—time slipped past, but still she ran on.

Until she approached the looming silver construction that was the Winter capitol. The body of the horn melded into the cliffs behind it. At the open end stood two massive doors. She monitored from the safety of the trees, monitoring the routines and patterns. When the doors swung open, and two guards who'd been patrolling were replaced by two others—faeries wrapped in fur and leather. She recoiled at their clothing choices. What forest friends had been sacrificed for their comfort? She'd heard the rumors of strange Winter practices, but it was hard to stomach the idea that faeries could be as cruel as humans.

After a quick circumnavigation through the trees surrounding the structure, Dewy confirmed that the doors were the singular point of entry and exit. She sent her feelers out to the water running under the earth, but the reports were the faintest of whispers and revealed nothing that she would be able to access. Grates of hard metal blocked the drainage channels running below.

No point trying to sneak in.

Dewy called up her watery friends. It was like hollering down a long tube, but she pulled and pulled until the water responded. The air around the entry thickened with mist. Fog rolled in curling waves until there was little visibility. She waited until she heard the faerie guards mutter to each other in frustration, and then she tiptoed next to the first. She didn't need to see him. The water told her.

And when she felt the guards' exhalations, she moved. Before they could take in the next breath. A simple twist at the right point, and two faeries lay unconscious at her feet. They would wake, but with brutal head pains. She didn't envy them that.

In the next moment, she secured the hawthorn key from one of the guards, opened the massive oak door, and slipped inside.

The cavernous entryway—formed into a large half circle with concentric layers of felled wood—was dark. Few lights flickered. She sensed pine and edelweiss and felt for any water inside the horn. Though there was much outside, the fires indoors burned away most of the moisture from the air.

The little whispers she sensed were muted. But they were enough.

She followed them through a long western corridor and deep into the horn. She scanned arched passages and hollow doorways that were open to empty chambers. At some point, the Winter Fae must have hosted many guests or a much larger court. She spared a thought to wonder where everyone had gone.

Near the end of the corridor, a torch flickered outside of a closed door. One tug proved it to be locked. Dewy laid a palm on the wood and let her awareness extend. She cried in relief as she sensed the contours of a Spense-shaped body, a warm steady presence.

"Spense," she whispered, nearly chocking on a sob.

Dewy heard a shuffling from inside the locked chamber. The warm presence came closer, until she knew that Spense pressed his hand against the opposite side of the door from her.

"Dewy?" Spense's voice was rusty with disbelief.

"I'm here," she gasped.

"Is it really you? Not some faerie deception?"

"Really me." She choked out a laugh. "I'm getting you out of here."

Dewy heard Spense take a deep breath. Something thunked against the door.

"Dewy—the door is locked with magic. You shouldn't be here—you don't have to try to save me. I would never ask—or command—that of you." Spense's voice was missing its usual hopeful quality. Even when he was spiked like a porcupine with pine needles and trying to convince her to leave him, he hadn't sounded so…lost. *What had happened with the Winter Fae?*

Chapter 70

Dewy's words were sweet and fragrant to Spense's cold-numbed senses. If it were a deceit, a new attempt from Lumine to break him or manipulate him, at the moment, Spense didn't care. *She* was here and breathing sunshine into a cold, dim room.

"Don't talk like that—of course you're getting out of here—and of course I am helping you. Tell me what they did to lock the door." He heard her—or whoever was convincingly masquerading as her—give it a demonstrative tug. But to no avail. He knew from frustrated experience that there was no trick to it. No combination of narrow objects positioned in just the right way could pick this lock.

There was only one person who could enter or exit. His jailer and tormenter. Lumine.

"Are you sure they used magic?" He could hear Dewy moving around on the other side of the door. Her voice came to him near the keyhole.

"Pretty sure." In between his time with Lumine, he'd spent plenty of time examining the lock. It's not like he'd anything else to do with his time. While it looked mechanical, it was locked by a magical key. "Lumine waves his hand when he leaves our…conversations, and the lock releases. He closes it up again when he is on the other side of the door."

Spense slid down the door, searching for her

278

presence, getting closer to her voice.

"Lumine comes to visit you himself?"

"Hmm…" Spense closed his eyes and rested the back of his head against the sealed door.

When they first brought him to the small, simple quarters, he'd paced, kicked the edge of the tidy bed, and swore colorfully.

But then minutes passed. And hours. He couldn't be sure. Lumine came. Sometimes with faerie attendants. They brought hard, brown bread and more of that sharp, mineral-infused water, that never quite seemed to quench his thirst, and always left him craving more. And they brought questions. Lumine was frustrated by Spense's limited knowledge, his inability to give more information. Spense reciprocated the feeling.

When he wasn't angry with his captors, he was irritated by his own inability to resolve the situation. His head spun, but he couldn't find sleep.

And his mind circled back to Dewy. He had no idea what she must have thought when he didn't return. Not that he had a choice, but still. It was another loss. The death of her parents. The Claiming and subsequent expulsion from The Vail. And now his apparent abandonment.

His heart ached. Spense rubbed his chest. Too much didn't make sense. What had his father kept from him? Maybe he hadn't expected him to go past The Vail and hadn't considered that he might need to know a little something about the Silver Horn and the Winter Fae. And what was Lady Radiant's role in his current predicament? What did that letter say? Whatever it was, it was the cause for his condemnation and imprisonment, but also the reason he was still alive. Lumine expected something of him, but he had no idea what.

He thought of the night that he Claimed Dewy and how he'd reached out with his senses and felt her watery, living spirit. How he had ever mistaken that for the long-felled timbers of an old bridge was inexcusable. She was alive in every pore, every whisper of breath. She was not frivolous—she was vivacious.

He extended his consciousness. Maybe, even if she wasn't real, he could find a little of her energy. Maybe the illusion would comfort him.

Spense rotated his hands so that they faced each other, as if he were blowing into a pile of tinder like he'd done a hundred times. But then, he shifted his hands and imagined he was holding Dewy's face instead, whispering to her. Because she was not a collection of dry sticks, but a magnificent creature of sunlight and sparks.

Chapter 71

Dewy scowled. "Spense? Do you hear me?" She grasped for the core of Spense's person. She could feel him—his warmth—puddled at the bottom of the door.

"I hear you. You're lovely. You always have been." His voice drifted and spun away from her.

What was Lumine doing to him? She didn't know what it meant that the king took so much time with Spense, but she knew it was significant. What did he want from him, other than to imprison him and deaden his warm spirit? She knew too well what it was to have her spirit quenched. She would not see it happen to Spense. She would not see that warmth cool.

Warmth.

A thought sparked.

"Spense, you have fire magic."

"What? No. A little. I can do a few fire-starting spells...it's not like you and water. And anyway, what does that matter?" Spense was muttering—not a good sign.

Dewy slammed her hand on the hard oak door. *Daft human. Wake up. Come back to me.* "It matters," she explained, "because we are in Winter, and what combats the cold of Winter but heat...warmth...fire?"

"I'm not...I don't have enough magic. I'm not strong enough. Dewy—this is Lumine's magic—the *King* of the Winter Fae."

"You were powerful enough to Claim me, remember? And now, you're not alone—you have *me*." Dewy peered closer at the lock, analyzing what held it fast. As she expected. Ice.

"We can do this, Spense."

"Dewy...I..." Spense's voice drifted off, protest unfinished. He didn't even muster the energy to argue with her.

"Spense, listen to me!"

"I'm listening, Dewy."

"Put your hands on the door—like you did before." She waited until she could hear him rise and sense where his hands were splayed. She placed hers opposite. "Can you feel me? Reach out with your senses."

Silence.

"Spense. Stay with me.

"I'm with you." Another beat of quiet. "If this is an illusion, it's becoming more convincing."

He shifted. She heard the rustling, felt as he leaned against the hard wood of the door. She pressed her own hands flat, so that every knuckle touched the wood. And she knew the moment he connected. His presence was taller. He grew warmer. "I can feel you, Dewy..."

"Yes—I'm right here." Dewy smiled, tears leaking from her eyes. "Spense, listen to me. This lock. It's ice. Ice, Spense." She prayed he would understand and make the connection. "It's *water*. You may not be able to overcome Lumine's ice directly, but if you can heat...me, then I might be able to manipulate it."

"Dewy...you are a miracle come to life." She couldn't see his face, but she knew Spense was smiling. And she believed him, not because he told her to—it wasn't a command—but because it was Spense and hope couldn't die in him. "Let me know if it is too much. I don't want to hurt you."

"Don't worry. You won't," she said.

She heard the words of a simple spell—the same one he'd used to make a small fire in a cozy cottage and to heat a pile of stones in a forest cave.

She closed her eyes, sent her own will into the spell.

Sparks caught. Flame spread. His words grew stronger. Ribbons of caressing heat, bonds to connect them. As the heat built, the bonds grew tighter. The obstacle in between them grew thin, meaningless...

And kept building.

The heat grew and she stretched her senses to touch the water living in the wood and lock while Spense whispered the words of the spell. On and on. There was a natural moisture in the door, but nothing about the ice in the lock felt right. It was barren, inorganic.

Fire seared her palms where they lay flat on the door and slid up into her arms and neck. Dewy continued to reach out to the ice, letting Spense's heat move through her. It came at first in sparks, then waves of tendril flames. Dewy drew it from Spense and sent the heat out, spearing for the lock.

Rivulets of sweat dripped down the side of her face, but she kept drawing from the well that was Spense. His whispered spell continued, and the heat grew until Dewy shook with fever. But she wouldn't stop. She couldn't.

She poured fire and flame into the heart of the dark ice. She found its core, the point that held Winter, and she focused on it. She thought of the way Spense held her when she was exhausted, when salty tears gummed up her face, how he taught her about what it was to be cozy. She thought of fresh baked bread and the taste of it on her tongue. And she felt Spense's magic, searing through every vein. Dewy aimed it all at that bitter darkness in the center of the ice.

Something cracked.

Shards of ice splintered and erupted in fragile diamonds. Dewy blew out a final, fevered breath, and the ice crystals turned to a fast-flowing trickle of water, staining the door.

Her hands slid along the door. She tried the handle. It rotated, and she pushed the door open.

And *he* was there. Wan and haggard. But his eyes were bright and gleaming. Dewy's arms fell to her sides. Her mouth parted.

Spense lunged for her as she began to sway. He caught her body up in his arms. She knew she radiated heat, but he crushed her to him and absorbed it all. They'd burn together. He buried his face in her hair, and she soaked up the clean, pine scent that was Spense.

"Are you really here? Did we really just do that?" He breathed into her neck. His shaking fingers hovered over her hair and face.

Dewy pulled away enough to look at him. She didn't say anything. She didn't need to. Her arms tightened around him, and she answered his incredulous smile with her own.

"That's a fascinating trick. I didn't know my guest had such powerful friends."

They broke apart, and Spense drew Dewy behind him. She recognized that voice, and those too-familiar midnight robes. King Lumine shifted from the shadows of the corridor and into the full spectral light of the moon. It shone through frosted windows and onto his chilled, even features.

Chapter 72

The rains came down hard on the castle keep. Lord Ferrous's steadfast Telridge soldiers maintained their watch, the stretched-out silence punctuated with brief exchanges of fire. Their enemy was intent on siege, but the rains had hampered their efforts, giving Telridge a minor reprieve.

So far, the munitions supply had been sufficient to keep Verden at bay. And Lord Ferrous knew the smiths were laboring to keep the stockpiles full. He wondered how much of the castle cutlery had been melted down into arrowheads.

Ferrous stood in his study and rubbed the crimson and gold peace medals between his thumb and fingers. They were a gift from Verden a year before. Even then, they must have been scheming and plotting.

He wrenched open the window and hurled the brassy discs into the wild rains. He yelled—in anger and frustration—as he watched the trailing red ribbons sail through the air. When the medals disappeared into the dark and the downpour, he leaned against the window frame and bowed his head.

"Pardon me, My Lord?"

Ferrous lifted his head.

"Apologies, My Lord. I knocked, but…"

He swiveled his head and met Cait's kind, concerned face. "No, please, come in, Cait." He waved her over.

She nodded a curtsy. "I have the reports you asked for…about our stores, but if now is not a good time…"

Ferrous chuckled mirthlessly and collapsed into a nearby chair. "It's a rather *terrible* time, don't you think?"

She tilted her head. "As you say."

"Well?"

"As you expected, My Lord Not good."

He squinted, questioning.

"But not *terrible* either," Cait conceded. "As long as we are content with staples and can ration amongst the people, we should be able to hold out for quite a while."

Cait had always been a practical woman, never expecting much from him—even when he'd offered. It was his excuse for not seeing better to her needs or their son's. Irony had a horrid sense of humor, as this might be an opportunity for equitable treatment, as they would all struggle together. "So, you're telling me we'll be eating lentils and rice and dried mutton for weeks?"

"Not more than a few, My Lord."

"Wicked Winter, I didn't realize." Ferrous shook his head.

"There are many people to feed."

Yes, there were. Dirk and his Knights performed their job admirably, evacuating villagers and farmers via the tunnels, and sending them all to shelter inside the massive grounds of Telridge Castle before setting off on their own offensive mission. The castle felt a bit less massive at the moment, crowded with so many souls, and at the same time empty without his sons.

He sent up a prayer for Telridge, but especially for Dirk and Spense, each doing his own part to protect the people. "May Grace be upon them."

Cait murmured, "Upon us all."

Chapter 73

"And who do we have here?" Lumine ambled toward Dewy. "If I'd known I would be receiving more guests, I might have been better prepared." Spense was doing his best to block her from view, but she grabbed his hand, gave it a quick squeeze, and stepped up beside him. He hazarded a worried glance at her before she spoke.

"I am called Lady Dew Drop of the Summer Court, and you, King Lumine have taken my friend, the Ambassador of Telridge captive. I would know how you explain yourself."

Spense froze beside her.

Lumine cocked his head to the side, in speculation. "Bold words, *Lady*. I don't remember meeting you on my last visit to the Vail."

"I was otherwise engaged." Dewy remembered the whispered conversation between Lady Radiant and King Lumine. She'd eavesdropped on the end of the meeting, but had she not been gallivanting with the wood faeries, she might have been present for his reception. "I am sorry to have missed you."

"Likewise, my dear, for you present something of a puzzle to me." Lumine continued his analysis while drifting closer. Dewy's spine stiffened at his proximity. Spense reached out a hand, supporting her at the elbow. She was still weak from the magic they worked, and she leaned into Spense's steadiness, depending on it and him to keep her standing.

"Indeed," Lumine continued. "The missive that your queen sent to me via this human made no mention of a Summer Court alliance. And yet you seem quite comfortable together."

"Ambassador Spense is…a friend."

"And what kind of *friend* enhances a Fae's powers?"

Dewy frowned. She had no reason to think her power had been enhanced. The whispers of water had been undeniably faint—that is until she joined with Spense. But why would that make a difference?

She glanced at Spense. His eyes were wide and imploring as he grasped the change as well. It was something about their joined magic that disabled the Winter lock.

Lumine narrowed his eyes at the evident mystery she and Spense created. He was none too pleased that he'd been overcome. As he took two gliding steps toward her, she wondered if Lumine saw them as a curiosity or a threat.

He reached out his hand, as if he could approach any faerie he outranked with impunity, and she shrank back from his possessive touch. His fingertips caressed her face, but he snatched his hand away and cursed. His fingers were tinged red at the tips. He looked up and pointed at Spense. "You," he hissed. "Human. You Claimed this faerie?"

Dewy recoiled from Lumine's new wrath, her eyes panicked and pleading with Spense. There was no way to deny it, but how he answered mattered.

Spense hung his head. "Yes," he whispered.

There it was. The truth of Spense's mistake. Without

embellishment or apology.

"How dare you?" Lumine said. "She is Fae. I should kill you for that insult." He ripped a hawthorn knife from inside his robe and raised it, preparing to strike.

"No!" Dewy screamed. Lumine opened his eyes wide as she launched herself at him. "No, please. It wasn't his fault. He didn't mean to!" She grabbed his arm, reaching for the knife.

Lumine startled and shook off her burning touch. "Do you not understand how these spells work, girl? He has manipulated you—"

"No—he's been trying to find a way to release me," Dewy pleaded. "Lady Radiant said there was none she knew of, but still he tried. He only intended to Claim a bridge—to defend his country. I was just in the wrong place at the wrong time."

Lumine lowered his knife and flicked his gaze between them.

Spense pulled her away from Lumine. "Please, believe me. I never meant to Claim a person—I know it goes against *The Rules of Magic*—but there is nothing in magic lore to tell how to un-do this."

Lumine laughed humorlessly. "Of course there's not," he barked. "Because you humans banned all knowledge of what you called dark magic after the old wars—when you separated the faerie-folk from each other. Divided us into Winter and Summer."

"Please," Spense whispered again. Feeble hope played out on his face. "If there is a way, I would do *anything* for her."

Dewy's heart broke at his words. Her chest tightened, but not in response to a compulsion. It was something else, new, raw and tender.

Lumine narrowed his eyes. "Really, human? *Anything?*"

Surely Spense knew better than to make a promise to a Fae, that bargains struck with faeries never worked out well for humans. Spense turned to Dewy as if she were a bright ray of light and hope given to him in the darkness of a hopeless prison. As if she were more precious to him than his magic, his status, or his family. As Spense looked at her, she knew what her mother and father must have felt when they looked at each other. She knew how the world could fall away. Because of Spense, she been banished, and yet she had found home.

"Anything." He turned and met Lumine's steel gaze with his own.

Chapter 74

"Spense," Dewy whispered. "You can't."

He reached for her hand, linking it with his, and held on. She squeezed back, and he felt pressure from her long, thin fingers. Whatever despair seeped in while he moldered in a Winter prison fled from him. Because of Dewy. She ignited him and his magic in a way he'd never seen or experienced. She had sacrificed so much because of him. If he could give any of that back to her—her home, her people—it would be worth the cost.

Lumine contemplated. "Perhaps Radiant was right, and there *is* a purpose for you. If you can best my magic in partnership with the Fae you control, you may not be as useless as I previously thought."

Dewy sputtered. "*What* did Radiant say?"

"It's not important," he whispered to her.

Spense raised his chin and looked Lumine square in the eye. "No. Not her."

"No? I thought you said 'anything.' " Lumine pretended disappointment, but as he turned to look at Dewy, his expression shifted into disdain. "It seems you have allied with a fickle man, Lady Dew Drop."

Dewy started to protest, but Spense stepped in front of her. "I will make a bargain with you, Lumine, but you must release Dewy first. She must be set free before I will serve you. I said anything. And I mean it, but she comes first."

Lumine brought his hands together, causing his robe to shimmer in the moon rays, and emphasizing to Spense how powerful Lumine could be. He towered over Spense, an ethereal and ancient being. Spense was less than nothing in Lumine's eyes, as he'd been reminded over their recent conversations. Spense prayed that the offer of himself—of one so insignificant—would be enough to bargain a favor from the King of Winter.

"Yes," Lumine drawled.

Spense locked gazes with Lumine. He would not flinch. He had to show he was worthy if only in this small way.

"I will give you the tools to release her. Then you will remain in my service until the mission I have for you is complete."

Spense nodded. His fate was sealed. He knew that. But he also knew that it was worth it if it meant that Dewy would be free. "I agree to your terms. Show me how to free Dewy so that she can be released—unharmed—from the Claiming and from these lands, and I am at your service until the mission you have for me is complete."

"Spense, no!" Dewy cried.

He turned to face her. "It's the right thing to do. The only thing, if it means you will be free."

Spense let go of Dewy's hand and offered his own to Lumine. "In the human world, we grasp hands to form a contract."

Lumine arched a brow. "Of course." He extended his own pale fingers. His grip was strong and cold, icy bones beneath a thin layer of pale skin.

And in the small space of that hand grasp, it was complete. Spense felt the magic of the bargain click into place, a cold mantle upon his shoulders, a weight pressing down, heavy but bearable.

"Are you ready, human?"

Spense nodded.

"*Tell* Lady Dewy that you release her of your Claim." Lumine gestured at Dewy.

"What?" Spense furrowed his brow. "It can't be that simple."

"Much of the most powerful magic is. Simple, but not easy. Speak the words to let her go and *mean* it with all of the truth in your heart, and she will be free of you."

Spense opened his mouth. He desired Dewy's freedom from the moment he realized what had happened, but he'd never said the words. He could have released her at any time if he'd but known. Instead, he dragged her into his people's conflict, used her to fight their battles. He knew what Lumine was implying, that he didn't want to let her go.

Spense withered in dismay and realization.

Lumine was right. At least in part. Spense compelled Dewy to the point of causing her pain on more than one occasion. And at least once, it was not done in innocence and blunder. He knew exactly what he was doing in the cave when he pushed her to speak about The Vail. Maybe it was done in her best interests. Or maybe that was just what he told himself.

And hadn't he *liked* having a beautiful Fae princess fawning over him? When would that have happened in his small, ordinary life?

Spense swiveled his gaze from Dewy to Lumine and caught the king's smirk. He thought back over the words of their agreement. Lumine knew Spense might hesitate, but he'd owe him his service regardless. Lumine had already honored his part in the bargain. He'd shown Spense *how* to release Dewy, but it was up to him to do it.

Lumine's eyebrows lifted in pretend patience. All the while, his real expectation was clear, that a human would never act against his own selfish nature.

Spense faced Dewy, cupping her shoulders with his hands. He looked deep into her mossy green eyes, welling with un-shed tears.

"Lady Dew Drop, I, Spense of Telridge, release you of the Claiming I have put you under. You are free." He relaxed his hands and dropped them. He took a step back, and then another. He waited.

Her smile was watery. "Thank you."

Spense nodded. Something hot and stinging formed in his eyes. He bowed his head and looked away.

Lumine's mouth dropped open. "I don't believe it…"

Dewy moved to stand between the ruler of the Winter Fae and Spense. She grabbed the king's hand. He didn't pull back. Her touch hadn't scorched him. "It's true. I am free."

Lumine frowned. He withdrew his hand from Dewy and pinned Spense with cool assessment.

Dewy turned to Spense, tears streaming, and said, "Tell me to do something, give me a command."

Spense shook his head, his mouth opening and closing. "I don't know…umm…hop on one foot?"

She crinkled her forehead. "Really?"

"Yeah," he laughed. "Dewy, hop on one foot."

She laughed alongside him, and more tears ran freely. "No," she said. "No!"

Instead, Dewy reached for him. In less than a

heartbeat, she was wrapped in his arms. They held each other, shaking.

Lumine cut off their celebration. "Say your farewells, and then find me, human. Don't make me wait long." His words were clipped and impatient and yet, solemn. Out of the corner of his eye, Spense saw the king drift away down the shadowed corridor, granting them privacy. It was an act of decency that surprised Spense.

Soon, Spense would follow Lumine, because he was decent, too. He had an obligation, his part of the bargain, and he would fulfill it.

But not yet.

He closed his eyes and tilted his head until his brow connected with Dewy's. He drew in her sweet, floral scent. And savored it, like the last piece of a delectable dessert that he may never taste again, or the final, winking glance of the sun before it set.

Chapter 75

Dirk had never been fussed over. Maybe from his mother, but she'd died when he was small. And his memories of her were few. Since he was a child, he'd trained first as a squire, and when he was old enough, a Knight. There was never time to spare for extra rest or to lie indolent as he recovered from minor injuries.

But Flora was fussing. She found him old blankets to lie on and propped his leg up on a well-used saddle to keep it elevated, mentioning something about blood flow.

She'd also coaxed him to drink the same liquid she used to clean the wound, and the details became fuzzy after that. He dozed when the potent drink took effect, waking to a cool cloth on his head and Flora's worried face hovering over him.

Familiar voices drifted to him from a few feet away.

"Flora?" he croaked.

"Yes, My Lord?" She continued her ministrations, pressing the cloth to his brow. The whispered conversation stopped.

"Are you awake, My Lord?" Lady Xendra's serious face came into view, accompanied by Sir Gervais. Their features were haggard. Xendra had a bandage wrapped around her upper arm and a cut on her face.

"More or less. Report?"

The Knights looked at each other before answering.

He couldn't recall a time when either of them ever hesitated to respond to a direct question. "Report," Dirk repeated. "Gerry? X? What do you *not* want to tell me?" He attempted to sit up. It wasn't graceful.

Gerry cleared his throat. "The girl's farm is surrounded, sir." He glanced at Flora. "Most of the Knights are holed up in the house or here in the storeroom."

Dirk heard a slight pause when Gerry said "most." Some of his elite Knights hadn't made it.

But that made no sense. They'd driven back the Verdenian forces, thanks to the lethal combination of Flora's traps and Spense's explosives. When he was injured, they were winning. "Who surrounds us? Verden or Dark Fae?"

Lady Xendra said, "Both, sir. Reinforcements arrived."

Dirk fell back against the rough pile of blankets. "Wicked Winter. I don't suppose anyone has tried to retreat via the tunnels?"

Lady Xendra nodded. "We lost two Knights in the attempt."

It wasn't uncommon for there to be injuries and casualties during battle. Everyone knew this. It didn't make it any easier. His Knights were his closest friends. Like family. Maybe closer. He thought of his father, who he spent more time reporting to than talking with, and Spense, his brother who he didn't understand half the time and ignored the rest. The Knights were the family he chose. Dirk's jaw tightened.

"Have any good news?" He found himself looking at Flora.

She said, "It's still raining."

He heard the constant pattering against the barn roof. "How is that good?"

She shrugged. "Our elevated visibility is better than theirs, and they can't use flaming arrows against us."

Dirk didn't like that his Knights were dependent on something as fickle as the weather, but at this point he guessed he'd take what he could. "How are *we* stocked for arrows?"

"Haven't run out yet," Gerry assured him.

Dirk closed his eyes. "Then tell the Knights to keep firing."

"We'll keep them off as long as we can, My Lord."

Dirk nodded. "Grace be upon you."

"Upon us all."

Chapter 76

"I have to go," Spense said, "And so do you. You need to return to Summer."

Reluctance was written across his face. She understood his frustration. There were no words adequate. She was free from him, but she didn't want to leave.

Dewy nodded, but she didn't release him. Not yet. She needed another heartbeat. Another tick of stolen time. She slid her arms up Spense's chest and wrapped her hands around his neck.

He sucked in a shaky breath and let it out. His clean soap scent mingled with traces of forest washed over her. "Dewy..." he began, and then shook his head.

She waited.

"I'm sorry. For everything. For the spell and for all you had to endure because of me, but—" Spense's voice cracked. "I will never be sorry that I met you."

"Nor I, you." She attempted a smile. "I can say that with assurance now—thanks to you—I know how I *actually* feel about you."

"And what did you figure out?" Spense whispered. They locked gazes and didn't flinch.

She used her newfound leverage to pull his face down and pressed a kiss to his lips. A real one. Not an act of curiosity or mere flirtation. She let him interpret.

He got the message. And he kissed her back.

Thoroughly.

It was a kiss to capture all they had been through. Of goodbye. Of kindness. Of loyalty. Of love. It was a kiss to re-write the world, and everyone in it. Or maybe that was just how it felt to Dewy.

But it led her to a decision.

She knew there was something powerful in the love and light her parents shared. All of her pursuits to honor them with dancing and flirtations had been frivolous—a mockery of whom they'd been. It was her aunt, who Dewy derided for her cold adherence to duty who honored them. Radiant had taken up the mantle of her older brother and became first the Crown Princess, and when it was time, Queen Regent. Radiant had been born with a different name, meant to play the eternal princess, as frivolous and free as any common faerie.

Dewy pulled Spense closer and wrapped her arms tighter. He'd saved her. She wanted to save him.

When they drew apart, she said, "I think you forgot something."

Spense's cheeks grew a charming shade of pink and his forehead creased. His chin did that funny thing. He started to ask, but she anticipated him.

"I am a faerie. And I am much faster than you."

She barely saw Spense's eyes grow wider as she bolted away from him and fled through the corridors of Winter.

Chapter 77

It wasn't hard to find the king's Receiving Chambers. As in Summer, all paths led there. When Dewy arrived, her breath coming in rapid pants, she found Lumine lounging on his great, fir tree throne. He didn't show the least bit of surprise that it was she and not Spense. As if he'd been waiting.

"I suppose you're going to do something brave and reckless." He shook his head. The gesture was almost paternal.

"I don't believe it to be reckless." She lifted her chin and strode toward the Winter King.

"No, you wouldn't. You're like your parents, I suppose."

That gave her a moment of pause. One heartbeat. "You knew my parents?"

"Of course I knew them—they were Summer Fae—and I know who you are, too, Crown Princess. Like you—" He pointed a demonstrative finger. "—your parents would do anything for the one they loved. No matter how foolish."

Dewy's eyes pricked. Lumine had known her parents. At least he'd known the most important part of them. "You don't seem surprised."

Lumine grimaced, a dark slash of a smile across his moon-pale face. "Your human had the opportunity to compel you. Forever. He didn't take it. Not only that, you

302

came to find him. On your own. That wasn't from any command." He pushed forward in his chair. "Don't you even want to know what the task is? Before you take on *his* burden?"

Dewy opened her mouth and closed it again. She shook her head and smiled.

Lumine snorted. He rolled his wrist in her direction. "Get on with it, then."

She steadied herself. "I want to take Spense's bargain."

"Yes, I know. Anything else?"

"You have to call a truce with Telridge."

He tapped his finger on the arm of his throne and pursed his lips. "Fine. Agreed. If you perform this task, then my grievance with Telridge will be moot anyhow."

Dewy didn't pause to puzzle out that comment. Instead, she faced him and declared, "King Lumine of the Winter Fae, I freely take the bargain you made with Spense of Telridge. To serve you until the task you would have given him is complete."

Running footsteps echoed in the corridor and came to a skidding stop. "Dewy, what have you done?" Spense cried.

Lumine rose and stalked to Spense. "She has taken your place. Your bargain. You should be thankful." Spense's face became a thing of anguish as he found her gaze. He shook his head, mouthing the word "no" over and over again.

"Tun, are you lurking about?" Lumine called. A blue-gray goblin appeared from behind one of the full-grown fir trees. His toothy grin took up half of his face.

"Yes, Your Majesty?"

"Our human guest will be leaving us now. Would

you care to show him the way out?"

The goblin's grin grew wider.

"Wait...no..." Spense stuttered.

"You have said your farewells, human. And I've grown rather tired of you." Lumine leaned into Spense until they were nearly nose to nose. "It is time for you to leave."

Spense gritted his teeth. "But *what* is the task? Can you at least tell me that?"

Lumine drew himself up to his full menacing height. He towered over Spense. "It is no more than what I asked of *your* king and *her* queen. They both refused me. What a delightful turn of events for Radiant—she handed me this human to serve me—and instead it is her own niece who takes his place. I am tickled with the irony."

Spense stumbled back from Lumine and shook his head. "I don't understand." He had no more knowledge of what Lumine spoke of than Dewy did. What had Lord Ferrous and Lady Radiant *both* refused to do?

"That is clear enough. You consumed enough of our truth waters to loosen the tongue of even the strongest Fae, and yet you revealed nothing of import. Your sovereigns send you forth and yet prepare you so poorly." Lumine scoffed. Let me enlighten you. Like you, dear Dewy, years ago, my own daughter, Princess Snow became entangled with a man beneath her. She gave birth to a child. Of course I could not acknowledge the child, and sent it and its half-breed father into exile. But with Snow's recent passing, I have no choice but to accept the child in my lineage."

"The faerie Courts *must* have a Named Heir," Dewy whispered.

"Yes," Lumine hissed. "To preserve balance. The

nature of the Courts abhors uncertainty."

Spense thought back to the way the trees and foliage reacted against them, and how it nearly killed him. If what Lumine said was true, then it had started already, the fraying at the edges of the faerie lands.

Lumine lifted his brows and spread his hands out before him. "There are those in this Court gifted with skills of the Sight. I know the child to be living among the humans—in Telridge to be exact—but when I asked for aid from Lord Ferrous and from the Summer Court, I was denied. I will not be denied now, Dewy, because you will find my Heir."

Chapter 78

Before Spense could take in all Lumine said or implied, the goblin grabbed him. He attempted to struggle for a moment, but it was no use. The most he could do was turn his head and get a last glimpse of Dewy, standing calm and fearless, as silent tears tracked down her freckled cheeks.

Spense scrambled to get his feet under him but the goblin marched him through the corridors. He yelled for Dewy. He screamed her name again and again. He knew it didn't matter and wouldn't make a difference. He yelled for her all the same until Tun's rough, blue-gray hands threw him out the front doors of the Silver Horn and into the snow.

"Well done, human. You've saved your kingdom." Tun cackled. Spense's eyes narrowed. He'd come to hate that goblin.

Less than a heartbeat later, a murder of crows flew from the doors, whooshing out into the forest of Winter. Spense ducked and fell to his knees onto the icy earth, throwing his hands over his head. He heard the giant oak doors slam with cold finality.

He peeked an eye out when the flapping and cawing grew distant and looked up into the cold forest beyond. He wasn't sure how long he sat staring at nothing but snow-encased tree limbs—his breeches had grown cold and damp—when a form emerged from the trees and he met the eyes of Thorn, Lady Radiant's steward, lounging in a cluster of saplings, his arms folded over his chest—nearly hidden by the shadowed patterns on his green cloak.

"I take it that it didn't go so well, human?"

Spense shook his head. "What...are you..."

Thorn picked his way through the snow. He offered his hand and pulled Spense to his feet. The faerie's grip was warm and strong. "You think Radiant trusts just anyone to gather intelligence for her? I was sent to see how things were getting on. Looks like I arrived just in time."

Spense's head was ringing. This was not how it was supposed to go. He couldn't reconcile what happened, what had been revealed, what Dewy had done for him or his abrupt ejection, despite the clear, cold evidence all around him.

"Why don't you tell me all about it on the road? We don't want to get caught out in deep Winter at night. You can explain how it is that a goblin of Winter said you saved your kingdom and sent out a fleet of Winter messengers on your behalf, and furthermore, how it is that the Lady Dew Drop is no longer in your company."

Spense's face crumpled, but he nodded and held in the sobs. "You don't seem...disappointed."

"Oh I am. But not in you." Thorn took several long strides into the snowy trees before speaking again. "You did find a way to free Lady Dew Drop?"

"Yes."

"Then, our alliance with Telridge is renewed." Thorn leaned over and whispered his next words. "Though it looks like we have a new matter to deal with regarding our Winter friends. But that is a matter for another day."

"I can't leave her."

"You will do no one any good—least of all, Dewy—if you freeze to death in Winter."

Spense hung his head. He knew Thorn's words were true, but he wasn't inclined toward rational thinking, not when it came to Dewy. "I let her go. I gave her freedom. And she used it to save me." Spense shook his head. "Why would she do that?"

"Come, young human. You know the answer to that. And if you care for her as well, you still have work to do." Thorn placed a gentle hand on Spense's shoulder.

Spense brushed away the tears already frozen on his upper cheeks. He took one last look at the Winter doors slammed shut to him, behind which Dewy was trapped until the bargain—his bargain—was fulfilled. He considered the cold doors and the words of the agreement. There was nothing in it that forbade her from receiving help. And help her he would. As Thorn said, they had work to do.

Spense nodded, rose, and turned from the Silver Horn. He trudged behind the faerie, and together, they made their way out of Winter.

Chapter 79

The hammering beat of rain droned on for hours and hours. It was the sound of salvation—or at least an extended reprieve—for Dirk and his Knights. During that time, he managed to get himself upright and even hoisted up into the main part of the storeroom. Flora argued that he needed rest, but not with much conviction. They both knew that he would have plenty of time for rest soon, one way or another.

He even took a shift with the bow, firing at anyone bold enough to approach and foolish enough to be seen. Dirk hadn't lasted long. His wounded leg started to cramp, and his body was weak.

It was Flora, again, who helped him back to his sidelined position amongst the smooth old saddles and worn blankets, who gripped his hand when his wound was cleaned and bandages changed. She didn't flinch when he squeezed hard enough to break bones and seethed as the last of the liquor sent cleansing fire along his swelling cut. She stayed with him still, shoulder to shoulder through tedious, tension-filled minutes and hours.

"Do you hear that?" Flora asked. Her gaze stretched up to the ceiling of the storeroom.

"The rains are slowing." He'd been listening for that for a while, dreading it.

"No...not that. It sounds like...birds."

He cocked his head to listen better. Dirk heard the distinctive clamor of crows cawing, shrill and emphatic. Lots of them. "Let me see." He looked around. "Gerry, are you near?"

Sir Gervais moved to his side. Dirk flung an arm around the Knight's shoulder and pushed off with his other hand, until he was able to get up on his one healthy leg and hop to a crack in the siding.

"Wicked Winter."

Scores and scores of crows swarmed the forest. They moved in bunches, congregating over a section, and then lifting off again, moving on to an adjacent area. Wherever they'd been, faerie warriors turned and disappeared into the trees.

"Are they leaving?" Flora asked.

Dirk nodded. "I think so."

"Why?"

Dirk laughed. "Because those aren't just any crows. My little brother might have done something right."

He watched as their enemy thinned until less than a company of Verdenian soldiers remained. Ordinary humans who were panicking as only ordinary humans could. His mouth lifted up in the corners.

"Gerry! X!"

"Yes, My Lord?" The Knights spoke in unison.

"Drive these bastards out of my forest."

"Yessir!"

Chapter 80

Spense marched his way through the fields and forests, past villages and farms. First through the harsh, windy lands of Winter, skirting through the borderlands in Summer and then on to Telridge. There was no farm that hadn't been ransacked, no glade untouched by battle. The rivers and streams worked to clear ash and bloody silt from their waters. The skies cleared and wind blew away the stench of battle.

On his way, he came across clusters of soldiers. Burying the dead. He bowed his head as he pushed through. They nodded in return. Some saluted. Spense offered the occasional healing spell, small easy remedies, perhaps a few words of meaningless comfort and walked on.

"It's not meaningless, Master Spense."

Spense swiveled his head. "What?"

Thorn, always calm, who walked alongside him through every battered forest trail and burned-out village, lifted his brows. "Your words. They mean something to the people, to the soldiers."

"Now you're reading my thoughts?" Spense scoffed.

"Hardly. They're written plainly across your face."

He grimaced. He was sure that Thorn could read that, too. Maybe he would be able to interpret for Spense. He'd thought the faerie spy and steward would leave him as they neared the Summer territory, but he hadn't. Instead, a fleet of sunset-hued butterflies joined them. Despite Spense's blusterous dismissal, he was grateful to have Thorn with him to make the journey. It didn't mean that his heart didn't ache for the sunlight-kissed faerie back in Winter, but the presence of another soul, especially one as even and quiet as Thorn, made every step away from her almost bearable.

"Without you, this would have been much worse." Thorn scrutinized the battered landscape.

"It's hard to imagine worse than this." Spense walked on, scanning broken branches and trod-upon shrubs. Where would the deer find berries? Where would the birds nest?

"The forest will heal. Your people will re-build." Thorn clapped a hand on Spense's shoulder and squeezed. "They have you to thank for that opportunity."

Spense shook his head. "It is Dewy they should thank."

Thorn nodded. "So you say. But they have you, too. And when you get home—to your people in Telridge— they will want to thank you. You should let them."

They continued their trek without speaking. In the quiet, there was healing, too. But he would try, as he had been, to offer what he could, whatever small peace. There was no true silence to be had, in the midst of their fluttering companions, but that quiet persisted, everywhere but inside Spense's head.

Home. Spense was going home, to his mum, his father and brother.

And yet, he knew he'd left his true home in Winter.

Chapter 81

Lord Ferrous waved away the summer flies that had decided to take part in the ceasefire negotiations. He supposed that was one of the inconveniences of meeting beneath a large tent in a field distant from the castle. In truth, he preferred the company of the flies to the collection of scowling Verdenian dignitaries. King Tempra had sent his smarmiest negotiators. Alas, he couldn't wave *them* away, at least not until they'd signed the agreement.

He appreciated Verden's reluctance. The terms were not favorable to them. But they'd been the aggressors, and they'd also been soundly routed once they'd lost their faerie allies.

Except for the crows, there'd been no word from Spense, but Ferrous knew the feathery messengers were his doing. Ferrous asked his son to beg mercy and a possible alliance with the Summer Fae. He'd gone further and made peace with the Winter Fae as well. It was more than Ferrous had even attempted for nearly two decades.

One of the Verdenians growled over a provision, a particularly distasteful ambassador named Rascamouth, but Ferrous paid his complaints no more heed than the buzzing flies. The Telridgian ministers of finance and agriculture were arguing a point regarding realized costs. Ferrous let his mind drift, as his input wasn't necessary, and he formed the opinion that he was more intimidating when he said nothing.

His minister of finance was sharing a complex calculation regarding grain prices Ferrous wasn't entirely sure he understood—judging from the Verdenians' vacant expressions, he was sure they absolutely did not—when a single, orange-hued butterfly landed on the negotiation table.

He looked up.

Another landed on the minister's chair and another on his neighbor's plumed hat. Outside, a small swarm flew towards the tent. They played escort to a pair of larger beings. Ferrous caught Dirk's eye and jerked his head in the direction of the swarm. Dirk whipped his head to follow Ferrous's hint.

He knew the second Dirk recognized his brother. Dirk's mouth parted and he muttered a curse, which caught the attention of the negotiators.

"Excuse me." Dirk cleared his throat. "Lords and Ladies, I'll be just a moment." Dirk hobbled off without waiting to hear if the gathering of nobility, officials and ministers had indeed granted him pardon. Ferrous lifted the corner of his mouth.

As Spense came closer, accompanied by a dusky male he guessed to be from the Summer Court, Dirk picked up his pace, labored though it was. He watched his sons' exchange, animated on Dirk's side—his arms gestured wildly, clapping Spense on the shoulder. Spense was more subdued, ducking his head at Dirk's praise.

And the unthinkable happened—a miracle of sorts. Dirk limped one step farther toward Spense and embraced him, as a brother and an equal.

Epilogue

Spense perched on an outcropping of rock over the River Selden. Its waters sparkled clear and blue in the mid-morning sun. His thoughts couldn't be darker.

This wasn't how it was supposed to work. He'd won the heart of the princess. And together they had saved the kingdom.

But he didn't get to stay with the princess? What heroic tale ended *that* way?

Spense rolled a pea lily in his fingers, the delicate flower that he could crush with no more than a clench of his fist seemed stronger than the fragile state of his heart. He looked down at the river, followed its wandering path from the White Rock Mountains to the sea, leagues beyond. The river carried snow-melt and spring rain across stones, through silt plains, over misty falls, and kept going. Every day. Every year. Its story did not end.

Spense pulled a linen cloth from his pocket and tucked the pea lily into it. He reverently placed the package into his alchemy journal, closed the book, and put it in his satchel. He gave the river one last glance before hefting the worn leather bag to his shoulder and rising. The river's story did not end. Theirs wouldn't either.

Acknowledgements:

So many people have gone into the making of this book, from the nascent idea stage to the final copy, and I am so grateful for the encouragement, advice and helpful nudges at every step along the way.

First a huge thank you to Val Mathews, Rhonda Penders, RJ Morris, Amanda Barnett and the team at Wild Rose Press for making this book a reality. Jennifer Greeff, this cover is gorgeous. I can't wait to see what you do next.

To my agents and dear friends, Shannon Orso and Lizz Nagle, thank you for caring as much about these characters and this story as I do, and for wanting to see this book out in the world. We miss you, Shan.

Our Victress Literary community of writers and readers—you all make me laugh and keep me sane. I trust each of you to prod me to "do better" and cry with me when the words are hard. I can't thank you all enough for the countless hours you have given. Stephanie Scott, Josh Corneil, Laura Reeves, Josh Roots, Anne Belen, Kimmie Cooper, Adriana Allegri and everyone who has been a part of this community, you are all rock stars.

I am so thankful to SCBWI and PNWA for all that they do to help writers become authors, from honing craft to learning professional skills and understanding the marketplace of publishing. It was at an SCBWI conference where I first wore a badge that said "author." I owe a debt to the talented people in the Germany, Oregon, Texas (Southwest and Austin), and Western Washington regions. The joy of moving so much has meant that my writing community spans the globe, and I have critique partners, who have become friends and confidants, all over the world.

Angela Cerrito, Joy Thomas, and Jodi Corey, you saw something in Spense and Dewy when they were barely ideas and urged me to "keep going," even checking in on me, when I'd already moved at least twice, asking when that book was going to be finished. Shannon Rigney, Sonia Acharya, Lisa Lee, and Carrie Sturrock, my Portland ladies, thank you for the glasses of wine, the truffle fries, and the thoughtful encouragement. Thank you to Deb Yates, Kimberly Kisner, Arti Kvam, and Eric Taylor, for offering helpful critique and needed perspective. And to my Tacoma critique partners, Stephanie Scott, Mary Boone, Wendy and Joe Wahman, Adria Goetz, Paula van Enkevort, Jessica Froberg, and Elizabeth Scherman, thank you for teaching me how to write to non-fantasy readers and keeping me caffeinated and smiling during this process.

To all of the beautiful souls at the Glen Workshop, Image Journal, and The Madeleine L'Engle Conference, you are my people and my tribe. Thank you for speaking my language and giving me permission.

To my family, I am so blessed to be surrounded by readers, artists, musicians, and teachers. I love you all for being my fans, even before there was an actual book to hold in your hands. Mom and Dad, you get credit for pushing me to write when I still had baby teeth and for pushing Tolkien, Lewis, White, and so many others into my hands and into my heart, even if you called it "required reading." Jeff, thank you for leaving those paperbacks laying all around the house when we were kids, and for getting as excited about my characters and worlds as you were about Xanth, Narnia, and Middle Earth.

Molly Cullen, I'll never be able to say thank you enough, for the read-throughs, the hard questions, and the enthusiasm, for knowing when to kick my ass and when to give me encouraging words, for eighty-nine days in Germany where you gave me a little space to write and for showing up in Texas with a box full of my favorite chips.

Scott and Paige, your bright-eyed, endless creativity and imagination astound me. Thank you for loving faerie stories and inspiring me to write them, and for coming up with back histories for goblins.

Jamison, I couldn't be a writer without you. Thank you for dreaming big, being my first encourager and co-conspirator. Thank you for not only understanding when I needed to lock myself in a room with my computer, but for facilitating it. Thank you for everything—especially for reminding me when it was time to celebrate and pouring me a shot of brown sugar bourbon.

And I thank God, above all, for giving us words and the desire to be image bearers, to be creators.

A word about the author...

J.A. Nielsen has spent most of her professional life in education—as a therapist, teacher, administrator, and librarian. She holds an M.A. in Counseling and an M.Ed. Though she spends much of her time writing, she can still be found teaching art, shelving library books, and occasionally, choreographing school musicals. In all of these endeavors, she is driven by stories.

Her own story has led her to live all over the world—on a tropical island and in the shadow of a crumbling Rhineland castle—but she has always considered the Pacific Northwest corner of the United States home. When not writing, she is most likely playing with her family in the forest, on the water, or in the mountains.

In 2020, she won the Pacific Northwest Writers Association Literary Contest for Young Adult literature.

The Claiming is her first novel.

Thank you for purchasing
this publication of The Wild Rose Press, Inc.

For questions or more information
contact us at
info@thewildrosepress.com.

The Wild Rose Press, Inc.
www.thewildrosepress.com

CPSIA information can be obtained
at www.ICGtesting.com
Printed in the USA
LVHW051825250123
737935LV00007B/357